an eminent national danger

THE PARAPONERA

perry d. defiore

THE PARAPONERA
AN EMINENT NATIONAL DANGER

iUniverse books may be ordered through booksellers or by contacting:

iUniverse
1663 Liberty Drive
Bloomington, IN 47403
www.iuniverse.com
1-800-Authors (1-800-288-4677)

ISBN: 978-1-5320-0930-3 (sc)
ISBN: 978-1-5320-0929-7 (e)

Library of Congress Control Number: 2016920095

Print information available on the last page.

iUniverse rev. date: 12/15/2016

PROLOGUE

RICHARD SPENT EVERY SPARE HOUR IN HIS BASEMENT LAB, which was unknown to his closest friends, colleagues, and even his neighbors. He worked there to the point of exhaustion. The thoughts of his creation haunted him until he fell unconscious, trying to chase the horrible possibilities out of his mind with help from a green bottle he had come to know all too well.

His arms formed a pillow upon his desk for his head and perspiration soaked his body. Beads of sweat were trapped among the hairs of his short-cropped hair and salt-and-pepper whiskers of his unshaven face. His legs crossed under a wooden straight-back desk chair with weakened cane webbing, something he had picked up at a garage sale when he built his lab, an antique older than his forty-five years.

Mixed feelings pulled at the very fibers of his brain. He knew he had broken through a scientific threshold that could possibly win him a Nobel, but he also feared his creation, which worked diligently, incessantly, in large glass aquariums not five feet away from him, a product of his genius and something that was a lifelong obsession.

It wasn't the present that held him in terror—he had that under control, at least up until now. It was the future that gave him the incredible nightmares ... nightmares that, with one small error, could give the world nightmares and "day-mares."

He had not permitted any meaningful personal relationships,

even allowing the love of his life to walk out of his life. He imagined he understood how the scientists had to have felt when they discovered the neutron in the thirties only to have its discovery used in the making of the atomic bomb. Chadwick had to have gone through this, and didn't Einstein even warn them?

Nobody was warning anyone about his creation though. The secret wasn't out yet. Sleep escaped him most nights as he battled with himself about the morality of what he was doing.

It was all science at first, but now, after seeing his creation develop, he wondered how it would end. How could he control the creation that lived with him in that private, secluded world of no more than four hundred square feet? Even worse, how could he stop it if it ever got loose? How could he righteously account for such a creation?

Had he turned into a modern-day Frankenstein?

CHAPTER 1

━━ ━━ ━━ ━━ ━━ ━━ ━━

THE MOUNTAINS OF KENTUCKY ARE A BEAUTIFUL SIGHT during the early fall when their leaves lavishly paint the countryside with carelessly stroked yellows, oranges, browns, reds, and evergreens; for the tiny village of Smithtown, the anticipation of the onslaught of its bitter winter obscured nature's beauty from its residents.

A large three-story house stood isolated on the south side of FM19, just where the meandering, barely two-lane road with a ditch on each side for shoulders leveled out for a quarter mile at the top of the mountain. A couple wooden exterior boards appeared as if they would fall from their places at any moment, and the white paint was worn thin and blistered, taking on a grayish tone of white.

A small broken window on the third floor faced the road. Blue wasps, a family of goldfinches, and a variety of rodents and insects shared the floor.

Mary Sue and her family of twelve lived in the house. Five years earlier, a large, happy family lived there. Pretty white embroidered curtains hung at all the windows instead of the motley soiled sheets that now covered the first-floor windows and the soap that covered the second-floor glass windowpanes.

It was a hot August night when Mary Sue's husband told her he needed to go to Maysville to see about a new, high-paying job at the Browning Manufacturing plant. Tyrone never returned. Rumor had it he ran off with another woman from Aberdeen, Ohio, but

Mary Sue never believed such "bull wash." She waited faithfully for him to come home.

The handful of local married men, including relatives, who knew of Tyrone's demise had no qualms about approaching her to give her their most intimate attention, but she shunned them with disgust.

Only six months after her husband's disappearance, Tyrone's best friend, Mitchell, had pulled her into the bathroom of his own house while ten other couples were in the living room celebrating Mitchell's forty-first birthday. She could have screamed out, but in her town, she would have been accused of enticing him and been called a slut. Mary Sue never attended another "get-together." The memory of that white commode and the small green wall tiles constantly reminded her of that dreadful experience.

The months crawled by for Mary Sue. The late October sun had disappeared three hours earlier, and man-made light flowed softly into the dead blackness around the house.

This was a large corn and tobacco farming region, so it was no surprise a large cornfield was next to Mary Sue's house. The scattered residents of Smithtown, all 212 of them, consisted of large families. Mary Sue's closest neighbor lived a good country mile away.

Mary Sue put all the children to bed and sat on a brown couch worn so thin the color had vanished from the cushions. A black-and-white, thirteen-inch portable TV sat on the coffee table accompanied by empty soda pop bottles, old newspapers, and plastic plates with remnants of tonight's macaroni-and-cheese supper.

The station went off the air at one in the morning, which was Mary Sue's nightly signal to go to bed. Another alarm would interrupt her peaceful silence at five thirty, and she would face the chaotic environment of getting her children fed and ready for school.

She lifted her feet off the table and slid them into a worn pair of furry pink scuffs her husband had bought for her six years earlier.

Half-asleep, she shuffled her way to the large bedroom with ten beds to check on the kids.

Mary Sue pulled her heavy red duster tightly around her as the wind sang its song of autumn through the windowpanes. She let out a long sigh and turned back the blue wool blanket and faded pink sheet. As she swung her legs into bed and slid them under the covers, she thought of the snow that would be coming soon.

It was about time to break out the nineteen-gallon white plastic paint cans for those who had to get up in the middle of the night to use the bathroom. Mary Sue always left the kitchen light on during those times and placed the bucket close to the door. The winter was just too cold to send the children to the outhouse.

She had just wormed her way under the covers when the urge to use the bathroom hit her. A small curse word escaped her lips in a whisper as she swung her legs out, donned her housecoat, and slid her feet into her slippers once again.

Mary fought many periods of severe depression. Sometimes it got so bad she would take long walks, disappearing at erratic times for hours on end, but she always came back to the same dreary life she led, day in and day out, waiting—waiting for her world to come back to her, to bring the joy she once had back into her life.

As she unconsciously made her way to the kitchen door that led to the outhouse, she thought of how everything that could possibly go wrong had gone wrong and that God had not yet found it in his heart to answer any of her prayers.

■ ■ ■ ■ ■

The family of Paraponeras increased rapidly. They worked feverishly from sunup to sundown, building deep, intricate tunnels in a soil still moist from the abundant rains over the last four weeks. Now that the rains finally stopped, it was time to forage. They were hungry, and the queen had to be fed—and fed well. Their numbers were great now, and they depended on the queen for nourishment.

The scouts sent word and marked a trail to follow. A sense of something really big filled the nest to the deepest chamber. The construction crew surfaced first like molten lava flowing from a volcano, then the kitchen crew came, and finally the nursery personnel that could be spared broke into the damp, brisk, cold night air, leaving only a skeleton crew for guard and nursing duty. Of course, the small male population would continue feeding and remain at home, allowing the females to do all the work. Their short lives were limited to a single function.

Initially, they seemed to be confused. They ran into each other, and the occasional fight broke out over the frustration. Within a few minutes, they organized and began to move as if they were on their way to the biggest sale of the season at Bloomingdale's. (Come one, come all … everything is being given away at 75 percent off! Supplies limited!)

Their preparation and discipline for combat showed an expertise the United States Marines would envy. Up until tonight, the edge of a nearby cornfield had been their northern boundary. The landowner had become seriously ill and had not turned the field under as of yet, providing them with a great tall forest of dried corn stalks.

Local domestic animals had already learned to keep a distance from their territory. Not unlike their African relatives, they left various skeletons of small rodents near their home, a clear warning to any who approached.

The dry cornstalks stood like a gigantic black Redwood forest in the moonless night. The cool, damp wind rustled the dry leaves of cornstalks as they silently marched in columns of four in five different paths toward their enemy.

The cover of their forest, the black night, and the noise of the dry stalks in the wind drowned out any noise from their movements. Upon reaching the edge of the field, which spanned twenty yards, the forerunners halted. The ranks of female warriors thickened behind them until their bodies covered the ground below them like a blanket. They waited in disciplined silence.

A small structure, silhouetted by the soft yellow light emanating from a light on the wall of a much larger building that stood among the bluegrass already moist from the night's condensation, rose out of the ground. The Paraponeras waited patiently until a lone human figure had entered and settled into the small wooden construction in front of them.

The right flanks began to move toward the small building from the north, not hindered in the least by the wet grass. The middle flank moved in from the east, and the left flanks moved in from the south.

They noiselessly scaled the walls and squeezed through the cracks between the old worn wooden planks as well as the ample opening where the roof met the walls.

Sensing the enemy, they began to feel the hunger for battle. Fearless excitement rushed through their bodies, but discipline remained throughout as they continued to position themselves on the roof and walls inside the lightless small room, moving with incredible silence.

They stood motionless, knowing the signal would come soon to engage in battle with their largest prey ever. It would be a fight to remember, and they were confident they would conquer. Victory would be quick, and the ceremonious feast immediately after would take many hours this time.

■ ■ ■ ■ ■ ■

The late hour brought a brisk wind and cold dampness that penetrated Mary Sue to the bone the moment she stepped into the night. Her mind told her to run, but her aging muscles stiffened, keeping her progress to a fast walk of short steps.

She could feel the ground's dampness through her slippers, and the wind rustling through the cornstalks made it feel even colder. She pulled her robe as tightly as she could around her body.

She never noticed the unusual quiet since the constant rattling of dried leaves filled her ears. If there had been no wind, she would have noticed the crickets weren't singing, the night owls weren't hooting, and there were no barking dogs or screaming cats. It was just the night zephyr in a moonless ebony night. Perhaps if she had noticed—if she had had a clear head and had not been feeling so sorry for herself, drowning herself in her misery—things might have turned out differently. If she had pulled the large paint can out tonight and used it as a toilet instead of just thinking about it, perhaps what was to happen in that small dark wooden room would not have happened.

She pulled the outhouse door open and stepped into the black room. The closeness was suffocating, but Mary Sue had spent many years coming to this room and knew every inch of it by heart.

She latched the door, reached for the wooden toilet seat, and raised the cover, releasing an immediate unpleasant odor to which she and her family had also become accustomed. She opened her duster and pulled her black knit slacks down in a painfully exhausted manner. Her white briefs with a hole worn through on the left buttock were lowered next, and she eased herself over the wooden hole like releasing the pressure on a hydraulic jack under a car after changing a tire. A soft sigh escaped her.

The wind gusted and howled as it found its way through the cracks in the wooden boards, giving her goose bumps from her shoulders down to her ankles where her clothes tied her legs together.

She held her head in her hands, her elbows resting on her thighs, and sighed again while she waited for nature to run its course. Thoughts of Tyrone filled her mind. *Where are you? It's been over a year. When are you coming home? Are you even alive?*

Despite the cold, she almost fell asleep during the several minutes needed to eliminate her body's waste.

Without thinking, Mary reached for the roll of toilet paper on the wooden platform beside the toilet seat. Her eyes had become slightly adjusted to the darkness, and she felt a slight sensation that the walls were moving. She tossed the thought aside.

Her instincts made her feel the presence of something unknown, and her adrenaline begin to flow. Something was eminent. Mary slowed her reach for the toilet paper.

When her hand found the roll of toilet paper, her skin felt movement—and she screamed. The scream shook the outhouse, but the gusting wind's song smothered her scream. Only a muffled sound could be heard outside the walls of that little room of terror.

She jumped to her feet a split second after her scream, but the signal had been given and the attack had begun.

The female warriors came from all directions, showering her with their bodies from above, swarming her body, and totally covering it within twenty seconds. The first of the warriors crawled over her hands and legs and thrust their spears into her skin, hundreds at a time at first, and then thousands.

Mary Sue wanted to pull up her clothes and run, but her limbs wouldn't respond. She fell back into a sitting position, killing a few of her attackers. Her back fell against the back wall, killing a hundred more. Her mouth formed a permanent zero from whence the attackers poured inside, tearing at her tongue and cheeks.

Mary Sue felt them enter her ears, her mouth, her eyes, and her nostrils. She felt them tearing at her legs, but she couldn't move. She screamed inwardly with desperation, but no sounds escaped her mouth. She was frozen in place by the thousands of injections her attackers had given her. Her larynx was silenced forevermore. Her body began to tremble, and she fell into the bliss of unconsciousness.

Their mandibles sunk into her skin and pulled tiny chunks of skin and muscle from her throat, her legs and arms, her chest and cheeks, and then they tore at her eyeballs. They bit through her eardrums and slowly dug through its canals toward the delicious brain matter. They traveled up the opening between her legs and made their way to the inner organs in a maddening frenzy.

In just two and half minutes, Mary Sue lay against the wall in the corner of what was now her tomb. Her figure changed quickly as the hundreds of thousands of soldiers feverishly ate and drank in glorious victory. Only a few hundred were sacrificed in the battle, and most of them were eaten by their fellow soldiers.

Mary Sue now rested in peace, a horrendous end to her recently miserable life, and her children's fates now rested in the hands of the Commonwealth of Kentucky.

CHAPTER 2

— — — — — — —

RICHARD SAT IN HIS BEDROOM WITH HIS NOSE IN A BOOK
about the *Siafu* ant when his father burst through the door into his
sanctum.

"I should've known! Got your nose in a book about those damn
ants! What the hell's the matter with you! Every other kid's playing
football or baseball or basketball—or even getting laid, for Christ's
sake! Not my nerd brainchild! He's got his damn head in a book, and
his room is a damn insect museum! Your mother won't even come
into this room anymore!"

Richard sucked in a large amount of air and sighed heavily.
He was used to his father ranting and raving about him not being
interested in sports and not running around with any friends. He
tolerated his father calling him a nerd and an insect, but this thing
about not getting laid was new. Maybe it was because he had just
turned fifteen in December. He closed his eyes and waited for the
storm to pass.

"Get your ass downstairs! Your mother's got dinner on the table.
If I don't see you down there in two minutes, you and I will be going
round and round after dinner, hear?"

"Yeah. Okay, Dad. I'm on my way." Richard marked where he was
in his book and rose. His father, an ex-marine, enforced his strict
regulations with physical force, never asking questions. If he was
one minute late, Richard would feel his father's large fist on his face,
followed by the simple, highly intellectual statement: "You're late."

His mother was a great cook, especially her pastries and peanut butter fudge. Richard was glad he exercised a lot each day, something no one except his mother seemed to notice. He didn't want to get fat like his father.

He was greatly enjoying a piece of his favorite rhubarb pie, thinking he had made it through the meal unscathed, when his father began once again. "When are ya goin' ta get interested in girls?"

"He's only fifteen," Richard's mother interrupted.

"When I was fifteen, I had one in every town—and I didn't just kiss 'em either!"

"Not everyone is like you, dear. Besides, times are different."

"There you go butting in again! Times never change when it comes to sex. But you're right. He's not like me. He's a wuss. You queer or something?"

Richard's anger cup boiled over. He could take no more. He shot from his chair and gave his father a right to his left cheek that sent him out of his chair to the kitchen floor. He glared at his father on the floor with his fists clenched.

"No! Richard, please!" his mother pleaded.

"That's it! You want a piece of me? Well, c'mon. Let's see if you're a man or pussy, boy!"

Ross Denton shot to his feet and lunged at his son, lifting Richard over his head and throwing him into the refrigerator. The refrigerator sported a dent from Richard's body, but that was just the first of many battle scars it would receive during the next few moments.

Richard responded, and their sparring finally left the kitchen. In the dining room, the large table was turned over—and three chairs found new resting places in motley positions. The scuffle rolled into the living room, overturning the sofa and breaking the lamp on the end table.

After more than thirty minutes, both father and son were panting and breathing heavily on the living room floor. Richard's father nodded from his place on the floor, leaned against the overturned sofa, and waved his right hand to signal the fight was over. He painfully got up and slowly left the room.

Mother rushed to her son's side. "Oh, my God! Are you hurt?" She touched his cheek, and he winced. "Let me get some ice, sweetheart."

Richard remembered all the times his father had hit his mother in the car. "I'm okay, Mom, but I'll never let him hit you or me again." He ran his tongue around his lips, tasting the sweet blood, got to his feet, and went to his room.

His mother remained on her knees, sobbing into her hands.

Richard's older sister controlled their dad, but to Ivory's good fortune, she was at a pajama party with her friends. Her laughter filled the room whenever she entered, and she always had stories to tell her father. She loved her brother dearly and did more to protect him during his younger years at home than he did to protect her, but that would change from this day forward.

By the time Richard was a senior in high school, Ross had sent Ivory to study business at Carnegie Mellon in Pittsburgh, a short distance from their hometown of Aliquippa, Pennsylvania. He had always reminded his son that Ivory was the smart one in the family. Richard accredited his father's sour mood to his sister not being around.

Ross hadn't punched Richard since that fight three years ago, and over time, Richard's body had matured into a muscular, athletic one. Although he didn't participate in sports, his disciplined exercise and long runs would keep him in shape for a lifetime.

"I'm going to the University of Kansas, Mom," Richard announced one evening at dinner.

"That's wonderful, sweetheart! What are you going to study?"

"Bugs! Right?" his father said with disgust.

"Entomology. It's called entomology, Dad. And, yes, I'm going to specialize in ants. The University of Kansas has what I think is the best program for what I want."

"Well, I am *not* paying for you to study bugs!"

"Don't have to, Dad. Never expected you to. I got a scholarship. That's what *nerds* do, Dad. They get scholarships. You won't have to spend a dime on me!"

"That's wonderful! Oh, I'm so proud of you!" Mother exclaimed.

"Huh!" Ross snorted without looking up.

"Well, you won't have to shell out the fortune we have to for Ivory, dear," she offered softly, smiling endearingly at her son.

"Ivory will make an income with six digits a year! What's he going to make? Forty grand?"

"How much do you make, dear?" she said softly.

Mr. Denton was an appliance repairman for Sears. He stared furiously at his wife, rose, and left the table.

Mother and Richard smiled at each other.

CHAPTER 3

━ ━ ━ ━ ━ ━ ━ ━

RICHARD FINISHED AT THE TOP IN HIS CLASS AT THE University of Kansas and obtained his master's degree in science in advanced evolution at the University of Kentucky in Lexington. For diversion, he watched the thoroughbred horses being groomed and trained. He was especially interested in their behavior, but he never went to any horseraces—not even the great Kentucky Derby.

He returned to the University of Kansas for his doctorate in entomology; his doctorate thesis explained his research in ant DNA. DNA work with insects has become quite common, particularly involving bees and flies. Mexico was successful in developing a fly that rendered the offspring sterile, and the United States had reduced the aggressiveness of the African killer bees. Richard had referred to the DNA changes as a form of "cross-pollination."

Dr. Richard Denton worked at his alma mater—not so much for his loyalty to the university, but for the access to the advanced laboratories.

━ ━ ━ ━ ━ ━

Ann Kreindler pushed open the classroom door with "Bioscience" painted on its window. Three of her close friends followed at her heels, but they would soon split up because Ann always sat in the front row—and they preferred being farther back.

"Why don't you just send the professor a love letter and be done with it?" Charlotte said.

Ann gave her a disgusted look, and the others giggled.

"She'd be wasting her time," Taylor interjected. She was the serious one of the group.

"Yeah," Carol added. "He's untouchable."

"Or maybe he's just a fag," Charlotte said with a smile in Ann's direction.

Ann stopped walking, and the others stopped a step ahead of her and turned. "He is not a fag. Have you no respect for a man of such genius?" she hissed, and her eyes darted around the room to see who else was around.

"Ooh," they all chimed in response and then giggled some more.

"You be careful, Ann. You have a bright future. You're pretty much a genius yourself. You wouldn't be the first to destroy yourself by getting involved with a professor," Taylor said.

"Well. Maybe she could turn him. He does have a good body," Charlotte said.

"Oh, so you noticed?" Carol teased.

"Don't pay no mind to them, Ann," Taylor said. "He is the best professor at this university. More than half the students in this room are here because of his reputation—not because they really have such an interest in bioscience."

Professor Denton entered the room without looking at anyone and headed straight for his pulpit.

"Spread your legs nice and wide—and see if he notices. I hope you're wearing nothing at all," Charlotte whispered.

Ann huffed and took her seat while the others giggled and found theirs.

Richard gave his morning lecture, looking at everyone and no one, and then he headed to the university's park to relax, eat his daily peanut butter and jelly sandwich, and smoke two or three cigarettes before he continued to the university's bio lab to do the boring research they required of him.

— — — — — —

The lab phone rang, and Richard welcomed the interruption. The wall clock above the door read 4:12.

"Hello?"

"Richard?"

Silence ensued.

"It's Mike. How about a coffee? I'm buying."

"Oh, hi, M. Sure. Why not? Where?"

"Seattle's?"

"Okay."

"Are you okay? You sound … off."

"Yeah. Everything's fine. Just boring research is all."

"Ha, ha. Of course it is. Okay. Leave now. I don't want to be on my third cup by the time you get there."

Richard nodded and said, "Okay. I'm on my way in five."

"Good! See you there." The phone went dead.

Richard had few friends and wanted fewer. Dr. Michael Morton could be construed as his closest colleague (he had called him M&M once in front of others, and it had stuck—but now it was reduced to just M). Despite their relationship, Dr. Morton was more of an acquaintance to Richard. He really only had one person in the world he could call a friend, and he didn't live in town.

As he entered Seattle's Best Coffee Shop, he noticed Dr. Morton waving at him. He held up a coffee cup, and Richard joined him straightaway.

"How the hell are you? It's been, what, a month?"

"Yeah, I guess," Richard shrugged. He hadn't counted and really didn't care.

"Getting voluntary conversation out of you is difficult, so I'll just ask. What have you been doing besides working?"

Richard jerked his head up and looked into his friend's light blue eyes for a moment. "Besides work? Nothing." He shifted his gaze around in silence.

"Oops! Naturally. Silly question. Sorry. Haven't you even gotten laid?"

"Haven't found anyone since Linda," Richard responded flatly.

"Well, you don't have to marry them to have sex."

"I didn't. But I would've. I really blew that one."

"Yeah. At least you admit it. Your work was too much competition for her. But you got tons of girls who would jump in the sack with you in a second right in front of you every damn day. Give one or two of them a break."

"Yeah, sure. And lose my job in the process? No, thanks, M. I need the money. Besides, it's against school policy."

"What the hell you keep working out for then? Drink beer and eat pizza. Have fun! Let go a little! Let yourself develop the traditional beer barrel!"

"What's with the sex interrogation? You're married. The old lady cut you off or something?"

"As a matter of fact, she did." Michael chuckled. "Some stupid little bitch sent me a letter in the mail. Can you believe it? In the mail! My wife opened the letter, of course, since she doused the damn thing with perfume! Need I say more?"

"Nope. Enough said. Not the first time, either, is it?" Richard chuckled.

"Yeah, I know. Belinda is really in a huff. Haven't figured out how to get out of this one yet, but I will."

"I guess you'll just have to keep it dry for a while." Richard laughed out loud, and Michael joined him, bringing attention their way.

"Did you ever come up with a safe poison for that Japanese beetle plague in Nebraska?"

"Yes. As a matter of fact, I did. I'm working on a compound for the University of Texas right now. Oh, not to change the subject, but have you paid your electric bill this month?"

"Yeah," Richard said. "I think so."

Michael pulled out his cell phone and dialed.

Richard's phone rang, and he answered. "Hello?"

"It's me. I just wanted to see if you paid the phone bill." He laughed boisterously. "I'm still surprised you haven't been kicked out of that house you rented."

"Well, the rent I have on automatic payment."

"And since your check is automatically deposited, you don't have a problem with the rent. Good boy!"

"It's not all that bad."

"Yeah? Your car insurance current?"

Richard gave him a blank look.

"You are the model absentminded professor.'" He laughed. "The kind they write books about. Why did you ever move off campus? When you were in the Stouffer Place Apartments on Nineteenth Street, you were only a mile from work. You could have walked to work. And I'm sure it was cheaper than the house you rented with the discount you get for being a professor at the university."

"Simple. Privacy. There was always a lot of noise, lots of parties. You know, the life of the typical college student. The house is peaceful. The town population is sparse, and there's an open field in front of the house. It only has some kids playing baseball on the weekends every once in a while. It's quiet and peaceful."

"Yeah, but isn't it far away from everything? I mean, you've got to go twenty miles to see a movie. And how far away is the nearest grocery store?"

"I never go to the movies. I don't even watch TV except for the news every once in a while. There's a little grocery store right there in town. It's really convenient, and it has everything I need. Mary, the owner, is a real nice lady."

"A *real nice lady?* Do I sense something there? I mean, for you to say real nice about a woman is a lot!"

"No. Well. I never thought about it really. She is very pleasant to talk to. She extends me credit whenever I need it."

"Extends you credit? Extends you credit! Hey! Wake up and smell the coffee, my friend! She likes you. Invite her out to dinner. Get a life! Wow, look how red you turned."

"She's not that kind of woman. Her husband died a little ways back. I don't think she's interested in any kind of relationship."

"Oh, God! You are hopeless!"

Michael's phone rang, interrupting his thoughts.

"Well. Boss called. Gotta go. Got to watch my p's and q's for a while. Know what I mean? Really good to see you, Richard. And take that lady out. I'm serious."

"Yeah. Maybe I will."

Why did M really want to see me? She likes me? He smiled as he left the coffee shop, shook his head, and climbed into his white 1990 Ford F-150 pickup. He opened the glove box and pulled out the proof of insurance. Expired. He did mark his calendar to put gas in the vehicle each Friday. He was not worried about missing a class when Monday rolled around, but he was concerned about not getting home to continue his work in his basement.

Every spare penny he could get his hands on went toward the lab he had built in his cellar. The Maxwell House coffee cans with money rolled up in rubber bands had long been spent. He did, however, still enjoy the Maxwell House coffee and saved the cans, filling them with pocket change. On weekends, coffee constituted most of his diet.

He parked his truck in the driveway, picked up the mail from his black mailbox on the post at the front of the driveway, and made his way to the front door.

Richard tried the key and found he had left the door open again. He shrugged, stepped inside, and walked past the empty living room to the right. A noticeable haze of dust had destroyed the beauty of the dark hardwood floor. Light shone through the front window, which displayed no curtain of any kind.

He walked past the visitor's bathroom, which had been used no more than ten times in the past year—and only by him—and into the kitchen. He threw the mail on the table, and it landed on a pile of other unopened mail.

The door to his cellar lab was to his left. He placed a key into the bolt lock and slid the bolt to the right. After he placed a second key into another door lock, he opened the door. He turned and locked the door as soon as the threshold was crossed, descending the stairs into the world that awaited him below.

He spent quite a bit of money remodeling the basement to suit his needs, doing all the work himself for privacy. No one stepped into his sanctuary.

He walked across the white linoleum tiles with gold speckles to his office, glancing at the numerous large glass aquariums to his right. All seemed in order.

He walked past the white toilet in the back corner of his office and sat at his wooden double-pedestal desk he had bought at a garage sale. Four-millimeter thick glass covered the marred top. Two Dell computer systems occupied half of the desk; the monitors and keyboards side by side in the center of the desk, and the towers were on each side of the monitors. A Sony Vaio laptop sat on the left side of the desk. A cluster of notebooks, papers, yellow legal pads, and CDs haphazardly covered most of the remaining surface. A printer sat on the far right of the desk but was hardly noticeable with all the papers and books stacked on top of it. Two soiled coffee cups were atop the towers. A box of Kleenexes showed its existence only because of a tissue sticking up proudly from the box. A University of Kansas pencil box jutted from the papers, and a few pens and pencils waved their existence but drowned among the clutter.

He had installed an acoustical tiled ceiling and connected the house's central air ducts to the basement. It didn't work as well as the rest of the house, but it was satisfactory.

After a short while at his computers, he moved on to inspect his ant farms. He continued on to his lab along the right wall below and to the right of one of the cellar windows.

Black Formica-topped counters were crowded with Bunsen burners, Erlenmeyer flasks, large and small test tubes in their holders, and beakers taking haphazard positions on available spaces. A drying rack sat against the wall to the right of a stainless steel double sink. Scrub pads, sponges, and test tube brushes cluttered the sink. Two power scopes and an inverted scope sat patiently farther down on the counter. A box of coverslips and a box of new slides waited by each of the microscopes.

Under the lab counter, he had built wooden cabinets and painted them white. They held glassware, syringes, rubber gloves, and an array of glass-bottled chemicals that were each neatly labeled.

Richard worked till his eyes burned. When his watch read 2:05, he went across the room and heated up a cup of noodles in the microwave, which sat on a table made of pine two-by-fours with a half-inch plywood top.

He eased himself into a faded blue couch he had been given by a neighbor who was going to throw it in the garbage. A bed pillow at one end showed telltale signs of needing a fresh pillowcase. A small blanket was balled up at the other end of the couch.

He reached down to the floor absentmindedly and slid the button to the left to turn on the alarm on the floor. The alarm would go off at six, beginning another typical weekday for Dr. Denton.

CHAPTER 4

▬ ▬ ▬ ▬ ▬ ▬ ▬ ▬ ▬

ON SATURDAYS AND SUNDAYS, RICHARD NORMALLY SLEPT in for a couple of hours, made himself a hearty breakfast in his kitchen upstairs, and hid himself away in his den of ants.

His cell phone, which he had never taken off his belt, rang at 8:10. "Hello?"

"You up?"

"I am now. Who's this?"

"Bill Tucker."

"Bill!" He bolted upright. A smile spread across Richard's face in recognition of his only real friend from Maysville, Kentucky. They had met years ago at a tractor pull event. He shook the cobwebs out of his head and began putting a pot of coffee on to start his weekend.

"How the hell are you? Haven't heard from you in a while. What's up?"

"How about breakfast, genius. Think your ants could spare you for an old friend?"

"Only for you." He chuckled, but he meant it. "You're here in Lawrence?" He stopped his process of coffee preparation.

"Yeah. Had one of those boring law enforcement conferences in Topeka. It ended yesterday, but I told the old lady I wanted to stay over and see my Dr. Ant buddy since I was so close."

"Glad you did. Where are you?"

"Where else would a hillbilly stay? At a Motel 6 on I-70. I'm not a high roller like you."

"Motel 6s are just fine for me. Believe me. You know you could stay here. Save you some bread. Where should I meet you?"

"Thanks, but I thought maybe I could convince you to go to Kansas City with me. Haven't been to a big city in a while. Maybe get us some poontang while we're there."

"I don't think Sue Ann would appreciate that. You mean the whole weekend?"

"Hell, yes! The whole weekend. It's only one night, Doc. C'mon! Don't spoil my once-a-year weekend. Knowing you, you haven't got your dick wet in a while with your nose in your labs instead of where it should be. I don't see how you can resist all that young stuff around you. God, I'd be divorced in a year."

"You'd also lose your job in a month. And you wouldn't do that to Sue Ann, either."

"Yeah, maybe, but I'd sure be happy until I was caught. So pack an overnight bag and get in that old pickup of yours and get out here and have breakfast with me. We'll leave for Kansas City after breakfast. I don't want to hear any excuses, hear? See you in what … half an hour? I'm in 106."

The phone went dead. Richard smiled. That was Bill. He left him no choice. Richard dropped a field mouse in his main aquarium, which he had positioned directly under the cellar window so it would get direct light. In seconds, his best creation swarmed the squealing mouse, but it only suffered for a few seconds.

He told himself he could use the break—and didn't M just tell him he needed to get out? Jesus, it has been a long time since he'd seen Bill.

He shook his head, and a chill went down his spine while looking at his creation work.

"If you all ever got out," he whispered, "I don't even want to think about it."

There were five new giant queens and two dozen males on top of the mound, drying their wings and ready to mate. They would probably mate tomorrow. He would have to make another aquarium when he got back.

"Just how long are you going to let the colony grow, Richard? When will it be enough? You already have five colonies. And what now, genius?"

He climbed up the cellar stairs, locked both locks, threw a change of clothes in a KU tote bag, grabbed a KU coffee cup for Bill, and climbed into his pickup.

Maybe I should get myself some poontang. He smiled to himself and shook his head.

He stopped by an ATM and withdrew a hundred dollars. His balance showed $274.83. Payday was still another week away. He felt a pang of guilt about how he had handled his credit. He had credit cards once, but he kept forgetting to pay them—and they canceled his credit. Collectors sent lots of mail and kept calling him, but he rarely opened his mail and didn't return calls. They finally filed suit against him. He could have paid them, but there was always some lab equipment he needed that was more important. And then there was that trip to Africa to get his *Paraponera* queen and *Siafu* male.

When he arrived at Motel 6, Bill was waiting outside with a small suitcase. He had already checked out. "Hi, Doc," he said as he hopped into the truck, throwing his bag in the backseat. "There's a McDonald's just up the road here. A couple of Egg McMuffins will hit the spot. My treat."

"McDonald's?"

"Yeah, that's so we don't waste a lot of time. I've got a surprise for you, Doc. You'll see."

"McDonald's is just fine with me," he said with a shrug.

It only took twenty minutes to devour two McMuffin Trios each while they began to catch up on each other's lives.

Sue Ann had just gotten a hysterectomy, which was why Bill was thinking about looking for some relief. His youngest son, Charlie, drove a tanker for BP and spent most of his time on the road. Bill's two girls were still just housewives and took care of his grandkids. His oldest, Bill, Jr., recently became the chief accountant for Browning Manufacturing in Maysville. There didn't seem to be much to catch up on with Richard.

As they arrived in the city, Richard asked, "Are you going to tell me where we're going—or are you going to keep it a secret until we get into Missouri?"

"Exit on Argosy Parkway."

"Argosy Parkway? Okay, I'll bite. What's on Argosy Parkway?"

"You'll see. Patience, Doc."

They turned on Argosy Parkway, which was actually in Riverside, Missouri. A little ways down, they came to a large lighted sign that read "Argosy Casino."

"Turn in here," Bill ordered.

"A casino? Whoa, Bill. I don't have money for a casino."

"Relax, Bubba. The room's free, the meals are free, and you only spend what you want to spend on the slots. Neither one of us has the money for the tables. I even have coupons they sent me for fifty bucks to play the slots with."

"Since when do you gamble, Bill?"

"Since last year when a guy at the convention took a few of us here. I won $1,800; can you believe it? Don't you tell Sue Ann. They sent me a card telling me I could stay a night for free, and they would give me fifty bucks to play with—and the buffet would be free. I know you hardly go anywhere. Have you ever been to a casino?"

"Well I'm not exactly dead, you know. I went to Las Vegas with Linda once … back when we were together."

"That's it? That was what … eight years ago? For Christ's sake."

"Well. I'm not into casinos."

"You're not into anything, Doc … except ants. One of these days, you're going to turn into one. You're going to live a little tonight though. Guaranteed. Don't worry. It won't kill ya. And your ants will be there when you get back."

Richard smiled and nodded as he pulled up to the hotel

entrance. Bill was just what he needed right now. Bill insisted on valet parking.

While Bill took care of the room arrangements, Richard looked around at the elegant pink tile floor with wine curved designs in it and the chairs upholstered with fabrics of green, wine, and pink. The large windows curved at the top. The wrought iron reminded Richard of Bill's jail cell.

Bill opened the door to their room, stepped aside for Richard, and said, "Well, Doc. What do ya think?"

"Wow. Elegant, isn't it?"

Two queen-sized beds with white plush comforters lined one wall, a brown easy chair with matching hassock sat by the window, a maple wooden desk and wooden high back chair upholstered in yellow fabric sat along the left wall by the window, a flat-screen TV was hung on the wall and was surrounded by black rectangles of wood, which had absolutely no function, and the pink carpet featured a wine-flowered pattern.

He walked into the bathroom, noticing a marble countertop, yellow-patterned wallpaper, and a large glass shower stall with yellow tiles, including an inlay of tiles that formed a huge flowerpot with a plant growing out of it. Another door led to a white commode.

Bill turned on the TV and found the Pittsburgh Steelers/Green Bay game. Even though the Bengals were closer, Bill was an avid Steeler fan. Richard really didn't care about any team, but since he hailed from Aliquippa, he felt obligated to share Bill's enthusiasm for Pittsburgh.

Richard pulled his wrinkled change of clothes out of his bag and placed it in the top drawer of the black dresser under the TV.

Bill threw his clothes in the second drawer, pulled out a twelve-pack of MGDs, a bag of Ruffles, a bag of Fritos scoops, and a jar of Fritos red salsa, and placed it all on the nightstand between the two beds.

"Plop yourself down, Doc. I'll get the ice. Do me a favor and put the beer in the sink."

Bill came back shortly and poured the ice over the beer. Richard tried to explain his project to the only living person he felt he could trust, but Bill's attention was distracted half the time with the game. Bill would nod or grunt every once in a while, but he did catch some parts.

"You mean to tell me you have man-eating ants in your house— and you sleep there?"

"They're not man-eating ants, Bill. They're carnivorous. They eat rodents and small animals."

"And if I sat on their mound, they would just say, 'Hello, there'?"

"Well, of course they would attack—just the same as a fire ant would attack anyone who disturbed its mound."

"There ya go! Man-eating ants."

Bill's simple comment made Richard pensive.

When the game finished (Pittsburgh 27, Green Bay 21) they showered, changed clothes, and made their way to the Terrace Buffet. Bill insisted on paying half of Richard's $21.99.

Full to the point of feeling sick, both friends, intent on enjoying their rare jaunt of freedom and "wildness," although for different reasons, made their way to the casino. Five tall columns made of three pillars each reminded them of the Roman coliseums, but the archways joining the columns had some kind of Indian design. Neither had any idea of worldly architecture like Vegas. A stained-glass dome made both look up and take a moment to comment on how much it had to cost to build.

Going through the doors, they stepped onto a carpet of oranges, browns, and blues. Rows of slot machines sang constantly with green- or brown-cushioned seats with matching backs.

In the middle of a sectioned-off area, there was a large lighted sign that said Double Diamond with multi-pointed stars that shone in reds and blues. Bill explained they were progressive twenty-five-cent slots (the pot read $1,313.48), but you had to bet the max of three coins to win.

They meandered about the casino, found two vacant machines, and took a seat. Bill inserted two twenty-dollar bills, and Richard inserted one. Bill bet two coins, or fifty cents a throw, while Richard bet one coin.

"Drinks, gentlemen?"

A cocktail waitress stood between them in what resembled a black Playboy outfit, showing her natural abundance. Bill ordered an MGD, and Richard ordered a scotch and water.

"Like those boobs, Doc?"

"Sure. I'm not blind."

"Well, we'll see if we can't hustle up some to take with us in a little bit."

"Oh, yeah. I'm sure we'll be overcome with so many young chicks just dying for us to get into their pants." Richard chuckled.

They looked around the casino, and mostly elderly customers were playing the machines. They looked at each other and laughed.

"The night's young, Doc. Younger poontang will start showing up. Trust me."

The free booze and their good luck made them lose all track of time. Every time they changed machines, they would look for two more adjacent vacant machines.

When Richard began to drop his head while pushing the buttons, he began betting max on the three-coin machines. By four o'clock, Bill was up $180—and Richard had taken in over $300.

"The breakfast buffet opens at seven, and I'm starving," Bill said.

"I don't know if I can stay awake another three hours."

"Have some coffee then. We're on a roll. Besides, when's the last time you got out like this?"

"Not since Linda." Richard laughed softly, thinking back to how he and Linda walked the strip, wanting to see every hotel and as many shows as they could afford.

"Man, you gotta get out more. I'm serious, man."

"Where have I heard that before? What about that poontang you were talking about?"

"Someone finally feeling their oats?"

"I probably couldn't get it up in my state, anyway."

They both laughed boisterously and continued their play.

Breakfast sobered them up enough to call it quits before they gave all their winnings back. They retired and got in five hours of shut-eye before making their way back to Lawrence.

On Saturday afternoon, twenty boys were playing baseball in an empty field. Each team used four outfielders. The boys were mostly from the high school, and the few who were in junior high were brothers of the high school students.

They brought their own equipment: bases, wooden and aluminum bats, well-used hardballs, helmets, gloves, and cleats. They had even built a pitcher's mound the year before.

No fences surrounded the field, and Dr. Denton's house loomed across the street past left field as the only home around.

The baseball game ended around five, but a few stayed around to practice hitting flies. One of the boys got a good one off that landed on Dr. Denton's front lawn and crashed through his cellar window.

With that, the practice ended. The boys left the scene quickly, voluntarily donating their grass-stained baseball to Dr. Denton.

By the time he dropped Bill off at the airport in Topeka and returned to Lawrence, the bell had tolled midnight. Richard went straight to his seldom-used bedroom and crashed. Tomorrow, it was back to the grindstone for his Monday morning class.

As he turned on the alarm and closed his eyes, he thought, *I could never live a life like that.*

CHAPTER 5

■ — ■ — ■ — ■ — ■ — ■

ANXIOUS TO GET HOME TO HIS LAB, DR. DENTON CUT HIS afternoon lab time at the university down to two hours. He didn't remember ever leaving his life's work for so long.

When he arrived home, he hurriedly unlocked the cellar door and ran down the stairs. When he got to the bottom step, he froze. There were bits of glass around the largest ant farm that housed his prized hybrid.

His heart beat wildly as he realized the winged males and queens were gone. He looked around frantically and noticed the broken cellar window.

Guilt overwhelmed him, and he sunk to his knees. He put his head in his hands and began to sob. In the back of his mind, he knew this day would come, but he had continually erased it from his mind each. Every time, it resurfaced like a balloon of air pushed back down below the surface of the water.

He slowly made his way to his feet like a tired old man, his tears blurring his vision. He wiped the tears with the back of his hands, took a deep breath, and began to survey the damage in more detail.

The culprit, the grass-stained baseball, was in the aquarium with several pieces of glass around it. The ants seemed at ease now, still repairing the damage to their chambers. Thank God he had a lot of glass above the dirt line of the mound and had thought about coating the glass with graphite.

He had a window screen that was much too large for the

aquarium, but it would do to protect the farm until he could make another piece of perforated glass. This time, he would use a thick acrylic and glue screening over the ventilating holes. He had thought of this before (many times), but the acrylic wouldn't give him the clear view from the top that glass gave, especially after time.

I guess I should replace the other tank tops too.

He carefully lifted the baseball out of the tank with a pair of tongs, placed it on the counter, and used large tweezers to pluck the glass out of the tank. He let the pieces fall to the floor along with the rest of the broken glass. There was minimal disturbance. Some soldiers came out to check things out, but they didn't seem too excited.

After cleaning the glass from the floor, he fed his ants. The other two farms were different hybrids. They were less aggressive and not as large as the farm whose queens got away, which were a mixture of the *Paraponera clavata*, the *Dorylus* (driver ant), and the *Formicium giganteum* (giant ant).

The venom of the *Paraponera* paralyzed the lab mouse in short order. His experimentation with the giant ant's DNA allowed the new species to grow to five centimeters. He had been proud of his success in creating the largest ant in the world. The aggressiveness of the driver ant was nothing short of frightening. The colony population had grown enough to devour the lab mouse in approximately ten minutes, leaving only the skeleton for the doctor to extract.

He went over to the lab counter and examined the baseball with a large magnifying glass. He could see thousands of punctures in the leather covering.

Why didn't they build their way out of the aquarium, a common characteristic of the driver? He looked around the entire floor for signs of his creation. *Surely they would have found you by now, Doc, if any were free.*

Satisfied he had secured the situation, Richard went to his desk and plopped himself in his chair. He reached for the lower right-hand drawer and pulled out a fresh bottle of Glenlivet. He brought the bottle to his lips and began writing in his notebook.

He remembered there were at least five queens—all seven to eight centimeters in length. No telling where they would begin their nests. At their new size, they had the strength to fly hundreds of miles. He took another large swallow of his medicine. There would be no stopping these. He looked at the baseball on his desk.

"The catalyst of a holocaust," he whispered to himself and took another good hit on his elixir. The frequent shots of scotch began taking their soothing effect.

His classes became shallow over the next couple of months, giving students easy assignments, grading flexibly, coming to class with scotch on his breath, and practically avoiding any lab work at the university.

He found a note on his desk to see Dean Snyder after class on the last day of classes before the Christmas holidays.

When he arrived at the dean's office, the dean's secretary greeted him coldly. "Please have a seat. The dean will be with you in a moment." The young, attractive brunette with a good figure wore a tight coral-blue wool pullover sweater and a short black wool skirt.

Thoughts of some late-night work with the dean crossed his mind, and a thin smile crept across his face.

"You can go in now, Dr. Denton," she announced with a cold tone as if she knew what the purpose of his visit was.

"Thank you," Richard said and entered the dean's office.

Dean Snyder didn't get up to welcome Dr. Denton. He nodded in silence for him to sit in one of the brown leather chairs in front of his large oak double-pedestal desk. A wall of bookshelves held books Dr. Denton had no interest in.

Dr. Snyder was a Wharton graduate in business administration and had a doctorate in education. His wavy, silver-gray hair reminded Richard of President Clinton. His height allowed him to carry his excess weight well. His cold, hazy blue eyes centered on

31

Dr. Denton. "I won't waste your time and beat around the bush," he began.

"Please don't." Richard noted a red stain on the right shoulder of the dean's blue pinstriped suit. A picture of the dean in a football uniform sat behind him on one of the bookshelves.

"You are one of the most knowledgeable professors on campus … but you seem to have a problem lately."

"Problem?" Dr. Denton shrugged as if he didn't know what he was talking about. Inside he wanted to say, "You have no idea!"

"I have had numerous complaints by students and various comments by teachers about you lately … none good."

Dr. Denton sat in expectant silence.

"Do you have anything to say in your defense?"

Am I in a courtroom? A defense? "Defense against what? You haven't told me what the complaints or the comments are."

The dean nodded in understanding. "Okay, then. I'll spell it out for you. You come to class under the influence—a direct violation of policy—you miss classes, and you are not teaching. Instead, you are just giving them assignments to do. You haven't progressed in our research for months. Is that enough—or do you need to hear more?"

"I see. I have changed some of my tactics, yes, but I have never drunk a drop of any kind of liquor on campus. What else can I tell you?"

"Nothing, Doctor. I don't agree with your change of tactics, and I can't accept any professor coming to class with alcohol on his or her breath as you have right now. I can smell it from here. You obviously have some problems to work out. However, you're going to have to work them out on your own time—not the university's time. I'm afraid there won't be a position here for you next semester."

Richard looked down at his hands for a moment, puckered his lips, and shrugged. "Whatever." He stood and left the dean with his mouth open. As he went by the dean's secretary, he noticed her lips were red. "Humph! Whatever."

"Excuse me, Dr. Denton?"

He turned to face her after pulling the door open. The sign on her desk read Grace Kohler.

"Nothing, Grace." He smiled knowingly. "Enjoy."

He went to his classroom and lab to pick up his handful of personal items and left for his pickup.

He actually felt like a load had been lifted from his shoulders. His severance pay would be enough to last him several months at least—maybe even a year if he was frugal.

He stopped by a liquor store on the way home.

"Hi, Dale. A case of Glenlivet, please."

"Hi, Dr. Denton. We got Glenfiddich on special for almost half the price. It's also a single malt."

"Good deal. Thanks."

Richard stopped at the grocery store by his house. A little buzzer rang when he opened the door.

"Hi, Richard," Mary said.

"Hi, Mary. Going to do some serious shopping today. I'll have to write you a check."

"No problem. Want help?"

He handed her a list he had prepared before leaving the university.

Mary owned Mary's Family Groceries and lived above the store. It served the small community, and she did moderately well. Her husband had died four years earlier at the early age of forty-six in a car accident, and Mary had not decided to see anyone else yet, which was an easy task in a small town. She knew her clients on a first-name basis and served as the cashier most of the time.

"Wow, Dr. Richard. You stocking up for the winter?"

"Yeah, I guess you might say that," he answered.

"Everything all right, Dr. Richard? You look kind of beat … if you don't mind me saying so."

"Had a tough year, Mary. Going to take some time off. How are you holding up?"

"All right. Can't complain. Business is good as usual. Steady. You know, pays the bills."

"Don't you see your parents or kids?"

"My parents are in Philadelphia, too far away. My daughter, Mary, is in Florida. She got married. Had to, the idiot. He's an insurance salesman. Can you believe it?"

"Ha, ha. Wow. The stories really are true?"

"They painfully are." She laughed. "Anyway, she's too far away too. John's in Boston, getting his master's at MIT, costing me a fortune, but he works part time and helps … a little."

"Mom's left all alone to take care of the business. Shame," he said. He thought Mary was a really nice lady. She was nothing special in looks or figure—typically average—but she had a great personality. She deserved better. He enjoyed his visits to the store, and Mary was easy to talk to. M's conversation in the coffee shop popped into his mind.

"One gets used to it," Mary said. "You should know. Seeing anyone lately?"

"Naw. Who wants a boring professor?"

"Don't sell yourself short. You work too much, Dr. Richard."

"I guess I could say the same about you, Mary."

"And you'd be right."

"Well, I'm going to have some time on my hands now. Maybe we can take in a movie or something." He was surprised at how easy that was to say.

"I think I would like that very much, Dr. Richard." She smiled sheepishly.

"So would I, really. And please call me Richard."

"Okay," she said softly. "$142.56."

"What?"

"The food you bought. It's $142.56."

"Oh, yes … sorry. Thought you were referring to what it would cost me to take you to a movie. My mind was somewhere else." He pulled out his checkbook. "Do I owe you anything from the past?"

"No. That's all."

"I'll call you."

"I'll be waiting."

When Richard left, she put his check in her purse instead of the cash drawer.

▬ ▬ ▬ ▬ ▬

Sally had been working for Mary ever since her husband died three years ago while trying to put out a fire as a volunteer fireman for the town. He had left her with four children and no insurance. "Mary!" she said. "What are you doing?"

"What do you mean?'"

"You know he still owes you eighty-some dollars from last month."

"Richard? No, he doesn't. He paid me. I just forgot to note it."

"Well … he's … you know … a loner. One of those crazy professors."

"Why, Sally, I never noticed!"

"And he's not responsible either. Half the time, he doesn't pay for his groceries—and you know it."

"Dr. Denton always pays his bills, Sally. Sometimes he's late, but he does pay."

"Well, you can't go out with him anyway."

"Why the hell not?"

"Mary! You'd be the talk of the town. You know how people are. What if they stop coming to shop here?"

"I don't believe you, Sally. Where are they going to go? The closest store is a good ten country miles from here. Besides, everyone keeps telling me to go out. Maybe I just will."

"Well, they're referring to someone from out of town. I'm just trying to save you from a scandal, is all … as a friend. I certainly wouldn't tell anybody."

"A scandal? For going out with Dr. Richard?"

"Well, you know. They say he's, you know, homosexual."

"Homosexual? Where do you get that?"

"Well, that's just the local gossip. I mean, he never, you know, has any female company and all."

"And that's exactly why I wouldn't want anyone in town knowing my personal business. I wonder what they call me. A *dyke*? Dr. Richard is a very nice person, I'll have you know. He's extremely intelligent—"

"And available," Sally interrupted. "He does look like he's in good shape and all, but—"

"He's a loner and a crazy scientist. You told me. And homosexual, I almost forgot."

"I'm sorry. I guess it's not any of my business. It's just that I'm indebted to you. I don't want you to get hurt, you know."

Mary sighed. "That's very sweet of you Sally, but I can take care of myself. I have been for a few years now."

"Yes, you have. And well. They say the nerds are good in bed." She giggled.

"Sally! I really wouldn't know personally—and where do you get these ideas from?"

"I guess when we need to get laid, it doesn't really matter what they are, does it?"

They both laughed.

Mary shook her head, and then the phone rang. It was back to business.

— — — — — —

Richard checked his Internet twice a day for news. He didn't want to, and he never used to, but he felt obligated now. When his existing inventory of mice ran out, he stopped feeding his ant farms. He fed himself a constant onslaught of his elixir.

As time went by, unshaven and unbathed for weeks on end, he lived in a stupor of floating misery. He slept on his couch or at his desk and lingered like a fall leaf waiting for its final moment to float to the earth. He was oblivious to the messages on the phone he had unplugged from the wall and the mail that was screaming for space in his mailbox.

The February cold penetrated his box of wretchedness through the broken windowpane that was patched with a piece of cardboard. Snow covered his house and the surrounding land like a blanket covering up his deep dark secret—even his ants seemed to be hibernating deep in their chambers.

An array of cans of Campbell's baked beans, Libby's baby lima beans, Spaghetti-O's, Del Monte peas, and corn were scattered about the desk and floor along with three empty boxes of Oreo cookies, various bottles of Gatorade, water, and Cokes. Half a loaf of moldy bread sat on top of the small refrigerator. Packs of crumpled Marlboros cluttered the floor with an opened carton on his desk and two unopened ones on top of the filing cabinet. A few petri dishes, which had been used as ashtrays, were on his desk, but many of the butts had made their way to the floor.

Where are you? Maybe, by some miracle, they all died.

CHAPTER 6

━━━　━━━　━━━　━━━　━━━

"MARY'S GROCERIES."

"May I speak with Mary, please?"

"This is she."

"Mary. You don't know me. My name is Bill Tucker. I'm a very close friend of Dr. Richard Denton."

"Dr. Richard. Yes, of course."

"Has he been around lately?"

"Around? Well, actually, not lately. As a matter of fact, I haven't seen him for a few of months now. He came in and bought a lot of groceries a while back and hasn't been in since."

"I've been trying to call him for a week now. I really need to talk to him. It's really important."

"Well, to tell you the truth, Dr. Richard said he was going to call me, but he never did. Not surprising, really. He's a scientist, and he does a lot of research or something. He took some time off, he said."

"Time off? What do you mean?"

"Yes. He said he was taking a year off ... if I remember correctly. He looked really worn, too, if you know what I mean. I told him he looked like he needed a rest."

"I don't know how well you know him, but it sounds like you do. What are the chances of you going and knocking on his door? Tell him to call me?"

"Well, I know where he lives, of course. It's a small town, but I've never been inside his house, Mr. Tucker."

"I'm sure you haven't, Mary. Knowing Richard, no one has. But I do know that Doc thinks very highly of you, and I know he likes and respects you. As a matter of fact, you are the only female name he has mentioned to me. I wouldn't ask you the favor, but it's a matter that's really important. It's scientific."

"Oh. Well … uh … I guess I could do that … being scientific and all,"

"Mary. Believe me, I know Richard very well. He's a loner. He gets out very rarely, but he's really a nice guy. Women don't get much of a chance to know him. He lives in his ant world."

"Ant world? Is that what he does? Researches ants?"

"Yes. And he's the best there is, Mary—internationally."

"Oh. I see."

"Will you do that for me? Just knock on his door and tell him to call me?"

"All right. What's your number?"

"I assure you he has it. Just tell him Bill Tucker called and that he should call me immediately. It's *extremely* important. You could even say it's a matter of life or death."

"It's not really, is it?"

"What?"

"A matter of life or death?"

"No, Mary. Well, it may be actually. But it may be necessary to say that to get him to stop his research long enough to make the call."

"Oh, I see." She chuckled. "Okay, I get you. I'll run up there and see if he answers."

"If he doesn't answer, go in. He won't mind. I wouldn't be surprised if the absentminded professor left his front door open."

"Really? He leaves the front door open?"

"Not intentionally, but he has on several occasions."

"Wow. Okay. Uh … why don't you give me your number so I can call you if he's not home."

"Good thinking, Mary. Oh, and Mary, my friend says you are the only woman he feels totally comfortable talking to."

"Really? He really said that?"

"Yes. And that's a lot for him. Believe me. He's not much on socializing, and he's very shy and awkward with the ladies, but he's one of the smartest guys I know. He's a real quality guy."

"Yes. He is kind of a loner, isn't he?"

"Yeah, but only because of his dedication to his work. Get him out of town—and he'll loosen up."

"I guess you're probably right."

"I know I am. Will you do me the favor?"

"Tell him to call you? Sure, Mr. Tucker."

"Please call me Bill."

"Okay, Bill. I'll go within the hour."

"Thanks, Mary. Bye."

— — — — — —

Mary knocked on the door and waited for an answer. She tried again. After the third time, she tried the doorknob and smiled. The door was open. She shook her head, stepped inside, and slowly closed the door behind her.

"Richard?" No answer.

"Dr. Richard?" she repeated louder. No answer.

The living room had no furniture, and the hardwood floor looked like it hadn't been cleaned in months—or longer. She chuckled softly and shook her head. "Typical man."

The kitchen table had a large pile of mail. She added the large stack of mail she found stuffed in the mailbox to the pile, being careful it didn't fall off. She ran her finger along the tabletop, shook her head, and stacked the mail by envelope size.

She opened the refrigerator timidly, a little fearful of what might be there. She found half a head of lettuce—still in the plastic and soggy with mildew—several cans of V8, a tub of margarine, and two tomatoes with white mold on the first shelf.

The contents in the refrigerator door showed signs of more

frequent use. Eggs filled most of the spaces designed by the refrigerator on the first shelf. The second shelf boasted a collection of KFC ketchup, Taco Bell hot sauces, and an array of other small plastic envelopes of mayonnaise, relish, and mustard. She wrinkled her nose and closed the door.

"Richard?" No answer.

She looked around the kitchen and explored some drawers until she found a package of unopened washcloths. In twenty minutes, the refrigerator was respectable again, the countertop was bright, and the kitchen smelled clean.

She tried a door off the kitchen, but found it locked. She knocked hard.

"Dr. Richard?" she yelled out bravely.

"Hello?" A voice barely discernable came from below and beyond the locked door.

"Hello? Richard!" she yelled out with more confidence.

"Who is it?" The voice seemed to be coming closer.

"It's Mary ... from the store."

"Mary?"

Mary heard him climbing the steps and the lock being opened. She waited nervously for Richard to appear.

"Mary! What a nice surprise," Richard said as he turned around and locked the door. "What brings you here?"

She was taken aback by his appearance. "I'm really sorry for barging into your home. I knocked several times. The door was open. I yelled out several more times—"

"No problem." Richard held his hands up to stop her. "You are welcome any time you want. I left the door open again, I see." He laughed. "The absentminded professor. At least it was fortunate this time."

"Your friend Bill called. He said it was a matter of life or death that you call him. I would never have entered your home otherwise."

"Bill?" Silence ensued for a long minute that felt more like five.

"I see," he said slowly, his smile turning into a painful expression. His clothes were badly wrinkled, his face was unshaven, and his body odor was offensive. "Sorry. I, uh, get carried away in the lab. Haven't been upstairs really in a while. You don't want to see downstairs. It's a mess. Thank you for coming though. I, uh, will call him right away."

"Okay," she said. "I guess I'll be going then." She quickly made her way toward the front door and stopped. "Oh, by the way. You never called."

"Called?"

"The movie?"

"What? Oh, yes! The movie! I'm really sorry. I ... uh." He shook his head.

"Umm, if you want, I could help you clean up a little here."

Since he didn't answer, Mary left.

He watched the door close behind her. He wanted to stop her, tell her he needed her, and tell her he had stood her up. He had never needed someone to lean on more than now—a companion, someone he could share his burden with, someone who would want to share his problem. He shook off the wave of feeling sorry for himself and reached for his phone.

"Doc? Thank God!"

"How did you know it was me?"

"Modern technology. Caller ID. Ever hear of it?"

"Oh, yeah. I never really look at who's calling." He thought for a moment. "I get very few calls, anyway."

"Ha. Amazing. Yeah. Listen, Doc. I need you to get down here to Maysville."

"Okay. Why? Is something wrong?"

"I know you are wrapped up in your lab, but I don't want to hear any ... what?"

"I said okay. I will need some money for the flight."

"I think you'll be here for a while, Doc. I'll deposit some money for gas in your account. Pack a suitcase. You'll stay at my place."

"What's it all about, Bill. Something wrong? Sue Ann all right? Mary mentioned something about a life-or-death situation."

"That's exactly what I need you here for. You need to tell me. All I can tell you is it's about ants."

"Ants? What about them?"

"Are you okay, Bubba? You sound really on edge."

"Yeah. I'm fine. Just send me the money. I'll take off tomorrow morning."

"Great. See you the day after tomorrow. My house. Remember how to get here?"

"Yeah. Sure."

"Okay. Thanks. See ya."

"Yeah. Bye." *Maybe you should put me in your jail cell.*

Bill snapped his phone closed and pondered.

CHAPTER 7

━━ ━━ ━━ ━━ ━━ ━━

RICHARD TOOK A DEEP BREATH, LET OUT A LONG SIGH, AND shook his head. He went to the refrigerator to see if there was a bottle of water left. No water, but his refrigerator was clean. *Mary.* He closed his eyes. He had a flashing thought about Ann, but he shook her out of his mind. She would understand the science, but she'd report him to the authorities in a minute.

He climbed down the stairs, shuffled over to his desk, and pulled out the familiar green bottle.

He walked over to where his creation had escaped from, took a long draft, and coughed. Salty tears welled and made their way down his cheeks to the corners of his mouth.

I should have destroyed those months ago. He then told himself to destroy what was left of them now. *I'll do it as soon as I get back.*

He felt old and weary. After this nightmare ended, he would make good on his offer to Mary. It would be nice to have someone to share his life with, if she would even see him, and that would be a big if. What life, Doc?

He went upstairs to his bedroom that he had estranged, showered, shaved, and threw some clothes into a suitcase. It had been just about a year ago that he and Bill had gone to the casino. He'd been drunk ever since. He couldn't even remember when he had his last meal—or even snack for that matter. Should he leave his medicine? Naw. He was sure he would need it even more soon.

He stopped by the grocery store on the way out. A customer had temporarily attached herself to Mary.

"Can I help you, Dr. Denton?" Sally asked menacingly.

Richard was somewhat taken aback. "Uh. No. No, thank you. I, uh, need to speak with Mary for a second is all."

Sally looked into Richard's eyes with intensity and then said in a low voice, "If you ever hurt that girl, I will kill you with my bare hands." She then stalked away, leaving Richard with his eyes wide and mouth open.

"Hi, Richard. Well, we look a lot better this morning. Everything all right? Were you able to get ahold of your friend? Bill, isn't it?"

"Yeah—yes. Uh, I got to go to Maysville, Kentucky."

"Is that where the life-or-death emergency is?"

"Yes. It is."

"How long will you be gone?"

"Oh, I really don't know, to tell you the truth." He shrugged his shoulders. "Maybe a week?"

"Did you lock your door?"

Richard rolled his eyes and winced.

"Give me your key. I'll lock it for you. And take a vacuum with me." She smiled.

"You don't have to do that, but that would be great." He chuckled as he took off his house key and handed it to her. "It's the only one I have—never bothered to get a copy."

"You didn't use it much anyway from what I hear, but I'll take care of it. You just do what you got to do. I'll be here when you get back."

"Uh. You can't go into the lab. It's not that I don't trust you …"

"Don't worry. I'll leave your lab alone. I don't want anything to do with ants, anyway. And you got enough locks on that door to keep everyone out. I bet you didn't forget to lock that door."

"Well. Yeah. It's uh … well it can be dangerous … and I wouldn't want you to get hurt in any way."

"Well now. Isn't that sweet."

"You know … you are one of kind, Mary," he said tenderly.

45

"So are you. I think. But you definitely need someone to take care of you. You've lost so much weight. I can see your bones through your shirt."

Richard chuckled.

"You're driving?" She had looked past him and noticed his truck parked in front of the store.

"Yeah."

"Why don't you take a plane—or a bus? That's a long way."

"Uh … I … uh … need to take some equipment with me." It wasn't a complete lie. He did pack some small lab equipment in his suitcase.

Mary moved closer and whispered, "Richard, if you need some money, I can help you."

"Oh, I couldn't do that, Mary. But thanks anyway. Appreciate it." His face reddened.

"Well. You have my number. If you need anything, call me. Even if it's just to tell me how things are going, all right?"

"Yes. I will … really, this time, I will. And I am going to take you to dinner when I get back, okay? Promise."

"Okay, but if you don't, I'm going to cook you one—in your place."

He chuckled. "Well, that might be a little difficult."

"Oh, don't worry. I'll bring the necessary ingredients."

Richard smiled and nodded. "I bet you will. I think I'd prefer that to a restaurant."

"As you wish." She smiled.

"Well. I better get going."

"Drive careful." She had the word *darling* on her lips, but she held it back.

He noticed Sally's stern face staring at him on the way out. He waved and nodded at her.

Bill said it had to do with ants. He wouldn't call about a normal ant. Is has to be one of mine.

CHAPTER 8

━━ ━━ ━━ ━━ ━━ ━━ ━━

RICHARD KNOCKED ON THE DOOR. SUE ANN ANSWERED.

"Hi, Richard!" She stepped back and took a moment to study him top to bottom. "You look terrible. C'mon in."

"Hi, Sue. Thanks. Bill in?"

"Not at eleven in the morning. He works for a living." She led him into the kitchen.

"Right. Sorry. Forgot about that."

"Hungry? Got my chili con carne fresh off the stove. Looks like you could use some."

"Sounds wonderful, Sue. You're right. I guess I could use a little fattening up."

"That's calling the kettle black. What you could really use, though, is a good woman."

"Yeah. That too. Not too many candidates though."

"Well, they're not going to just pop out of the wall and bite you, Doc. You got to do your part, you know. What about that nice lady that Bill told me about? Owns a grocery store in your town?"

"Mary? Yes. She's really nice."

"Have you taken her out?"

"Uh, not yet. I plan to when I get back."

"How long have you known her?"

"Oh, uh, nigh on three years, I guess."

"And you still haven't asked her out? Men!" Sue Ann threw her hands into the air.

"Well, I did, actually. But I forgot."

"You for … I give up. You're impossible, Richard."

She served him a large bowl of chili and placed two individual packs of saltine crackers beside the large spoon. She placed a large glass of Coke in front of the bowl. "Or would you rather have a beer?" she asked suspiciously.

"No, this is fine. Thank you." *How does she do that? She sees right through me!*

She sat in a chair to his right.

"So, last year, you guys had a wild time up north, huh?"

"Up n—? Oh. You mean when we went to the casino. Well, I don't know if you could call it a wild time."

"Bill told me about the girls. You don't have to cover for him."

"Girls? There weren't any girls. We played the slots and drank free beer all night. That's all, I'm afraid. We did talk about them though," he said with a chuckle.

"Ah, c'mon, Richard. I know my stud."

"Bill thinks the world of you, Sue. He just wouldn't do that. We both talk about it like two studs, but I'm afraid we are disappointing."

"I guess he was just pulling my leg then. Don't mention our conversation to Bill. I don't think he remembers what he said a year ago. Sometimes even last week. I think Alzheimer's is creeping in. I'll let you eat in peace. I got some clothes on the line I got to get in. Bill will be home around five. Go take yourself a nap after you eat. The back room is set up for you. Serve yourself all you want. Don't be shy. Good to have you here, Richard." She bent over and gave him a small peck on the cheek.

"Thanks, Sue. That's exactly what I'll do." He noticed she was a lot more cheerful now, bubbly even. *How can women change their moods from one second to the next?*

━ ━ ━ ━ ━ ━

"Where's Doc?" Bill called out as he opened the door.

"Hi, hon. He's still sleeping in the back room." She placed a strong kiss on his lips and grabbed him between the legs.

"Whoa, girl! Been watching porn or something?"

"Nah. Just missed you, you big lug."

"Can we continue that later this evening? I'm starving, and I smell your chili."

"That's what Richard ate. I doubt he wants to eat chili again so soon."

"Your chili? He will. Did you make some macaroni?"

"Of course. I'll go heat some up. You can wake up your friend."

"No need to. Hi, Bill. And I'd be glad to eat your chili again, especially if you add some macaroni to it. Sounds delicious."

"Hi, Doc. Wow. You look like you've been to hell and back."

"He looks better than he did when he got here though," Sue added.

"Wow. I must really look like shit."

"You do, Doc. But Sue here will put a little meat on those bones for you. Si'down, partner."

"So what's so important that I had to come down here?"

Sue looked back at Bill with a questioning look.

"Tomorrow. Had a case recently that was really strange."

"You referring to that poor woman in Smithtown, hon?" She set large bowls of chili and macaroni in front of each of the men, and then she went for a bowl for herself.

"Yeah, babe. Charlie?"

"Went out with Carol Ann. Poor lady." She turned to Richard. "Had a bunch of kids—and her husband had left her for another woman in Aberdeen a few years ago."

"We don't know that to be true, hon." He turned to Richard. "Her husband disappeared a few years back, and no one has heard hide nor hair from him since. She had twelve kids."

"We all know, dear. Shame. Tyrone was a hard worker. But now she's living on welfare, poor thing."

"Was."

"Yeah. Was."

"She was found dead in her outhouse a week ago."

"In her outhouse? Heart attack?" Richard asked.

"Well. That's what I think, but I need your expertise to confirm it." He gave Richard a wink.

"*My* expertise? For a heart attack?"

"Yeah. Well, you see, I found a bunch of ants around the crime scene."

"Ants? I see." He nodded to Bill. "So tell me what's all the local gossip, Sue Ann? Charlie going to get married to this … uh … Carol, is it?"

Sue quickly and happily followed Richard's cue and began informing him of all the goings on in town and with the kids and grandkids. She didn't let Bill get many words in edgewise, but Bill didn't mind. He busied himself doing a six-pack in during their conversation.

Bill looked closely at Richard. Something was awry. He looked like he'd been on a yearlong binge—a look he had seen only too frequently in others, including himself some few years back. That was when Sue Ann came into his life and saved it.

Richard didn't sleep well that night. He knew what he would find in the morning. He touched his bottle more than once, even uncorked it a couple of times and took a whiff, but he resisted. It was time to sober up.

CHAPTER 9

THE AROMA OF GOOD, FRESHLY BREWED COFFEE DRIFTED its way up Richard's nose and filled his head with delight. He opened his eyes sleepily, stretched in different directions, then sat up and swung his feet over the side of the bed. He felt refreshed. He couldn't remember the last time he felt so good in the morning. He may not have slept long, but he slept hard.

He showered, shaved, and changed into jeans and a University of Kansas sweatshirt.

Bill sat at the table, sipping on a coffee, and Sue Ann stood at the stove stirring up a big breakfast of scrambled eggs, thick country ham, freshly cut thick bacon strips, and grits.

"Coffee's over there." Bill pointed his cup toward the kitchen counter. "Milk and sugar's on the table."

"Good morning, Richard. Sleep well?" Sue Ann cheerfully greeted without turning around.

"Morning, all. Coffee smells great, and breakfast smells even better. You always get up this early? It's not even light yet."

"Will be by the time we finish breakfast," Bill said.

Sue Ann brought the pan of scrambled eggs and ham first and served both men amply. Then she returned with the bacon strips, placing three on each plate. She served the grits in another small bowl. "Butter's on the table for the grits. Want toast? Bill doesn't eat toast, but I'll make you some if you like. Only take a second."

"Oh, no. Please, don't bother. There's plenty right here on the table."

Sue nodded. "There's more where that came from. Help yourselves. Eat up!" She retired to her bedroom, and that would be the last Richard would see of her until later that day.

"Sleeps in after breakfast. Plenty of time to do her chores in the afternoon. She says it gives her something to do while I work."

Richard nodded and returned his attention to the food on his plate.

Bill said very little during breakfast. When he excused himself to make a visit to the john before they left, Richard decided he'd better do the same.

"You hunting for bear?" Bill joked when he saw Richard slide into the front seat of his pickup.

"Just some lab stuff to investigate. The jacket's especially designed to hold test tubes and such."

"Test tubes. Thought you had twelve-gauge shotgun rounds in there. Fancy. What you're going to see ain't."

"What am I going to see exactly?"

"Hard to describe. You'll see soon enough. Won't be long. Twenty minutes tops." He reached into his shirt pocket for a cigarette and cracked the window.

Bill brought his pickup to a stop in front of a dilapidated house on top of a hill along a country road.

"Now your fun begins," Bill said as he got out of his car and lit a cigarette while Richard caught up with him. He nodded in the direction of the house and led Richard around the side. A cornfield of dry, brown stalks stood sadly a stone's throw away. Bill led him to the outhouse.

"This is where it happened." Bill pointed at the outhouse. Yellow plastic tape stretched from the cornfield to the house.

"In there. I got a call from the kids. Couldn't really make out what they were saying, but it was clear they had a problem. I came in a hurry. What I found was a skeleton dressed in a pink, blood-stained robe. White panties and black stretch slacks were around the ankles of the skeleton. I had to remove the skeleton 'cause of the kids. I'll show it to you later."

"Skeleton?"

"Yeah. That's all there was left."

As they lifted the tape and walked under, Richard said, "How come the tape doesn't have 'Crime Investigation Scene' on it?"

"'Cause I don't get the same funds those big city slickers get, wise guy."

They approached the outhouse.

Bill grabbed the door handle, took a couple of steps back, and extended his arms as a signal for Richard to enter.

Richard felt the dampness in his feet from the morning dew. He warily stepped into the outhouse door and stopped in his tracks. His heart was pounding so hard he could swear Bill could hear it. His breathing became difficult.

"Are you all right, Doc? They're just ants. Big ones, I grant you, but they're dead."

Richard nodded and picked the large tweezers from his right breast pocket and a test tube from his left breast pocket. He unscrewed the top of the test tube, knelt down to pick up a couple of the large ant specimens, and nervously glanced around and above him. Blood had soaked the wood and made it look black. He made his exit quickly.

"There were hundreds of them. I swept most of them down the shithole. Then I thought of you. I mean, these look really different than any ant I ever saw!"

Richard gingerly stepped back into the outhouse, gently lifted the lid, and peered down into the cesspool. It was too dark to see anything. He hastily made his retreat.

"Never seen any ants that damn big before. The poor lady was sitting on the crapper. You should have seen the bones. Well you will soon anyway. They shine! I swear they do!"

"The giant ant from Africa grows to five centimeters." Richard looked on the ground around the outhouse.

"African? Jesus! How the hell did they get here?"

"Your fire ant came from South America on a cargo ship. Infested half the United States already—and it will be in just about every state in the southern half of the US in a few more years. All you have to do is import one queen. The rest will be history."

"Jesus! So, tell me, Doc. Are they meat eaters? Or am I looking for a real sick son of a bitch?

"Whatcha lookin' for, Doc?"

"Their nest." Richard found five different paths they had traveled.

"They're carnivorous, aren't they, Doc?"

"Won't know till I get to the house with my field scope." He hadn't actually brought one.

"Well, I got to make a report on this thing. I've been holding it up, pending your investigation, but I've already got tons of calls."

"I can imagine. What are you telling them?"

"I suspect she had a heart attack—and the damn ants ate her. I didn't include how completely they ate her though. I told the kids as little as possible and told them to put a lid on it until I finish the investigation."

"The kids actually saw her in the john?"

"The oldest. She kept the rest out."

"Poor girl. Thank God."

"Where ya goin'?"

"To find the nest. Where else?"

"Oh, shit," Bill said softly. "Think it's close?"

Richard began following the trails, and Bill followed behind until Richard stopped at the cornfield's edge.

"Found it?"

"Not yet. Smart. The five trails merge into two." Richard looked back at how the trails divided and surrounded the outhouse. He nodded.

"Well planned."

"Sound like you're proud of these sons of bitches, Doc."

He stood up and looked Bill straight in the eye. "They've been around a hell of a lot longer than we have, and they've survived disasters much worse than we. They're well disciplined. You have to respect them."

"Jesus, Doc. You make them sound human. You're scaring me."

"You have to respect the ocean, don't you? They're like robotic warriors. No emotions. If they could think like us, we wouldn't have a chance."

"Ah, c'mon, Doc. You're exaggerating. Right?"

"I don't think so." He turned back to the field. "These were smart. They surrounded the outhouse before they attacked."

"Attacked? You mean like intentional?"

"If they are carnivorous, the poor lady was simply prey for them—no more, no less."

Richard slowly spread the cornstalks and stepped into the cornfield. After a few steps, he looked up and scanned the area above the stalks. He stopped his search when he spotted a large maple tree about fifteen yards ahead at two o'clock. He looked at the ground again. "Go slow. Try to make as little noise as possible, Bill. We're going in the direction of that tree."

"Roger that, Doc. I'm right on your heels."

Approximately five yards from the tree, the cornfield opened up to a large clearing that surrounded the tree.

Richard stopped, and Bill ran into him. "Tell a guy when you're gonna stop, will ya?"

"Shh." Bill pointed at the tree.

"Is that it? The nest?"

Richard nodded. The mound totally surrounded the tree and stood a good three feet high.

"Holy shit, Doc! There's got to be thousands of 'em in there," he whispered loudly.

"I'd say their population has passed a million."

"A million?"

"Quiet!" Richard whispered loudly.

"What. They got ears, too?"

"They feel vibrations, my friend. And that, over there, is a scout."

He pointed to the right side of the tree where a single large ant made its way down the mound in their direction.

"Think we better get outta here, Doc? I got a bad feeling about this." Bill began walking with his eyes on the mound. He tripped and fell to the ground. Thousands of ants poured out of the mound.

"Damn! Run, Doc!"

They made haste through the cornstalks and didn't stop until they were in the truck.

"I don't see them, Bill."

"Well, I'm not waiting, Doc. I'm outta here!"

"Is there anyone living in the house?"

"Not anymore." He threw the truck in gear and floored the gas pedal. "Social Services came and took them. Let's get to town. I'll show you the remains. My God, Doc! Did you see how them sons of bitches came at us?"

Richard pulled his test tube from his pocket and looked at the specimens through a magnifying glass. "Yeah."

"Yeah? Just *yeah*? We could've been their next meal, Doc! How can you be so cool?"

"What? Oh. Definitely carnivorous, Bill."

"So how do we kill 'em? Dump a ton of fire ant poison around the nest? Spray 'em with somethin'?"

"Not so easy. The queen will be deep. Their size may require a stronger poison. I need to classify this first. I'll call my friend at the university. Bill, you need to close off this whole area."

"Right, Doc. I'll call Jerome and tell 'em to be sure not to plow the corn under. I'll also tape off the area around the whole property." Bill shrugged. "With my luck, it'll attract people instead."

"Can't you post a condemned sign on the property?"

"Yeah. I guess I could. Good idea." He lit another cigarette. "House looks bad enough to condemn anyway."

"Got another one of those killer sticks?"

"This?" He held up the cigarette, handed one to Richard, and loaned his as a light.

"Here we are, Doc. Country version of a city morgue. I'll leave ya with the bones. I've got to make a few calls. And then I got to finish my report. There's going to be a lot of publicity on this one, Doc."

"Probably put Smithville on the map."

"Just the kind of attention I don't want. I'll come get you in a couple hours for lunch."

"Okay. I may need more time than that. Can I make a few calls? Long distance?"

"Sure, Doc, as long as they're in the US. Just come up with a way to get rid of those."

Richard spent most of the day with the skeleton. His ants' mandibles had even scarred the bones. He took lots of pictures, made several slides that he looked closely at in his field scope, and verified what he knew from the very beginning. The specimen was one of his hybrids.

"You're mighty quiet, Doc," Bill said while driving home.

"Just thinking is all."

"So how we gonna kill 'em?"

"Patience, my friend. I already made the calls. M will be calling me to give me an answer to that one."

"M?"

"Dr. Michael Morton. I call him M."

"Hopefully you get that call soon." Bill lit a cigarette.

"Give me one of those, will you?"

"A cigarette? Sure, Doc. Want me to buy ya a pack?"

"Just one. Your fault you smoke my brand."

His ants had traveled more than six hundred miles to nest. *Where did the rest go? And in what direction? How many queens left this nest—and where did they go? And the queens will produce more queens.* He had to do something quickly. The nests had to be eliminated as soon as they were discovered—and before they mated again.

— — — — — —

Sue Ann had thick pork chops, real mashed potatoes, cream gravy, corn on the cob, and fresh cornbread on the table when her men arrived.

"Jesus, Sue. I would've been happy with just another bowl of chili."

"Got to keep my men healthy," she said cheerfully.

"You eat like this every day?"

"Of course, Richard. What you need is a woman. Put some meat on those bones of yours."

"And get a pot gut like Bill's?"

"Hey! I invested a lot to get this. Took years!"

"I think the beer had a lot to do with it, hon."

"That's an investment, too."

Richard felt uncomfortable with all he ate. Sue could really cook. He and Bill excused themselves and sat outside. Richard helped himself to his elixir while Bill treated himself to his. He bummed a couple more cigarettes.

Bill said, "I don't mind feeding a man, but each man has to buy his own vices."

"Read you loud and clear. Now give me another one."

Bill and Sue retired around ten, but Richard burned the midnight oil. He looked up maps of all the states within a six hundred-mile radius, which was well over a million square miles. He wasn't worried about killing one nest. It was the propagation of the species he feared. *If these spread like the fire ants—with colonies in the millions?*

58

CHAPTER 10

■■ ■■ ■■ ■■ ■■ ■■ ■■ ■■

"DR. MORTON? YOU HAVE A CALL, SIR."

Dr. Michael Morton waddled across the teacher's lounge to a gray metal desk and picked up the phone. He pressed the flashing button. "Dr. Morton here," he said in an uninterested voice.

"Hi, M. It's Richard."

"Richard? What's going on? Thought you were dead or something. No calls—not even an e-mail."

"Yeah, I know. Sorry about that. Been out of touch for a while."

"The booze?" he said softly.

"Well, getting canned can get to you."

Dr. Murphy nodded. "Yeah. I hear you. Always live in fear about that around here—lots of spies too."

"Look. I need a favor. I'm in a small town in Kentucky. A friend of mine called me down here. There was an incident. A woman was eaten by carnivorous ants."

"Really? Great! I mean—not great for her, of course—but you've got to be excited! What kind are they?"

"*Paraponera clavata*, I believe."

"Here? In the US of A? My God. That is a find. Are you sure? Of course you're sure—you're the expert. Sorry."

"No. I'm not positive—not without more research—but I do need to eradicate the nest."

"Well, that shouldn't be too difficult. They don't make very big colonies."

"Uh, I'm afraid this one is."

"It is? How big is it?"

Richard let out a long whistle.

"That big?"

"My guess is about a million."

"A million! Paraponeras don't colonize like that! That would be really dangerous! It can't be … it just can't be."

"I assure you they are."

"Can you send me a specimen?"

"Naturally. I'll send it FedEx tomorrow—along with a bunch of pictures. In the meantime, I need you to tell me what to use to get rid of it. ASAP. You're the expert in that area. I don't want anyone else to be a victim. There's a family with twelve kids living there."

"Ouch! Okay. Quite a challenge. Their venom is a lot stronger. Tree nest?"

"No. Well, it's a mound around a tree."

"A mound around a tree? This gets more interesting by the minute. This has got to be a hybrid if it's Paraponera, Richard. I've got to have that specimen ASAP. You won't be able to buy anything that'll do more than piss them off over the counter."

"That's why I'm calling."

"Okay. I'll brew up a concoction—maybe a carbon sulfide with something. You can add muriatic acid at the site when applying it."

"Uh. I need to apply it from a distance. They're super-aggressive."

"Maybe I should come down there myself, Richard."

"No! I mean … it's not necessary. I'll be your eyes. I need you in the lab."

"You're really whetting my curiosity, my friend."

"I'm sure your curiosity will be satisfied when you see the specimen, M."

"Yeah. I guess you're right. You got the area closed off, don't you? It's not in a populated area, is it?"

"No, thank God. A single dwelling. All have been vacated. I'm with the sheriff here. Everything's under control."

"Good. I'll get right on it. You get the specimen to me, and I'll send you my brew. I'll include instructions."

"Send it FedEx, okay? I'll send you the address."

"Sure."

"Oh, and M?"

"Yeah?"

"Can we keep this under our hats for a little while?"

"Absolutely! Better we have all the info before we go public with this. Just in case there are others. I don't think you'll be able to keep this quiet for long though. You won't have much time. Have you found how it got here, yet?"

"Exactly what I'm working on, M. We'll stay in touch."

"Okay, Richard. Oh, and Richard?"

"Yeah?"

"Why are you there?"

"The sheriff I told you about is a close friend of mine. He asked me to help him."

"I see. Lucky you, right? Be careful. Wouldn't want the top ant scientist to be eaten by ants."

"Yeah. Very funny. Thanks."

■ ▬ ▬ ▬ ▬ ▬

Richard went to Maysville to send the specimen as he promised.

Bill found an old condemned sign in his office closet, posted it on the property, and roped it off with wooden stakes.

It took four long days for Dr. Morton's solution to arrive—about the same amount of time that Bill could delay sending his report to Lexington.

When Bill got home on Friday evening—he always worked later on Fridays to tie up loose ends at the office—he found the FedEx package on the kitchen table.

"Where's Doc?"

"He left for Cincinnati this morning, right after you left."

"Cincinnati? Say what for?"

"I don't know. Said something about the university, needing to research or something, I guess. Didn't really tell me, but I wouldn't understand anyway."

"Ha, ha. Yeah. Know whatcha mean, babe. Got a buncha smarts, that one has."

"Well, he looks a lot better now though. Looks healthy."

"Thanks to you, babe." He wrapped his hands around her ample waist from behind and slid them up under her blouse to her abundant breasts.

"Don't start something you can't finish, Sheriff."

"Oh, I have every intention of finishing, babe." He pulled her long, wavy brown hair back and began to nibble at one of her erotic zones.

"Richard may get here any minute, stud."

"He won't see anything he hasn't seen before—I think."

"Oh, you are cruel!"

"You have no idea, babe." He lowered her black stretch slacks to her knees.

Just then, Richard's truck pulled up.

"Damn!"

"Told you! But don't worry. I'll take care of that big boy later. You better be ready." She reached between his legs and squeezed his bulge.

"Hi, all," Richard said as he made his way into the kitchen." What's for dinner? I'm starved!"

"Ha, ha. Yeah. He's definitely better," Bill commented.

"Roast beef, roasted potatoes and carrots, gravy, dinner rolls, fried okra, and freshly baked apple pie for desert," Sue announced proudly and began to set the table.

"Your package arrived, Doc."

"I see." He reached for the package and started opening it.

"Not now, boys. No business till after dinner."

"Beer, Richard?"

"Just what I need right now, Bill. Thanks."

"We'll be outside, babe. Call us when dinner's on the table."

Bill sat down at the redwood picnic table and lit a cigarette. Richard sat opposite him and pulled out a Phillies vanilla cigar, put a lit wooden match in front of it, and drew the flame into the tobacco, sending a cloud of smoke around his head.

"Ah, we've graduated to cigars now."

"Don't inhale these. And they last longer."

"And cost more."

"I believe you smoke a lot more of those than I will of these."

"That package from your friend in Kansas?"

Richard nodded. "I read the instructions, and we'll apply it tomorrow."

"I don't know if I like that *we* word, but I'll be glad to rid the town of those. I won't be surprised if I hear from Lexington tomorrow. I couldn't delay the report any longer. They should've received my report this afternoon."

"They probably think you have everything under control, Bill. And you do."

"I really think they are going to get excited about this. Send someone out. Check it out for themselves."

"I hope it stays just like it is," Richard said.

"Dinner's ready!"

"Up! Better get in there—or there will be hell to pay," Bill announced.

They marched into the kitchen and threw their empty beer cans in the white plastic bag hanging from the doorknob.

Richard decided to wait till Bill and Sue Ann went to bed to open M's package. The three of them watched *CSI* and an old John Wayne movie. Bill and Sue excused themselves, and Richard went to the kitchen table to open his mail.

M had sent two half-liter plastic bottles of a clear solution along with instructions.

They didn't sound so good. He would have to get right next to the mound and walk its circumference. M said if he moved slowly, the fine spray would not alert them. The solution would produce a gas that was heavier than air and sink through the nest—all the way down to the queen. He found sleep evasive and kept pondering how he was going to get all the way around that nest without them flowing out by the thousands.

He couldn't let on to Bill that just one bite from one of these ants would paralyze their legs and arms in a matter of seconds. They didn't eat dead meat—it had to be alive.

CHAPTER 11

■ ■ ■ ■ ■ ■ ■

BILL AND SUE NORMALLY SLEPT IN ON SATURDAYS, BUT when Bill shuffled into the kitchen at seven, Richard was already sipping on a cup of java at the kitchen table.

"Whoa. Didn't 'spect to see ya up and around so early, Doc." He went straight for the dish drain, picked up a dry cup, and poured himself a cup of coffee.

"Couldn't sleep."

"Worried about how we going to do this?"

Richard nodded slowly. "May have to go to town to buy some things. Think Sue got a spray can for that Baygon you use?"

"Yeah. Keeps it under the sink. What else ya need?"

"A pair of those rubber gloves that go up to the elbow."

"Ain't got those. I'll go with ya ta town. We'll have breakfast at Sharon's. Give Sue a break."

Richard nodded. "Whenever you're ready."

Bill shot to his feet. "Let's go."

Richard explained the procedure for the nest during the short drive to town.

Bill pulled into one of the parking slots at Jimmy's Hardware in Maysville, and the odd-looking pair made their way into the store.

"I can't believe how early they open for a small town."

"Everything opens early and closes early. By five, they roll up the sidewalks. By six, it's a ghost town down here."

"Early to bed and early to rise makes a man healthy, wealthy, and wise."

"That's what they say, but I don't know about the wealthy part."

"Here are the gloves." Richard selected a yellow pair.

Bill reached into the bin and pulled out another pair.

Richard looked at his friend.

"You don't think you're doing this alone, do ya?"

"This has the possibilities of being quite dangerous, Bill. I'd feel better doing it alone."

"And I'd feel better doing it with ya. Besides, it's my town, 'member?"

Richard sighed in resignation, but he felt somewhat relieved.

"Now, the sprayers?"

"You already have that, don't you?"

"I thought about that. If I use Mary Sue's, she won't be able to use it afterwards."

"Right. They're in the back, Doc."

They finished shopping and went to Sharon's for breakfast. Bill had steak and eggs. Richard had scrambled eggs, an English muffin, and a coffee.

The drive back home was congenial, but the twenty-minute drive to Smithville found them both with little to say. The atmosphere in Richard's truck felt heavy and serious. When they pulled up to the house, Bill jumped out and pulled up a couple of the stakes that held the rope so they could drive onto the property. Bill slowly turned the truck around to face the exit, and Richard gathered the supplies.

They looked at each other in silence.

Richard looked around at the beautiful countryside, took a slow, deep breath, and exhaled slowly. "Cigarette?" Richard held out his pack to Bill and lit his.

"Yeah. Thanks. I see you broke down."

"You know you're my only friend in the world, Bill."

Bill looked at Richard in silence for a few seconds. "And all those ants you got in your basement?"

Richard nodded. "I'm going to have to eliminate them when I get back."

"Oops. Uh, well, thanks, Bubba. Hope you don't have to do that to all your friends. I … uh … well, when you get back, you see that Mary girl, hear? And that's an order!"

"Loud and clear, my friend. And this time, I'm listening." He pulled his phone out and dialed.

"Hello? Richard?"

"How did you know it was me?"

"Caller ID, you silly professor."

"Oh, yeah. Someone else told me that."

Bill had a huge grin on his face.

"How are you? Everything all right? Need anything?"

"Whoa. Slow down. Everything's fine. I have everything I need … well, maybe except one thing."

"Name it."

"You."

Silence ensued on the line, but Bill yelled out, "Yes!"

"Who was that?"

"That? That, my dear, was my best friend, Bill."

"Bill Tucker? The one I talked to?"

"Yes. The one and only."

He seemed very nice—and he was very concerned about you. I'm glad you men are having a good time."

"Yeah. We're having a great time." He looked at Bill. "When this is over, I want to bring you down to Maysville to visit him and Mary Sue. She's a great cook."

"Sounds great to me, darling."

"Well … I … uh … got to get back to work."

"How much longer will you be there?"

"If everything goes right today, I should be there by Monday night."

"Remember that you have to stop by here first."

"Well, I may get there kind of late."

"The hour doesn't matter. If it's after midnight, I'll make breakfast."

"And after breakfast?"

"Now that depends entirely on you, Dr. Denton."

"In that case, it may be a long night for you."

"I assure you I can handle it."

"Wow. Okay. Well … I … uh … really got to go," he said with a chuckle.

"Okay. I'll be waiting."

"Bye," he said sheepishly.

"Bye, dear. Oh! Remember, you don't have a key—and I do lock the door."

"Well. That certainly clears that up, doesn't it? Bye."

"Oh my God! I don't believe my ears! You actually had a conversation with a woman!"

"Wise guy!"

"Ha, ha, ha. Way to go, Bubba. Someone's gonna get some … finally."

"It's not like that."

"It's not like that? Hey! Boy meets girl, girl likes boy, boy gets laid. It's pretty basic. Doesn't take a genius like you to figure that one out."

"Okay, okay. Let's get this over with, shall we?"

"I can't believe I'm having a conversation like this with a man in his forties!"

Richard gave his friend a dirty look and slowly led the way through the cornfield. He constantly looked along the ground and glanced toward the tree between each tedious step until they came to the clearing.

They both looked at each other again. Richard put his index finger to his lips, and Bill nodded.

Richard slowly pulled out the two metal spray cans, put them on the ground, opened the lids and set them beside each can, carefully pulled out the rubber gloves, and handed a pair to Bill.

Bill's hands were trembling slightly, and Richard felt a pang of guilt.

Richard carefully poured a different flask of M's solution in each sprayer and screwed the caps on top. He reached into the bag of supplies, pulled out the surgical masks, and handed one to Bill. He pulled two transparent goggles out of his backpack and gave one to Bill.

He glanced at the nest that loomed in silence before them and nodded at Bill.

Bill nodded back.

"Remember to follow me exactly. Walk very softly. We *have* to make the complete circle—and you *have* to spray exactly where I do."

Bill nodded.

"If they start coming out, run like hell toward the truck."

Bill nodded vigorously. His heart was pounding hard against his chest, and his breathing quickened.

Very slowly, they made their way to the tree, trying their best not to make any noise. Upon their arrival, they stopped and looked at each other again. Sweat was beaded on their foreheads and cheeks, wetting their masks, even though the temperature was below fifty degrees.

Richard began pumping the fine spray onto the mound, which was up to their knees, and did his best to cover every inch of exposed mound.

Bill followed right behind, spraying the same area after Richard. They had practiced the procedure with water earlier.

Their breathing became heavy as they pumped as rapidly as they could, slowly circling the tree. Their arms began to ache, but they couldn't afford to slow down. When they completed the circle, they cautiously stepped back to the edge of the clearing and stopped, staring at the mound and waiting for something to happen.

Bill turned to Richard and took off his mask and glasses. His face was covered with a grin. Richard nodded and turned away.

Within a few steps, Richard slapped at his arm. He saw an ant inject him, but he got to it too late. He looked around and didn't notice any others, but he collapsed to the ground, his eyes wide with fear.

Bill quickly grabbed Richard by the vest and dragged him to the truck. He looked behind him. They weren't being followed. He stared at the cornfield for a minute to be sure. "Are you all right, Doc?"

Richard nodded. "Just one time," he whispered. "It'll pass."

Bill dragged Richard around to the passenger side and hoisted him into the seat, banging Richard's head on the doorframe. "Sorry, Doc." He anxiously buckled his friend into his seat and ran to the driver's side, glancing at the cornstalks one more time. He went to start the car and yelled, "Keys!"

Richard moved his eyes down.

Bill felt Richard's pants pocket and found the keys. "The closest hospital is in Aberdeen, Doc. Hold on."

"No," Richard whispered. "It'll … pass." Richard glanced at the clock on the car.

By the time they drove ten minutes down the road, Richard could move his arm slightly. By the time he got home, Richard could move his legs and arms, but he didn't have enough strength to support his weight.

Bill helped his friend into the house and set him on the sofa in a sitting position.

"What happened?" Sue ran over to see.

"Doc got bit by one of those ants."

"Their venom paralyzes the victim. I'll be okay. One's not enough to do any serious harm." Richard looked at the clock on the wall.

"Jesus, hon. We've got to get him to a doctor."

"No! He won't know what to do anyway, Sue. He wouldn't have the antibody. I just need time. It'll all pass, and I'll be good as new. Trust me. Don't worry."

"Jesus, Doc. If they could totally paralyze you with just one, imagine what it was like for Mary Sue, getting bit by hundreds."

"Try tens of thousands," Richard added.

"And they actually eat ya," Bill added.

"Alive?" Sue asked. "They paralyze you and then eat you alive? Oh my God! It just never … I mean I didn't think … oh my God! That's terrible!"

"But we got 'em, didn't we, Doc. We killed those sons a bitches," Bill said.

"Thank God. You're both heroes."

"Tomorrow we'll find out."

"What? You guys are not going back there! No way!"

"Got to see if the poison worked, Sue. I'll go. Bill can stay here."

"The hell you will! We're in this together, Doc—till the end." He turned to Sue. "Don't worry, babe. We know what we're doing now." He turned back to Richard. "We're the Ant Busters!"

That caused a burst of laughter from the both men.

"Men! You never grow up, do you?" Mary Sue stalked off to her bedroom and slammed the door.

"I think she's just a little upset," Richard said.

"She'll get over it. That was awesome. I mean, at the time, I was shitting in my pants, but now? Wow. What a rush."

Richard got his strength back within another hour and began to walk off the ants' poison. He and Bill were having a cigarette out back when Sue joined them and insisted they celebrate.

Her "brave ant busters" agreed to take her to Aberdeen for dinner and a movie.

Sunday morning meant a big breakfast before church. Richard joined them and did some serious praying for the first time in many years.

"Are you sure you need to do this, hon," Sue asked.

"Yeah, babe. Don't worry. I won't take any chances."

"We won't be long, Sue. Ready, Bill?"

"Yeah. Let's do it. Who're gonna call? The Ant Busters!"

Sue Ann clenched her fist and waved it at them as they drove off.

When they cautiously came to the clearing by the mound, they found no action. They looked at each other in silence. Bill picked up a small rock and threw it into the mound from the edge of the cornfield. They were poised to run. No movement.

Richard went back to the truck, grabbed the ground rake, and returned. He carried the rake over to the mound and pulled at the lower edge of the mound, but he found nothing. He continued trying to make a cross section by clearing the mound up to the tree. He pulled his magnifying lens out a couple of times and squatted down on this knees to get a closer look, which made Bill quite nervous.

"What're you lookin' for, Doc? A death certificate! They're gone, aren't they?"

Richard wrote something in his pocket notebook. "Gone? They went deep to escape the gas. I was looking for larvae."

"What gas?"

"What we sprayed created a gas that was heavier than air, and it sunk through the tunnels—hopefully to the queen."

"Hopefully? You mean she could still be alive?"

"I don't think so. We would've still had some visitors by now, even if they were deep. I think this battle's over."

"You talk like there'll be others, Doc."

"Let's hope not."

"Let's pray not. I really don't want to test my ant-buster skills again. No offense, Doc."

"No offense taken, my friend. No offense taken."

There are going to be other battles, my friend, and I'm afraid they won't be as easy as this one. Where are the others? Did they all fly in the same direction? Some had to have landed closer to home, but where? Where?

CHAPTER 12

RICHARD DROVE BACK HOME ON MONDAY MORNING, relieved and satisfied that the present crisis was over.

Bill, however, hadn't heard the last of it. A doctor from the University of Kentucky would arrive on Thursday afternoon, according to the call from the governor's office in Frankfort.

"Sheriff Bill Tucker in?"

"Yes. Just a minute." Bill's "assistant" got up and walked into Bill's small, cluttered office.

"Got some people here to see you, Chief."

"They have a name?"

"Oh. I didn't ask. Look like city slickers though. Definitely out-of-towners."

Bill nodded. He looked at his watch. *2:30. There goes my afternoon.*

A tall, thin elderly gentleman stood in front of Seth's desk. Two gentlemen in their thirties stood a few feet behind him.

"Dr. James Burton, I guess you'd be?"

"How astute, Sheriff. Allow me to introduce my two young assistants, Dr. Samuel Truant and Dr. Roger Smith. I assume you were informed of our arrival."

"How astute, Dr. Burton. Yes. You're from the University of Kentucky." *Arrogant Washington garbage.*

"Right again, Sheriff. Sam and Roger work out of Washington. I understand you have a quite interesting incident that occurred in your town."

73

"To say the least, Doctor, well, doctors. Let me get you out to the location right away. There's not much light left."

Bill escorted Dr. James Burton and his two sidekicks to the site, arriving while there was still a little more than an hour of sunlight left.

They had driven to Maysville in an unmarked van and followed Bill to the site. At the site, Dr. Burton excused Bill, telling him he would "take over from here."

Richard would never have kissed someone off like that who had been in on the job. They didn't even ask him any questions. They just told him to "skedaddle." Sue would be happy, of course. She had been having nightmares about losing her husband to man-eating ants.

━━ ━━ ━━ ━━ ━━ ━━

As Richard arrived in the small, sparsely populated suburb of Lawrence, he stopped by the grocery store to pick up his key from Mary. The sun was already setting.

"Hi, darling," Mary said. "Welcome home."

"Hi, Mary. How's everything here?"

"Same old, same old. But you, obviously, did something right. You look great."

"I do?" He looked at himself. His clothes were wrinkled from the long drive, and he hadn't shaved.

"Looks like you at least decided to eat. You look like you've been energized."

He chuckled. "Thanks, Mary. I ate way too much."

"Well, it certainly looks good on you. Maybe you should look for a woman who can cook for you like that as a steady diet."

"Kind of thought I had." He shrugged. "I'd probably get as fat as Bill. Don't know if I'd like that."

"Everything in moderation, my dear," she said with a smile.

"Got my key? Long drive."

"Everything go all right? Solved your friend's emergency?" Mary opened the register, lifted the cash drawer, and picked up a key.

"Yeah. Everything went very well, actually."

"What was the emergency—if I may ask, of course."

"Oh ... uh ... some woman was killed by some carnivorous ants. Had to eliminate the nest."

"Killed by ants? What a horrible way to die. Wait, did you say they were carnivorous?"

"Yes."

"They eat like meat ... flesh?"

"Yes."

"So they, uh, ate this woman?"

Richard nodded. "Down to the bone."

"Oh, my God! Poor woman! I hope she didn't suffer too much."

"Well, I don't think it was that bad. I'm sure their venom killed her quickly so she didn't really suffer from their feeding."

"Oh, you men! You have so little compassion. Poor lady. And did she have any children?"

"Yes. That's actually the worst part. Unfortunately, she had twelve. And her husband left her a few years ago without explanation."

"Oh, my God! What's going to happen to those poor children?"

"They are putting them in various foster homes. That's the tough part. They're going to be separated."

"Poor little things. Life is so tough sometimes."

Richard nodded. "Better get going. Thanks, Mary. How 'bout I call you tomorrow. Dinner?"

"Sounds great, but I thought I was cooking you dinner tonight at your place?"

"You still want to? I thought you might have changed your mind. But that's great! Nothing fancy now."

"You're the boss." She chuckled. "You really don't get out often, do you?" Her face was radiant, and her smile showed a nice row of small, even teeth.

Richard shook his head and left, closing the door behind him.

— — — — — —

Sally, waiting patiently in the dark in the back of the store, immediately closed in on Mary. "Be careful, honey. Don't let him use you. Know what I mean?"

"Yes, Sally." She laughed. "I'll make him work for it. Don't worry."

"Mary!" They laughed in a secret whisper and returned to their upstairs rooms after Mary locked the door. She was glad she had invited Sally to stay with her. They were good company for each other.

— — — — — —

Richard turned the key and stepped into the house. The hardwood floors shined as if they were just installed in the moonlight that filled the room. The house smelled of some pleasant fragrance he couldn't place.

Richard closed the door behind him as he made his way to the kitchen. He smiled. *Wow. You really put a lot of time in this place.*

He opened the refrigerator, and his jaw dropped. There were eggs, a large can of orange juice, a package of sliced ham, a package of bacon, hot dogs, bottles of condiments, onions, tomatoes, potatoes, a bell pepper, celery, and more. He grabbed the orange juice and took a long draw on it. "Oh! That's good!"

In the freezer, he found two New York strips, two packages of hamburger meat, and some pork chops.

"Man. You really spent some money here," he said out loud. "I don't know how much all this cost, but I will pay every cent back."

"There's no bill, darling."

"Oh!" Richard jumped and almost stumbled to the floor, a handy kitchen chair keeping his balance.

She slid her hands up his chest and around his neck, looking deeply into his eyes. She softly touched his lips with hers, and he pressed herself against him tightly, causing her to moan softly.

They went upstairs, and he shook his head when he saw that Mary had cleaned his bedroom too. Everything was clean and neat. His clothes were lined by category in his closet. The drawers of the dresser had his clothes neatly folded and orderly.

"Hey! How did you get in?"

"You left the door open, silly. But don't worry. It's locked now."

"Holy shit! This is nice," he whispered. "Looks like a real home." He laughed out loud.

"What?"

"This house has never looked so good is what! My God, woman! You are incredible!"

He took Mary into his arms and gently kissed her, holding her firmly, but not tightly. "I should have done this a long time ago."

"Yes. You should have. I have been waiting a long time for this."

"I ... uh ... I haven't been exactly, well, maybe poor is the word, with personal relationships."

"I know," she whispered. "Don't worry, darling. I'll take care of this one. Just relax and enjoy the ride." She gently pushed him into the bed.

It wasn't until after their lovemaking that he noticed the smell of the bed linen. They drifted off to that cloudy slumber land in each other's arms and felt nothing but air.

■ — ■ — ■ — ■ — ■ — ■

He awoke late the next morning, alone. After several minutes of stretching, he pulled himself out of bed and shuffled into the shower. He dried himself and let the wet towel drop to the floor as usual.

He shaved and was about to go get dressed, but then he stopped and looked around. Mary had straightened and cleaned his bathroom too.

He looked at the sink and decided to rinse the hairs and shaving cream down the drain. He looked at the towel on the floor, picked it up, dried out the sink, and hung it neatly over the shower stall.

He dressed and was about to leave the bedroom, but something pulled at him. He turned and saw the unmade bed. He sighed, picked up his dirty clothes, put them in the hamper he rarely used, and made his bed.

As he departed, he stopped at the bedroom door and looked back.

"The damn woman is domesticating me," he whispered. He shook his head and made his way to the kitchen to cook breakfast.

He opened the cabinet door to pull out a frying pan and noticed that all was neatly put in place. He grabbed three small frying pans and placed them on the burners. A smile crossed his lips; he couldn't remember the last time he cooked on a clean stove.

He opened another cabinet and reached for the cooking oil to find it was also well stocked. Mary had left a really high-quality virgin olive oil for him to cook with.

A good breakfast of diced fried potatoes, three eggs sunny side up, bacon, and toast made him feel like a king.

He went to his lab and stopped at the bottom of the stairs to look around. His creation was motionless. He shook his head. The place was a disaster. He thought about cleaning up a bit, but then he thought of Mary. Maybe he should have her come and do this. Of course, he would have to get rid of the evidence first. But not today, right, buddy?

He walked over to his desk and turned on the computer. While it powered up, he threw a few things in the trash and stacked a few papers in a pile to give him space. He rummaged through his papers for a blank piece of paper and searched for a pencil.

He brought up a US map, made some notes, and searched the map of Kansas in particular.

His creation was still out there—but where exactly? He didn't think they all flew down to Kentucky. There were four more queens out there, and there was no doubt in his mind he would find out exactly where they were in the not-too-distant future.

That afternoon, while Richard was reviewing his fresh notes, the phone rang.

"Doc?"

"Hi, Bill. What's up?"

"Just wanted to let you know the governor sent some guys up to investigate. I took 'em out to the site, and they told me to go home. Can you believe that? Conceited creeps."

"An entomologist?"

"A what? I don't know what you call him. Name's Dr. Burton. Know 'em?"

"University of Kentucky. Very knowledgeable."

"Yeah. That's right. That was his name. Arrogant son of a gun. Well, I don't know how smart he is. Anyway, he told me to get lost. That they would 'take over from here.'"

"Better for you to stay out of it anyway, Bill. He knows what he's doing. Keep me posted of any other news, okay?"

"Sure. At least the old lady's happy. Everything's back to normal now. Oh! There were two other doctors of some kind … from Washington."

"I'm sure she is. Washington, huh? The feds got their mitts into it too. Say, you know that lady I told you about? Mary?"

"The grocery store lady? Yeah. Get laid?"

"She stayed over." Richard laughed. "I'm taking her out to dinner tonight."

"Great. 'Bout time, Doc. She knock your socks off?"

"Pretty much. I don't kiss and tell—even to you. Well, I wanted to tell you that I left her my house key when I left. When I got back, she had cleaned the whole damn house!"

"Whoa, Doc! That's a keeper!"

"Not only that, she stocked up my fridge and cupboards. I've got food in the house! Can you believe it? And she put all my closets in order too."

"Oh, somebody's in trouble. Sounds too good to be true. That's a trophy fish. Maybe you should marry this one."

"Marry? Naw. I don't think so. I'm really not ready for that."

"Why not? Going to wait till you're old and gray and can't get it up anymore?"

"Well, that could be a problem in the future, but not yet. I need to get this problem taken care of first."

"What problem, Doc."

"Oh ... uh ... just a ... professional problem I have to take care of. You know? No job."

"Oh. Is that all? I'm sure you'll find something, Doc. With your smarts, that won't be a problem."

"Thanks. From your mouth to God's ears."

"It'll happen, Doc. Believe you me."

"Okay. Give my best to Sue Ann."

"Will do, Doc. Take care. Bye."

Richard let out a long sigh. He had almost blown it. He hadn't hung up the phone for more than a minute when it rang again.

"Hello?"

"Richard? M here."

"M! Your medicine did the trick. They're gone. Thanks." He didn't mention he had used it on his lab specimens.

"Richard. We need to talk ... privately."

"Sure. Whenever you want. What's the matter?"

"I asked one of your students to help me make the poison ... Ann Kriendler? Says she knows you well. Speaks very well of you. Actually, I think she's got a crush on you."

"I never did anything in any way with Ann. Besides, it wouldn't make any difference now anyway. They already fired me."

"I'm not talking about that, my friend. I'd get into her pants myself ... if I had the chance."

"Then what's the problem, M?"

"While we were preparing the solutions, she mentioned that you had asked her about the possibility of creating some hybrid species of ant."

"I just asked her if she thought it were possible. If I remember correctly, she seemed to think it was pretty impossible."

"Well, she thinks if anyone had the ability to do it, it would be you."

"Yeah, well, like you said … she has a crush on me."

"I don't know about that, Richard. I studied the specimen pretty thoroughly. It's a hybrid, all right, but a carnivorous hybrid—extremely dangerous. And the size!"

"And?"

"And I don't want to discuss it on the phone. Better we see each other in person."

"Your office?"

"Oh, no. Not here. How about Friday afternoon … say five-ish? Seattle's by Horton Park."

"Sure. Why not?"

"Good. See you then, Richard."

"Yeah, M. Bye."

He had been feeling so good, actually human again, but the pressure returned like a ton of bricks. Mary was the only positive thing in his life. He picked up the phone and dialed.

"Mary's groceries, may I help you?"

"Hi, Sally. Can I speak with Mary, please?"

"Whom may I say is speaking?"

"You know it's Dr. Denton."

"Oh. Okay. Just a moment," she said.

"Richard?"

"Mary? Hi. Is eight all right?"

"Eight? Sure. What shall I wear?"

"A dress. We're going to Chris's Steak House."

"Chris's? That's expensive."

"It's the least I can do for what you did for me. My Lord. The house never looked so good. It never looked so organized, and I have enough food for the next month."

"You weren't offended? I was so worried you would think I was a meddling bitch or something."

"Not at all. Of course, now I have to work at keeping it that way."

"Well, I can help if you like."

"Actually, I was thinking of my lab ... now that you mention it."

"You had the door locked with instructions not to touch, remember? I couldn't get in. Whenever you like, Richard."

"Not today. Maybe this weekend?"

"How 'bout we go to church on Sunday, have lunch afterwards, and start on it after lunch?"

"Sounds like a plan. We'll talk about it tonight, okay?"

"Okay. Picking me up—or do you prefer I stop by your place?"

"It would be easier for me if you came by my place ... say seven thirty? We have reservations for eight thirty."

"Seven thirty it is. See you then."

— — — — — —

Mary had always dressed in casual clothes that she covered with an apron at work, but Richard opened the door to see a woman with light brown hair in long, soft curls gently bouncing around her shoulders and a royal blue dress showing cleavage he had only recently become aware of.

His voice had trouble escaping his throat for a few long seconds. "You look ... very nice, Mary."

"Thank you. I'm a few minutes late. I'm sorry."

"That's okay. We have time." He started for the car, gently holding Mary's arm that was wrapped in what he believed was a fake mink.

"Richard, dear?"

He stopped and looked into Mary's large dark brown eyes.

"You want to lock your door?"

"Oh. Yes. Thank you."

Richard was glad he had washed his truck inside and out. Mary did most of the talking during the drive and dinner, telling Richard all about her childhood, college years, married life, and finally bringing him up to present.

Richard was comfortable with her talking and him listening,

although he told Mary more of his life's story than anyone else except Bill.

When they returned home, Richard awkwardly asked her to come in. Mary accepted and helped ease his awkwardness.

It was daylight when they lay exhausted against the pillows.

"I would much prefer to stay here and sleep, but I've got to open up the store." She rolled over on top of Richard and looked into his face. "I have never been with anyone who could last so long in my entire life. You were incredible!"

Richard chuckled. "That's probably because I haven't been with a woman in such a long time. Have a lot built up in me."

"And I am the lucky one to get all that built-up love. I hope you have enough to last a lot of years. Thank you, darling, for the best night I've ever had."

Richard nodded and smiled, feeling stupid for not knowing what to say. He felt like he just won the Boston Marathon.

Mary jumped out of bed. "Let me get you some breakfast before I go off to work."

Before Richard could react, he heard her footsteps going down the stairs. Seconds later, he heard the pots and pans.

Wow. She has so much energy!

CHAPTER 13

AS RICHARD MADE HIS WAY TO THE REGISTER, HE NOTICED all the tables were occupied.

"Yes, sir. What'll it be today?"

"Mocha, please"

"Hot or cold?"

"Sorry. Hot mocha … tall."

He paid the clerk and waited for his order to be prepared at the other part of the counter.

"Denton, hot mocha!"

Richard raised his hand, nodded at the clerk, and checked the cup for his name before he added some nutmeg and cinnamon.

Across the small room of undersized tables surrounded by four chairs, a couple rose from their places, taking their cups and trash with them. He quickly made his way in that direction, successfully overtaking three young ladies with laptops hanging from their shoulders, much to their disliking. *Age before beauty.*

He had just settled into his seat and cleaned his table with a couple of napkins when a burly, red-haired gentleman with a delicate white complexion, which didn't quite seem to go with his build, entered the establishment. Richard raised his hand like a student in class.

Dr. Murphy nodded, repeated Richard's earlier movements, dragged out a chair, and plumped himself down with a thump. "Hi,

Richard!" His smile showed beautiful big whites so even in length that Richard had always thought they might be false.

"Hi, M. Good to see you," Richard said. He read an ulterior motive in M's eyes. "Seems you put on a few extra pounds."

"Really? What're you up to, Richard. Find other work yet?"

"Naw. Haven't even looked, M." Richard chuckled softly, looking into his coffee cup. "I'm sure the dean has succeeded in blackballing me, anyway, don't you?"

He had always suspected Dr. Murphy of having something to do with his demise at the university.

"I really wouldn't know, Richard. The dean and I aren't close."

Richard nodded in silence. He knew it was a lie. The dean invited Dr. Murphy to every party he threw, and M had rubbed Richard's nose into that fact on more than one occasion.

"Well. Thanks for the quick response. I'm glad it wasn't windy."

"Oh, yeah. I forgot to mention that in my instructions, didn't I? Sorry. But it came out okay, you said, right?"

"Yeah. Great. Worked great. The cold helped. Less disturbance. So, what is it you need to talk to me in person about, M?"

"Uh, yeah. Cut to the chase. That's my Richard. That's why we're here, aren't we? You see, as I told you earlier, I had asked one of your *loyal* students to help me in the lab. Actually, I asked for volunteers, and no one seemed interested until I mentioned it was for you."

"So who were the brave ones?"

"Brave *one*. Ann Kreindler."

Richard nodded and smiled.

"Yeah. Thought you would enjoy that. She's quite a fox—and she thinks you are God!"

"Ann and I have never had any kind of personal relationships, M. Don't go reading things that aren't there. I will say, however, on her behalf, that she was my most promising student. Very astute."

"So, that's why you asked her opinion about creating a carnivorous ant eight centimeters in length? If she thought its exoskeleton could support the atmospheric pressure?" Dr. Murphy smiled broadly. "An original approach, I must say."

85

Richard shook his head and sighed heavily.

"Think what you want of me, M, but leave the poor girl alone."

"Protecting her, are we?"

"Dr. Murphy!"

"Okay, okay." Dr. Murphy held his hand up to stop Richard. "Just kidding. Don't be so delicate. Besides, I certainly wouldn't blame you if you did punch that. If I have the chance, I am definitely going to get in those hot pants!"

"Good luck." *Disgusting! Don't think she would stoop so low.* "So, what's your point, M?"

"Okay. Ann and I talked about you a lot." Dr. Murphy paused for a few seconds. "I put two and two together. Those specimens you sent me were hybrids, and you created them, didn't you?"

"*Moi*? There's absolutely nothing to support your theory, M. I'm sure you already checked my notes at the university."

"Actually, I have. But we both know the university would not approve such research, and neither would the federal government. Where's your lab, Richard? Your private one. The one you've probably been working in for the last, what, ten years? In that house of yours out of town? Is that why you moved out of town?"

"Sorry to disappoint you, M." Richard's stomach began to flip. Soon the evidence would be gone.

"Richard, I'm not going to rat on you. You can level with me. We've been friends for years." He leaned across the table. "As a matter of fact, I want in on it. Fifty-fifty. That's why you moved off campus, isn't it. I know you have your lab in your house, although that could be quite dangerous, considering what you're working on."

"Fifty-fifty of what?"

"Of what? Are you kidding! Don't take me for being naive, Richard!" He lowered his voice to almost a whisper. "There's a fortune in this, Richard!"

"A fortune?" Richard chuckled and raised his hands like a priest about to give a blessing while easing back into his chair.

"Sure. Don't you see? Look. Take the fire ants. How much fire ant poison has been sold since they arrived from South America? And they've already infested half the United States?"

"Hell, millions of bags, I suppose."

"And they spread more every year!"

"I see. You're talking about marketing your poison."

"Can you imagine? We will both make millions! Think about it. When word gets out—and it will—that there is a 'man-eating ant' out there, there will be a panic to buy the poison to kill them. And I will be the first one with the patent. I'll be ahead of everyone else. I'll have a ten-year head start."

"M, it's got to be in a form that can be safely administered by laymen."

"Exactly what Ann and I are working on as we speak."

Richard shrugged.

"Good luck. What do you need me for then, anyway?"

"Richard. I need your help. You've got to give me live specimens to test it on."

"Are you serious? Besides, where would I get live specimens? We just eradicated the only ones I know of. And that reminds me—we need to come up with an antidote to the venom."

"Richard, look. Wow. Great idea." Dr. Murphy turned serious. "I either get your help—or I let the world find out that your research created this monster."

Richard glared at his colleague and looked around the room. "No one will believe you, M."

"No? One of the world's most renowned entomologists who specialized in carnivorous ants gets fired from a university? Specializes in insect DNA?"

"I don't have any specimens of any kind."

"Okay, Richard. Let's say you don't—just for argument's sake— even though I know better. Repeat your experiment. I'd stake my life that you wouldn't throw your notes away."

"M, I wouldn't create such a monster."

"Ha! You already have! Somebody has, anyway—and you are

the only capable one in the world that could. These are your babies, Richard and you and I both know it!"

"They're all dead, M—thanks to your creation, remember?"

"Richard. You're not talking to an idiot on the street here. I'm a fellow entomologist, remember? There's no way you are going to destroy your work. Okay? Let's say you don't create any more? You know as well as I do that more will show up sure as I'm breathing, and they are going to spread just like the fire ants. We want to be able to stop their propagation. When the next ones show themselves, and they most certainly will, you go and get me live specimens."

"And if I don't?"

"You'll be the most infamous scientist in the world. No one will ever give you a job, and the government will be all over your ass. You'll probably even get jail time, not to mention the fines and lawsuits from the university. I can just imagine what the inmates will do to you."

"All right, M, all right. I'll get your damn specimens for you the next time they surface—if they surface."

"Now we're talking, my friend. I'm going to make you famous instead of infamous, okay? I'm going to make both of us multimillionaires!"

"Don't you mean the three of us?"

"Oh, yes, of course. A mere slip of the tongue."

Richard had little interest in continuing the conversation, but Dr. Murphy rambled on about his plans to develop and promote the toxins he was working on. He heard Dr. Murphy's words as distant noise as his mind took another course. He thought of how he was going to stop Dr. Murphy from involving him in his scheme of wealth, and more importantly, from telling the world he was responsible for creating his monster. A thought flashed before him of eliminating M. He would have to destroy the evidence as soon as he got home. He couldn't wait till Sunday.

He drove home with a troubled mind, and on a couple occasions, a horn from behind brought him out of his trance at a stoplight.

As he pulled into his driveway, he noticed he had left a light on.

He chuckled to himself and shook his head. He had even forgot to notice Mary's store as he came into town.

He pulled his keys out to open the door and decided to try the handle. It was open. He shook his head again. As he stepped in, he noticed the light was coming from the kitchen. He heard a sound coming from the lighted room, and Mary was cleaning and organizing the plates in the cupboard.

"Oh, thank God you're home. I was so worried." She scurried over and threw her arms around Richard's neck, giving him a hard hug.

Richard returned the hug in silence, a smile slowly creeping across his face.

"Where were you? I mean, you're always home. I noticed your car wasn't in the driveway, so I stopped to check the door—in case you forgot to lock it. You did." She caressed his face and placed a tender kiss on his lips. "Hungry, darling? I brought you a tomato macaroni and cheese casserole. Homemade. I can make a sandwich to go with it if you like."

"Just the macaroni. I'm not really that hungry." Richard plopped down on a chair at the end of the table.

"Is everything all right, darling? You look worried."

He wanted to tell Mary everything, but he didn't want to get her involved in such a scandal.

"What is it? You can tell me anything."

"Oh. It's just—work. A colleague wants me to do some work for him."

"Well, that's good, isn't it?"

"Yeah. I guess it is. It'll mean a lot of money, but I don't know."

"What's the matter? Is it something illegal?"

"Uh … no. It just could be a little dangerous."

"Dangerous! You told him no, then, didn't you? The money's not worth it. You're brilliant. You can get a good job, a safe job, just about anywhere."

Richard chuckled. *If you only knew.*

"You're protecting me?"

"Well, got to protect my—well, you're a big boy, I guess—a *big* boy. Got to protect that, you know."

They both laughed, the macaroni and cheese was abandoned on the kitchen table, and an hour later, their sweaty bodies were culminating the pleasure of his *big* boy, now dutifully named.

— — — — — —

Richard awoke to find himself alone in bed. He got up, eased into some jeans, pulled on a T-shirt, slid into his slippers, and went downstairs to the kitchen.

He noticed a note on the table:

> Morning, darling. Big boy did another hell of a job last night. There's an omelet in the microwave. Warm it up for just thirty seconds. Coffee's made. Enjoy! Left you the mac and cheese for later.

He finished his breakfast, debated whether to serve himself a plate of her casserole, and poured a second cup of coffee to take down to his lab.

He looked around and sighed heavily. It had to be done. He began to dig out his ant colonies. Salty tears rolled down his face when he looked at the empty aquariums.

He was soaked with perspiration, decided it was enough for one day, and made his way to the shower after placing the black plastic bags on the curb for the garbage pickup.

You really got yourself into quite a mess, haven't you, genius? You destroyed your evidence, but you can't destroy your notes, can you? Where will you hide them? And Mary? What if she finds out?

CHAPTER 14

▬ ▬ ▬ ▬ ▬ ▬ ▬ ▬

GOVERNOR SUSAN PERKMANN SAT BEHIND HER LARGE glass desk in her plush, high-backed leather chair and stared at a large glass test tube that safely encased a specimen. She gingerly reached for the test tube and held it between her right thumb and index finger, bringing it closer to her face. She rolled the test tube to examine her specimen carefully.

"Carnivorous," she said out loud. "My God. Huge!"

She carefully placed the specimen on her desk, opened a manila folder, and began to read.

> Estimated several hundred thousand—over five foot deep—average size 5.78 centimeters—queen measured 7.91 centimeters—several skeletons of small cats, dogs, and mice—woman's skeleton found in an outhouse and transferred to local morgue.

She closed the file and sat back in her chair, rolling the test tube over and over. She picked up the phone and waited a few seconds. "Barbara, get me the Animal and Plant Health Inspection Service, ASAP, okay?"

The phone buzzed, and the first button began to flash intermittently. She pushed the button and brought the phone to her ear. "Hello?"

"Hello. This is the Animal and Plant Health Inspection Service. How can we help you, Mrs. Perlmann?"

"Perkmann. I'm afraid I need to talk with your top dog on this one, honey. With whom am I speaking?"

"This is Linda Washington, ma'am. The top dog, Dr. William Overton, is in a meeting right now. Can someone else help you?"

"No. It has to be Mr. Overton, Linda."

"Dr. Overton. Can I tell him what this is about, ma'am?"

"Just tell Dr. Overton it's a case of life or death—of possible national security—and that this is the governor of Kentucky calling, not some attention-crazy citizen, okay?"

"Yes, ma'am. I'll tell him. He probably won't return your call till tomorrow though."

"Linda, dear."

"Yes, ma'am?"

"Just mention this to him: six inch carnivorous ants—a million of them. Can you remember that?"

"Yes, ma'am."

"Thank you, Linda. Good bye."

She hung the phone with a bang, shaking her head. *They even have morons answering the phone in Washington? Did she think I was calling to chew the fat? Damn!*

An hour later her secretary buzzed her.

"Dr. William Overton on the line, Susan. Line two."

"Thanks, Barbara." She pushed the flashing button and picked up the receiver.

"Dr. Overton?"

"Yes, Mrs. Perkmann. How can I help you? Linda mentioned something about a giant carnivorous ant—lots of them."

"Yes, Doctor. I have a specimen in front of me that I'd like to send you—accompanied by a report that I'd like to take the time to read you right now."

"I'm listening Mrs. Perkmann. Excuse me, and forgive my ignorance, who are you?"

"Oh. Sorry for assuming. I told Linda I am the governor of Kentucky. And, please, call me Susan."

"Thank you, Governor. Please call me Bill."

"Thank you, Bill." She read the full report and waited for Dr. Overton's reply. "Bill?"

"Yeah. I'm still here. I'm thinking. That's quite a report. How reliable is it?"

"Very."

"I definitely will need to see the specimen. You did the right thing to call me."

"Thank you, Bill. I'll FedEx them in the morning with the report."

"No, Susan. I'll send for them. Can you do me a big favor?"

"Sure."

"Now, I said!"

"What?" She held the phone away from her ear.

"Oh, sorry, Susan. I was talking to someone else. Mr. David Terrence will be there first thing in the morning—0800 hours. That all right?"

"Yeah. I'll have the coffee ready."

"He won't have time, Susan."

"Oh. Okay."

"I really must implore you to keep a lid on this until I investigate."

"I think we're too late on that."

"Probably. Write down anything else you can think of: who did the investigation, the names and addresses of every person involved, you know."

"Sure thing, Bill."

"I'll keep you posted."

"You better. Or I'll be calling you."

"Ha, ha. I bet you would, too."

"Damn right I will! Fair warning. This is my territory. My people."

"Gotcha. Really good thinking, Susan. I'd like to meet you someday."

"Looking forward to it, Doctor. You can take my husband and me out to the best diner in town."

"Done deal, Susan. McDonald's okay?"

"Only if I can order two Big Macs."

"You got it! Thanks again, Susan. We'll be in touch. Remember to keep a cap on this."

"Mum's the word, Bill."

"Thanks, Susan. Bye for now."

"Bye, Bill."

Does he really think we can keep a lid on something like this? If I handle this right, I might get a boost up the ladder in Washington.

CHAPTER 15

━━ ━━ ━━ ━━ ━━ ━━ ━━

JEFFREY E. DAVIDSON, KNOWN BY HIS FRIENDS AND WIFE as Jed, was a happy camper. He had recently retired from the Santa Fe Railroad Company after fifty years of service. The Santa Fe Railroad was his first and only employment.

He thought back on a conversation with his wife of forty-six years. "I want to move when I retire, honey. A small town where everyone knows everyone, you know? Tranquil—no discos, nightclubs, theaters, or fancy restaurants."

"Sounds kind of boring, hon. Sure you would be happy with that?"

"Me? Yes. It's you I'm worried about."

She had put her arms around his neck and placed her soft cheek against his. "I'll be happy anywhere you are, Jed, dear."

"I'll take you places whenever you want."

That was so long ago, but retirement was finally here. It was time to look for the town that had filled his dreams for so many years, but would his wife still go wherever he wanted?

A year before, Jed was on a run that stopped in Custer City. Normally, he didn't step off the train during stops in little towns, but they were loading cotton and broomcorn, and he decided to get off and stretch his legs about town to pass some of the three hours.

Main Street was only a couple of blocks from the rail terminal. He passed a couple of medium-sized homes with well-maintained yards, and one had a for sale sign. He stopped at a building that had a drug store, a restaurant, and an old-fashioned fountain store. He decided to have a cup of coffee; it was like going back to his youth.

"Can I get you anything, sir?"

"Coffee." Jed noticed the name tag on her dirt brown apron worn over a well-pressed white blouse and black slacks. Nancy Dobbs had short gray hair and looked like she had just stepped out of the salon.

"Just visiting?" Nancy placed his coffee in a large white mug in front of him on a thick wooden table.

"Yeah. Work for the railroad. Going to be a while seems like. They're loading."

"Well, we don't get many visitors here. Welcome, sir."

"Jed. Name's Jed. Say you don't get many visitors here? Why not?"

"Well, for starters there's less four hundred people in Custer." She smiled and sat across from Jed, placing the coffee pot on the table as if she'd known him all her life. The only windows were in the front of the building. The wooden walls were covered with antiques and pictures of the town's history.

"Really? Interesting."

"Interesting? Custer is a super tranquil town. Everyone's good Christian people though. All Caucasian. Can find everyone in town every Sunday at eleven at the church down the street."

"Really? I been through here many times, but I never got off the train before. What else can you tell me about your quaint little town?"

She was eager to share his company. She hadn't had a customer in two hours. "The only bank is the Southwest National Bank. Steve Pratt manages it. He's in his late forties. His wife, Carrie, is the town historian. She can tell you all about this place. It has a lot of history, you know."

"No. I didn't know."

"Well, it does. Anyway, Steve and Carrie have three teenagers. Nice people. Live just a block away."

"What do you do for entertainment, Nancy?"

"Well, there's really nothin' much to do here, but Clinton is just twenty minutes away. There's a lot to do there. They've got shopping, movies, a real theater." She leaned toward Jed as if to tell him a secret. "They even have a *casino*!"

Three refills gave Jed all the local gossip he needed.

Jed walked along the street. The building next door was J. H. Pyeatt's General Store, a historic landmark according to the signs. The large buildings were made of sandstone and brick with rectangular windows that lined the walls like soldiers. The First National Bank, made of what look like its original brick, was on the corner.

He fell in love with Custer City and made his decision. He had difficulty convincing Carol—even after he reminded her of her promise—until he took her to Clinton one Saturday.

In just a couple of hours on the streets of downtown, Carol discovered that the Southwest Playhouse only charged $9.50 a person to see its performances. The Western Oklahoma Ballet Theatre had perked her interest with their program, and the stop at the Route 66 Museum (at only $3.00 a person) delighted her.

Jed was not exactly blind himself. He noticed the Clinton Motor Sport Park and the Clinton Country Jamboree, but the real clincher in convincing Carol there was enough entertainment for them in this city close by was the Lucky Star Casino.

They spent the night at this "den of sin," and their comps paid for the room. They returned home late on Sunday evening, and on Monday morning, Jeffrey E. Davidson announced his retirement.

Jed was excited about starting his new life in Custer City, and his wife shared his enthusiasm, something neither had experienced in years.

It may have been the retirement, which meant she wouldn't be alone so much anymore, or it may have simply been the new change had stimulated their lives, but for whatever reason, even the sex reappeared in their lives, accompanied by laughter and playfulness.

Jed bought the house with the for sale sign. He repainted,

wallpapered, rebuilt, and landscaped his new dwelling to Carol's complete satisfaction without a single complaint.

They attended church every Sunday, and within four months, they had developed many friends and a full social life that surpassed the humdrum social life they had in Tulsa. They had lived for many years in the same house without ever being in a neighbor's house on the same street—much less knowing who they were or what they did.

Carol became close friends with Carrie and learned the interesting history of Custer City. She became active with the town's historical committee for the preservation of Custer City and its landmarks.

Custer City was founded in 1891 and was called Graves after the first postmaster until 1904 when the name was changed in honor of Lieutenant Colonel George A. Custer, the second postmaster.

Custer City was established due to the construction of two railroad lines by the joint efforts of five railroad companies. The construction of the railway routes through Custer City caused the nearby city of Independence to become a ghost town as its residents moved to Custer City for work.

Custer City's history has made its mark. The Broadway Hotel, the First National Bank, and J. H. Pyeatt's General Store were listed in the National Registry of Historical Places.

The history and preservation of the town was of particular interest to Carol; her frequent visits to Clinton, Weatherford, and Thomas kept her busy and content.

A week didn't go by without visiting the Lucky Star Casino. They liked going on Wednesdays. Without any crowds, they could play all the different slot machines they wanted, mostly the one-cent slots, and the restaurant always had a table available. They usually spent the night as their comps usually picked up the hotel and food tabs.

Jed and Carol, all things considered, emphatically concurred that life just couldn't be better.

CHAPTER 16

▬ ▬ ▬ ▬ ▬ ▬ ▬ ▬

HER LONG, ARDUOUS JOURNEY TIRED HER TILL SHE couldn't go on, but it seemed a good place to settle and raise her family. She found the land fertile and spacious—perfect for building her new home, which needed a lot of space for her numerous rooms. She would need to house many children.

In just three months, her family had begun. Her daughters worked diligently and incessantly, while her lazy sons just ate and lay around the house, trying to stay out of the way of their aggressive sisters who hardly noted their existence.

Her children built her a house that extended along a field's edge. The wild grass offered great protection and kept her clear of any nuisances or interference from neighbors. She was 100 percent family orientated and had no interest whatsoever in socializing with anyone outside of the family.

As the family grew, they added rooms along the field's edge instead of going up as a high-rise. They kept making more workrooms, storage rooms, and nurseries by going deeper.

They continually moved the mother's room deeper, and after several months, they had to carry her because she had gained too much weight for her own legs to carry her.

Her daughters didn't mind the extra work their mother caused and never complained. Every once in a while, a fight would break out among the sisters, just like in any other family, but it never lasted long. In quite a few occurrences, one of the sisters died.

Mother was never informed of these skirmishes or casualties, and the bodies were always disposed of quickly. She was immobile now and much too busy making food for all her children to notice.

Some of her children abandoned her and left to build homes of their own next door. Mother knew her sons that left would soon be their daughters' food. Her sons were too weak, lazy, and docile. Her daughters would use and abuse them, but there would be more sons.

The daughters that left home didn't travel like their mother. They began new lives nearby, sharing the wealth of the unused forest of grass, which extended for miles. Their entire community was hidden along the edge of a field in Custer City.

They had grown accustomed to the way the train vibrated their homes every time it passed.

━ ━ ━ ━ ━ ━

The United States government paid the owner of the field not to plant it. When he was offered the opportunity to allow a small herd of twenty cattle to graze in his field, he accepted the deal gladly.

Simon Schneider watched the train unload his new tenants directly into his field, ushered by four cowhands just like in the old western movies.

He smiled as he watched the cattle begin to chomp on the high grass immediately. They would eat their way to market weight. Herefords brought a good price.

Maybe the owner of Byson's Cattle Company would give him one of those cows—or at least give him a really good price on one when the time came. He could slaughter it and freeze all those steaks and roasts. He'd eat like a king for the next two years. Of course, he wouldn't share his prize meat with anyone. He would keep his stash a secret from the townsfolk.

Simon had maintained his bachelorhood for forty-seven years, and he had learned how to apply the word *frugal*—even with women.

—— —— —— —— —— ——

"Hi, Simon."

"Hello. Who's this?"

"What? You have so many broads after you, you can't tell the difference? It's Nicole."

"Nicole! Hi! I just didn't recognize your voice. What's up, babe?"

"That's my question to you, lover boy," she said softly.

"Ha, ha. Maybe if you come here, you'll find out."

"I got a better idea. How 'bout you take me on a Caribbean cruise?"

"Ha! You payin'?"

"As a matter of fact, yes. I won a cruise for two. We could leave this Saturday for Galveston. It sails Sunday."

"Really? Congratulations! Actually, it's good timing. Sounds good. Uh, you checked for those hidden costs and everything?"

"Yes, Mr. Splendid. I already paid the taxes. All the meals are free, and there's a free show every night. You just have to pay whatever you spend in the casino and shopping at the ports of call. And on board, of course."

"I've been on a cruise before."

"Well, then?"

"Yeah. Book me. We leave this Saturday?"

"I'll pick you up at 0400. Be ready. Oh, send me all your personal data. I need the name as it appears on your passport, addr—"

"Yeah, I know. Isn't this hurricane season though?"

"Why do you think they let me win? Don't worry. I checked the weather report and all. No problem, Mr. Valiant."

"Great. Okay, I'll send it to you right away. I'll even share the gas on the way down to Galveston."

"Ooh, how generous, lover boy. Just make sure you're generous with what's between your legs on board."

"Sex, sex, sex. Thank God that's all you think about."

After he hung up, he checked his red book to make sure he hadn't agreed to spend a week with a dog.

━ ━ ━ ━ ━ ━

"Jed?"

"Yeah?"

"I'm leaving on a cruise this Saturday morning ... early."

"Congratulations."

"I need a favor."

"Name it."

"I rented out the field to the Byson Cattle Company to graze around twenty head of cattle. Think you could kind of keep an eye on them while I'm gone? I mean, I have an automatic feeder and water for them. You really don't have to do anything. Just take a look out your back window every once in a while, okay?"

"Sure. That's why the wire fence."

"Yeah. I didn't want them grazing on my neighbors' lawns."

"That's a lot of fence."

"They paid for it."

"Good for you. You get a free fence. Sure the extra bucks will come in handy. How long will you be gone?"

"A week. Be back around noon on Monday."

"Okay. Have a great trip, Simon."

"Thanks. And thanks for the help, Jed."

━ ━ ━ ━ ━ ━

They sensed different vibrations than normal. Scouts from all six homes along two sides of the field made their ways through the forest of tall grass to investigate, marking their way as they went with their own special chemicals.

When the scouts discovered the abundant treasure, they excitedly returned home and broadcast the news. More than two million female warriors prepared for battle.

After four days of preparation, the soldiers began their march at first light. It was difficult to create paths to their targets, but diligence, perseverance, discipline, and superior engineering created ample paths for the hordes of warriors that would enter in battle that very night.

As the new day's sun climbed in the sky, the battalions began the daylong journey toward its targets and halted. The multitudes behind began to spread out until one battalion joined another. When all were in place, they stood in total silence, millions of soldiers at attention, motionless.

The cattle seemed to become a little restless as a scout informed the general and the silent command came, commencing the simultaneous attack of all battalions and the chaos of battle began.

The cries of their victims filled the crisp cool early evening air for a couple of minutes, dropping their victims with dull thuds.

A couple of households closest to the field were alerted at the distant cries of the cattle, but by the time they stood, silence ensued. They returned to their activities and television shows.

There was a frenzy only a witness of the African driver ant can imagine. Each battalion took its spoils to their perspective homes, tirelessly and with such rapidness and organization that one could only hold them in awe.

Climbing up the towering legs of the cattle proved no challenge for the warriors. Within seconds, tens of thousands of injections had been given and the giants fell, killing hundreds of the fearless warriors in the process, but there was no concern for such is the price of battle.

The loss of life did not deter or slow the soldiers. There were no skirmishes about who received credit for the kills or who shared the biggest slice of the spoils.

Not one battalion doubted the victory and not one soldier celebrated it. Victory was only the beginning of the arduous toil of transporting these giants, piece by tiny piece, to their individual homes, leaving only the bones, skin, and blood-stained ground for others to find.

▬ ▬ ▬ ▬ ▬ ▬

Halloween morning was cold, but the townsfolk had celebrated the previous day because Sundays were for church.

Jed looked out the back window. "Where the hell did they go?"

"Who, dear?"

"The cattle. I can't see hide or hair of 'em." He put on his rubber hip boots because the field grass was still wet from the morning dew. He really didn't feel like doing it, but he had given Simon his word—and his word was his bond.

"Really?" Carol looked out the window. "Well, you don't have to go right this second, dear. Wait till after church and the dew dries off."

"Naw. Might as well get it done and out of the way. It'll bother me throughout the whole service." He sipped coffee as he slowly made his way toward the center of the field. He couldn't see any cattle, but he saw the top of the feeder peering over the tall grass. He decided to walk a little ways more.

About a hundred yards into the field, he stopped. He squeezed his butt cheeks to try to stop the itch. He passed his cup to his left hand, reached down the back of his hip boots, and tried to slide his hand down the back of his jeans.

He set his coffee cup on the ground in front of him, slid the shoulder straps of his hip boots, and pulled them down to his knees. He unfastened his belt and unzipped and unbuttoned his jeans. He reached down inside his jeans until he found the spot, dug his fingers deep into the spot, and scratched.

He sighed as the burn substituted the itch and faded away. He fastened his trousers and belt, pulled up his hip boots, and picked his coffee cup. He took a big sip of his coffee, noting the familiar odor from his fingers, and looked around. There was not a single cow. Just tall grass.

He cupped his hand at his mouth and yelled as loud as he could. He made another 360-degree turn. *No noise. No cattle. Oh, the hell with it. She's right. Later.* The itch was returning.

——— ——— ——— ——— ——— ———

A couple of scouts noticed the tall fresh specimen. There was only ten feet to reach him as they steadily stalked their way toward him. They were just two feet away when their target turned and moved away. They followed at a distance until it disappeared into a large structure. They rubbed antennae and busily marked a path to the door. They slowly returned, exhausting their supply of chemicals before they reached home before they came across a path that led them the rest of the way.

——— ——— ——— ——— ——— ———

Oh shit. Simon's going to have a cow. He walked briskly toward the house.

After relieving himself of his itch in the bathroom, he looked up Simon's number and dialed. He either couldn't get through or Simon had turned off his phone.

"What's the matter, dear? You find the cattle?"

"That's just it. Not one."

"Well, they probably just wandered off behind Simon's house or something. It's a big field."

"With a fence around them? But just the same, I tried to call him. No answer though. I'll try again later. Probably no reception on the ship."

"Don't worry, dear. I'm sure they're all right."

Jed looked into a small telephone directory and picked up the phone.

"Byson Cattle Company."

"Hi. I'm calling on behalf of Simon Schneider here in Custer."

"Yes, sir?"

"Uh. How do I say this? Uh, Simon left on a cruise and asked me to keep an eye on the cattle you have grazing on his property."

"Yes. In Custer City, I believe you said. We have twenty Herefords there."

"Right. Well, uh, we may have a problem."

"Sir?"

"I can't find them."

"You mean you can't see them."

"Well, yeah. I can't see them either."

"Cattle move a lot when they graze."

"But the field is fenced in."

"Sometimes they all lie down to rest. If the grass is tall, you probably can't notice them."

"Ah. That must be it. The grass is tall. I'll check a little later. They do get up, don't they?"

"Yes, sir." She chuckled. "They do, especially when they're hungry."

"Okay. Thank you."

"May I have your name, sir?"

"Jed."

"Okay, Mr. Jed. Thank you for calling."

"You're welcome."

Jed felt a little foolish.

"Wouldn't it have been better to wait till you talked to Simon, dear?"

"Well. Maybe. I guess so. I just got nervous, I guess. Water over the damn."

"Yes, dear." She placed a plate with two fried eggs, sunny-side up, a large thick slice of ham, and a buttered English muffin. "Now relax and enjoy your breakfast so we won't be late for church." She placed a small bowl of grits with melting butter to his left and a large cup of coffee to his right.

"Oh, that smells delicious!"

CHAPTER 17

━━ ━━ ━━ ━━ ━━ ━━

"DO YOU HAVE TO BE SO STUBBORN?"

"I haven't seen them all day."

"Wait till you talk with Simon, dear."

"He told me to keep an eye on them. I just can't reach him. He must have his cell turned off."

"He's just out of range, dear. Remember, he's at sea. There's no reception. It's only another day."

"Naw. I gotta find out."

"You just stay put, Jeffrey E. Davidson!"

He knew that tone.

"Go get yourself a shower and get ready to have dinner with the Pratts. Those cattle are not your responsibility. And that Casanova Simon has never done you any favors. Tomorrow afternoon, you're taking me to Clinton—and we're not coming back until Wednesday evening. Tomorrow, you can call Simon. He'll be driving back by then. You said he'd be here by noon."

And that was that. Jed just relaxed and let the cattle walk out of his mind, which was easier than dealing with an angry wife.

━━ ━━ ━━ ━━ ━━

It would be a long march, but no one complained. The trail was faint, but still trackable. The scouts ran ahead, remarking the trail for the rest. It took them a day and a half to reach their destination.

The word went out, and they began to fan out along the shorter, softer, green grass until they completely bordered the yard of approximately one hundred feet in width.

The front line waited patiently for hours while their fellow combatants lined up behind them until not a spot of ground could be seen. They had filed in together so tightly that they were touching and overlapping each other.

The sun faded and disappeared into the western sky, and the cold night air fell on them like a weight. They crowded together even more, creating a blanket thirty feet long. They would rest for the night and delay the battle till daybreak.

— — — — — —

"As usual, you won and I lost," Jed said when they arrived home. They had gone to Clinton a day earlier.

"That's because you are so negative, dear."

"Yeah, sure! Negative, positive. I still lose."

"But we had a wonderful time, didn't we, dear," Carol said as he put the suitcase on top of the bed for her to unpack. She wrapped her arms around his neck and kissed him gently on the cheek.

"Yes. I guess we did," he said.

"You were really strong last night. How do you keep it up so long? I'm not complaining, mind you."

"Mother Nature, dear. Just Mother Nature."

"Think Mother Nature could repeat it tonight?"

"Tonight? Jesus, I give you an inch—and you want the whole mile!"

"Why not? You only live once." She reached between his legs and was a little disappointed.

"You have to unpack, don't you?" He pulled away. "I got to go to the john."

"Don't play with it," she yelled after him while she began unpacking. "I'll do that later."

"Woman turned into a freakin' sex maniac," he said to himself in the mirror.

"I heard that!" she yelled with a smile.

When they retired, she put her right arm across his chest, her right leg across his hip, and her head rested in his shoulder. His left arm caressed her forearm. This was the way they fell asleep each night, content and tranquil. Their nightly symphony began shortly, each playing their own song, forgetting about the promise of love for they had all day tomorrow and the next day. They would sleep in as they normally did after "casino night," Jed complaining about his back, tossing and turning, until sleep overtook him again.

■ ■ ■ ■ ■ ■

They could feel the heat of the early morning sun warming their bodies as they stirred to ready for battle, many scouts going ahead across the wet grass toward the house. They moved in five directions.

The order was given, and the mass of soldiers began to fan out in the directions marked by the scouts. When the three center flanks reached the house's edge, they stopped and gave time for the two end flanks to go around the house to the front.

When all was ready, they moved in. They entered the house through any and all cracks and holes they could find—and many were there to be found—covering the floors with their bodies. It seemed like they flowed across the floor until they reached the bedroom where their targets slept peacefully—mouths open and chests swelling and collapsing in a slow rhythm.

They scaled the bedposts and climbed up the blanket, replacing it with one of their own.

Jed and Carol never had a chance. Thousands of stings were delivered at once, and the venom triggered a heart attack in the two victims at almost the same instant. They were mercifully spared the horror of the millions of attackers fiercely chomping and tearing at their flesh.

CHAPTER 18

━━ ━━ ━━ ━━ ━━ ━━

AN ENTIRE WEEK WITH THE SAME WOMAN WAS REALLY TOO
much for Simon. He wondered how any man could marry and
spend the rest of his life with just one woman. It would be torture.
One became accustomed to the sex very quickly, and then all the
problems begin.

Nicole got out of the car with every intention of accompanying
Simon into his house.

"Thanks, babe. It was a great week, but I am absolutely bushed!"

She stopped in her tracks and looked at him like a child who
was just told they weren't going to Six Flags after being promised.

"Oh. Well, uh. Call me, huh? You did have a good time, didn't you?"

"Sure did! It was great. I ... u ... need to check on the cattle and
everything. You know. I'm taking care of them and everything. Got
responsibilities to handle, you know." *Good thinking, Simon.*

"Oh, yeah. That's right. You told me. Okay, then. Call me. You can
take me to Clinton for dinner."

"Will do," he said as he entered his house and closed the door
behind him. Escaped. He leaned against the door and let out a long,
slow sigh.

*Wow. I am so dad-gum sore! Whew! She is good, though. Great
body!*

The morning light on Tuesday morning entered through his
blinds, and Simon stretched and yawned out loud. He rolled over
and looked at the clock on the nightstand beside the bed. 10:10.

I guess I'll get up and make myself some breakfast. Tired, don't feel like doing anything.

He dragged himself to the kitchen in his underwear. He fried some eggs and ham and put some Pace salsa on top.

He picked up his cell and noticed Jed had called. He keyed in the phone number. No answer.

He had every intention on checking on the cattle after breakfast, but the "lazies" got the best of him—and he crashed for another four hours. *No wonder married men age so quickly.*

He got up, threw on some faded jeans and a gray sweatshirt, and made his way down to the restaurant. He didn't bother making his bed.

"Hi, Nance," he said as he dragged one of the chairs closer to the window.

"Hi, Simon. Welcome back to the real world."

"Thanks. Give me one of those Philly cheesesteaks and fries."

"Comin' up!"

She placed his order in front of him—along with the soda he always ordered—and plopped down next to him.

"So, how's Nicole?"

"Nicole? Fine, I guess."

"Aw, c'mon, Simon. Fine. What kind of answer is that? Spill the beans. Tell me how the cruise went."

Just then, another client a family of four came in.

"I'll be back." Nancy said.

Hope you don't, Simon thought as he bit into his sandwich.

— — — — — —

Darkness came early at this time of year, and by the time Simon got home from making the runs to the hardware store and the food store, it was too dark to check on the cattle—and not that he felt like it anyway.

He sat in front of the tube and turned on the recording of

Monday Night Football he had programmed before he left on the cruise. He never saw the end of the game. He fell asleep on the couch.

On Wednesday morning, he was up at daybreak. He made himself a good breakfast and put on some knee-high rubber boots to walk through the tall grass.

Halfway to the feeder, he still hadn't seen any cattle. "Lazy bums. Lying down on the job, I bet."

When he got close to the feeder, he stopped in his tracks. "What the?" He stared at the wrinkled skins draped over the large animals' bones. Cautiously he approached the large skeletons, his mouth still open with shock.

"Son of a bitch! Wow. Look at the size of those ants!" He noticed a bunch of dead ants, but his concern was not about ants at the moment. He reached for his phone and keyed in Jed. Still no answer. He turned on his heels and hightailed it out of there.

He sped over to Jed's to ask him what the hell was going on! He had left him to watch his cattle—and look what he came back to!

He jumped out of his truck, leaving the door open, and pounded on Jed's front door. He noticed Jed's car and knew he had to be home.

When there was no answer, he pounded again. "Jed! Jed! It's Simon! Open the damn door!" Still no answer.

He reached for the front door handle and turned it on the slim chance it was open. It wasn't. He saw one of those giant ants on Jed's doorstep. *Must've rained*, he thought.

He went around back and pounded on the back door. Still no answer. He noticed more ants on the doorjamb and on the ground. They looked like the ones around the bones in the field.

"Jed!" Still no answer.

He went over to a window and tried it. It moved. He raised the window.

"Jed! Carol? Anyone?"

He shook his head and climbed in the window, closing it behind him.

"Jed? Carol?" He yelled louder.

He looked around. All was quiet. He walked into the kitchen and then back to the bedrooms.

"Jed? Anyone home?" There were another few giant ants and some blackish red trails of something. "What the?"

The master bedroom door was open, and he cautiously walked in—not wanting to catch Jed and Carol in any hanky-panky. He stopped cold after three steps.

They were in blood-soaked sheets. Their hair was matted with blood, and they were dressed in blood-soaked pajamas. And were those bones sticking out of the sleeves of their pajamas?

"Oh, shit!"

Simon ran out, jumped in his truck, and drove off—and then he slammed on the brakes. *Where the hell am I going?*

"Lance!" He put the truck in gear and floored the gas pedal.

"Lance!" he yelled as he barged into the sheriff's two-room office building.

"Simon? What brings you here?"

"Lance, you've got to go to Jed and Carol's place."

"Whoa. Calm down, Simon. Jesus. I never seen you like this before. Sit down and try telling me what's going on."

"Jed and Carol! That's what's goin' on! Go to their place. Hurry! You won't believe it!"

"Okay, okay, Simon. I'll go see Jed and Carol. Just calm down. Comin' with me?"

"Oh, no. I been there. No way I'm goin' back there! No way! I'll wait right here, thank you very much."

"All right, all right. I'll go see what's going on. Take it easy, man. Make yourself comfortable."

"You won't see much of them," he said to himself when he heard the door close.

— — — — — —

Lance didn't say a word when he returned forty minutes later. He walked right past Simon and picked up the phone. Lance and Simon looked at each other knowingly in silence while he waited for someone to pick up at the other end.

"Clinton Police Department, Sharon Gilden," the police chief's assistant said.

"Sharon. Hi. Lance Compton here. Roger in?"

"Hi, Lance. How's Ellen? Better be treating her good."

"Sue's fine, Sharon. Thanks. Roger?"

"Roger? Yeah, he's in. Roger! Pick up line two. It's Lance!"

"Lance, my boy! Finally call to invite me to go fishing at that lakefront cottage of yours?"

"I wish. Oh, I really do wish that were the reason."

"What's up, Lance?" Roger sat up in his chair. "Sounds like you just lost your best friend."

"More or less."

"Jesus. Well, spill it, boy!"

"I need you to come down here to Custer."

"Something happened in Custer? Really? Custer?"

"Yeah. Custer. I told you about those newcomers, Jed and Carol. Remember?"

"Oh, yeah. That was a while ago now. Nice couple you said. Retired from the railroad. Bought that house in town that had been vacant for what? Eight years?"

"Yeah. Well. I'm afraid it's going to be vacant again." Lance paused a few seconds. "They're dead."

"What? Murdered?"

"I don't know. Jesus. I really don't know what to tell you. You need to get down here right now, Roger!"

"Okay, Lance, okay. Tell me what you can."

"Tell you what I can? Well, let's see. I broke into their front door, walked into their master bedroom, and found their skeletons. Didn't have to take any vital signs, Lance. No pulses or anything. They're dead. Oh, they are definitely dead."

"Skeletons? Did you say skeletons? Maybe it's some kind of sick joke some of the teenagers are playing on you."

"No. No joke." Lance shook his head vigorously.

Silence ensued.

"Roger?"

"Yeah. I'm still here."

"Get in your damn car and get your damn butt over here—now!"

"On my way, Lance." The phone went dead.

━━ ━━ ━━ ━━ ━━ ━━

Five hours later, Jed and Carol's house had yellow crime scene investigation plastic tape posted around their entire house. A coroner's wagon had carefully loaded the skeletons and sheets for transport to the crime lab in Tulsa.

"Well this is sure a weird case, Lance."

"That's calling the kettle black."

"Did you see these?" Sharon held up a small plastic bag with a large ant inside.

"They're called ants, Sharon," Roger said with a smile.

"I know they're ants, Chief, but look at the size of this one."

"Probably a queen," the chief said.

"I don't know," Sharon said. "I'm going to look at this under a microscope back at the office."

"You do that." Roger shook his head.

"I don't think the ant is exactly the highest priority here, Sharon."

"Probably not, Lance. But it'll give me something to do while we wait for the forensics report from Oklahoma City."

"Leave it to a woman to come up with something else to do, right, Lance?"

"Right."

CHAPTER 19

NEWS SPREAD THROUGH THE SMALL TOWN LIKE A SWARM of locusts coming down on a cornfield. It was the biggest newsflash in the history of Custer City. Although they didn't actually say it, the townsfolk were relieved it was the newcomers and not one of the regular townsfolk.

The Byson Cattle Company had sent a representative by helicopter to verify Simon's story about their cattle and made light of it. They didn't even try to get Simon to return the money they had paid him in advance.

"That's what insurance is for," the representative at the cattle company had explained to Simon. He told Simon an insurance rep may want to come out, but he thought the pictures from the helicopter would be enough.

Reverend James T. King's wife and two other ladies she had easily recruited distributed a special invitation by hand for Sunday's church service, which would be held promptly at eleven o'clock to honor Jeffrey E. Davidson and his wife.

A week later, scouts alerted the others about a location where they would find more food. It was a brick building. It didn't take long to put themselves in position in the freshly cut fields of hay that surrounded the isolated building, giving their advance great coverage.

— — — — — —

The church bell rang to announce the second of three services Reverend King planned for the terrible incident. Every woman, man, and child of Custer City and many from the surrounding towns had crammed into the wooden pews of the Custer City Baptist Church.

The parking lot was full, and many cars lined the street, reducing it to one lane.

All comments from the church members—and rare nonmembers—were about "poor Jed and Carol" and the herd of cattle.

"Oh, my God, honey. Every pew is full, and there are people standing."

"Yes. Isn't it wonderful? Shame it couldn't be like this every Sunday," Reverend King said. His eyes sparkled at the anticipation of speaking to so many of his flock. There would be more newspaper and television reporters again.

"Well, maybe it will in the future, dear. This really will put our little town in the news, dear, maybe increase the number of members, don't you think?"

"Maybe. I just want all the townsfolk to come every Sunday."

"You need to be more ambitious, dear. We need to increase the offering too." She looked at herself in the bathroom mirror, making sure she looked her very best for her grand entrance to her seat on the pulpit.

"This is the Lord's work. Not mine."

"The bigger your congregation, the more you make. I don't think there's anything wrong about eating well and living well."

"The Lord has provided us with a home with all taxes and utilities paid—plus a sufficient income to eat quite well, dear."

"You're hopeless, but I love you anyway. Ready?"

"Yes. I am." She made her entrance first, as always, and took her place to the left of the pulpit.

Reverend King made his entrance to his pulpit. Lorraine relished in the fact that the noisy congregation became silent when he entered the room. She saw some people in the back and sides with cameras. She took a second to check her hair and pressed out her black dress.

"First, I would like to thank all of you for coming for the second service of our dearly departed Jed and Carol. They were dear to all of us and will remain in our hearts forever.

"After the service, there will be a luncheon provided by the Pratt family on the lawn in the back of the church. I understand there will be hot dogs, ham sandwiches, potato salad, macaroni salad, and other snacks. Refreshments also. Now let us pray."

— — — — — —

The signal was given. All flanks moved forward like a dark brown wave, rippling with their movements. The organ music made them freeze for a moment, but on they continued. When they had the red brick building totally surrounded, they stopped. A few moments later, they all moved in unison.

— — — — — —

Little Sammy Shubert noticed them first. "Mommy, look!" he whispered.

"Hush, Sammy. Pay attention to the reverend."

He watched them advance for a minute, and then he said, "Ants, Mommy! Lots of 'em!" He pointed at the brown sea that had reached the back pews.

When Sammy's mother looked up, it was too late. Screams began to echo in the building, and all tried to leave. Many stomped on the ants that covered the floor like a blanket, but all they accomplished was blocking the exit from each other.

Reverend James finally figured out why everyone was jumping out of their seats and screaming with panic. "This way! Out the back door!" As he turned to lead his flock out the back, he saw the floor move. He tried to run through them and made it a few feet before he fell to the ground and was immediately engulfed by the ants.

In ten minutes, the roof-raising screams turned to a deadly silence. The brown mass rapidly reduced the people to bones, hair, and bloody clothes.

It had been their greatest victory. There was enough food to last them for a while. It would take them two days to finish there, but they were not disturbed. They would be able to rest and multiply into great numbers.

CHAPTER 20

━━ ━━ ━━ ━━ ━━ ━━

ANN BURST INTO DR. MORTON'S OFFICE. "GOT TO SEE THIS,
Dr. M." She placed her laptop on his desk and clicked.

What I got to see is under those clothes, M thought. With some degree of difficulty, he turned his attention to the screen. One eye stayed on the swells Ann was showing. What he saw made him immediately forget about sex and snapped to attention. "Holy shit! The whole damn congregation!"

"The whole town—every last woman, man, and child was in that church. They were having a service for an elderly couple found dead in their bed—just their skeletons."

"Now *they're* just skeletons." He picked up the phone.

"Hello?" a female voice answered.

"Who's this?"

"Who wants to know?"

"Dr. Michael Morton. Is Dr. Denton there?"

"Oh, yes. It's for you, dear. Dr. Morton."

"Morton? Hello? M?"

"Get dressed. You're going to Custer City, Oklahoma."

"What's in Custer City?"

"Your creation."

Richard took a deep breath and sighed.

"They just wiped out the entire town. Around 400, well, let's see, 367 to be exact. Turn your TV on. It's got to be on every channel by now. This time, there were hundreds of your babies left. Now it's killer ants instead of killer bees. Just like I told you it would be, my friend."

"Got your toxin ready yet?"

"Not commercially. I have the pesticide registration form all filled out—except for the method of application. OECA would be all over my ass if I sent you what I have to experiment with all the media that will be there. It's not a one-man show anymore, Richard. On the upside, I can now apply for an emergency exemption and get this through faster when I'm done."

"This is not going to be just a small nest like last time, M. There have to be millions. How much longer will it take?"

"You promised, Richard. Live samples, remember? I can move faster with live samples. You know how much a pesticide registration costs my friend? Around 135 grand."

"Just to register it? That's ridiculous."

"I'm going to try to get a waiver for at least 50 percent. I'd have to let the university get a percentage though."

"Whatever you've got to do, M. How do I get in? They're going to have the whole town blocked off. The feds will be there soon—if they're not already there."

"I'll get you in. I'll recommend your expertise. They won't refuse. Driving or flying?"

"Remember, I'm not working. Driving."

"Call me when you get there."

"Don't you want to join me?"

"Are you serious? Besides, Ann and I have to finish the toxin."

"Ann and you? She still working with you?"

"Yes. Jealous?"

"Not in the least. I have my own."

"The lady who answered?"

"Yes."

"Does she know about you?"

"She knows I'm an entomologist, yes."

"But she doesn't know about your killer ants, does she?"

"No. And let's keep it that way, shall we?"

"That's entirely up to you, my friend. Get me my samples."

"I'll be on my way within the hour."

"That's my boy. I'll call you as soon as I get you cleared. I expect there will be someone from the EPA there. This is big enough for Washington to get involved. You're going to be famous, Richard—just like I said."

"Yeah. Just get me cleared. Bye, M."

"Oh, Richard?"

"Yes?"

"Better stay in Clinton since they won't let anyone in town. Besides, it's a ghost town now."

"Yeah. Clinton. Got it. Bye."

"Who was that, dear?"

"A colleague from the university I used to work at. I've got to leave for a while, hon." He turned the TV to the news channel.

"What for? Oh, my God. Look!"

They listened to the news and watched the pictures. Close ups were taken of the "killer ants."

"Oh, those poor people! Where do you have to go?"

"Custer City," he said softly.

"Custer City? Custer City! That's where the 'killer ants' are!"

Richard nodded.

"You can't go there!"

"It's my field, hon. That's why they called me."

"But you … you … it's too dangerous!"

"Don't worry. I know my ants, especially the carnivorous ones. They're my specialty, remember?"

"I'm going with you," Mary said.

"No, Mary. I can't let you do that."

"Why, because it's dangerous? No, Mr. Denton. There's nothing to discuss here. I'm going with you—and that's that."

"What about your store?"

"Sally can take care of things. Just stop by the store on the way out. I'll pack a bag."

"I don't know if this is a good idea, Mary."

"You have the money to pay the expenses?"

Ouch! That really hurt. M's offer was getting to sound pretty good. "Okay, you win."

"Sorry, dear. I had to play hardball. I can't let the man I love just up and leave without a fight. Forgive me?"

Richard nodded. Now he would have to figure out how to keep her safe too.

CHAPTER 21

━━ ━━ ━━ ━━ ━━ ━━ ━━ ━━ ━━

THERE WAS A MOTEL 6 LEAVING THE LIGHT ON FOR THEM on Route 183 close to Southwestern Oklahoma State University.

"You're not going right away? At least get something to eat and three four hours of sleep first."

Richard was too tired to argue. He fell into the bed and was snoring in less than a minute.

"How do men do that?" Mary leaned over and kissed him on the forehead.

━━ ━━ ━━ ━━ ━━ ━━

He stretched and sat up on the edge of the bed. The digital clock read 2:00. He moaned and dragged himself into the shower.

Mary was still sleeping, so he left her a note. At least he wouldn't have to argue with her to stay at the hotel till he got back.

He turned off 183 onto 33 toward Custer City. State police had the road barricaded and were asking for the identification from every vehicle, turning them around, and telling them to find another route.

"Hi, officer. My name is Dr. Richard Denton. I was sent here."

The officer pulled a little spiral notebook from his breast pocket and moved a couple of pages. "Yes. Dr. Richard Denton. Entomologist. The ant doctor, right?"

"Right, officer."

"Got ID?"

Richard produced his driver's license and waited impatiently.

"I have instructions to have you report to the feds. They set up shop at the restaurant about two blocks ahead, sir. On the left. You were supposed to be here around ten."

"Overslept. Sorry."

He nodded and waved Richard on.

When he entered the restaurant, everyone stopped and looked up for a minute before putting their noses back in their laptops. Cups of coffee were scattered across the tables.

"Dr. Denton? Richard Denton?"

"That's me. You?"

"Lawrence Trexler. EPA." He stood a good head taller than Richard, and although his hair was solid white, he looked like he could still play football.

"Pleased to meet you Mr. Trexler." Richard offered his hand.

Lawrence grabbed his hand and nodded. "It's not dyed. Everyone stares. We were expecting you earlier. Have you been informed, Dr. Denton?"

"Please call me Richard. It's plastered all over the TV."

"All right. Let me take you to the church first. Hope you're not queasy. This is Dr. Ralph Mullen. He was sent by my boss."

"Pleasure to meet you, Dr. Mullen."

"Good to have you here, Richard. Please call me Ralph. Toxicology."

Richard nodded and noticed a small impromptu field lab he assumed Ralph was responsible for setting up.

"Crude but effective," Ralph said.

Richard nodded and smiled.

Lawrence and Richard crossed the street, ducked under the yellow tape, and entered the church.

Richard closed his eyes for a moment. Thoughts of a war movie flashed through his mind, and the skeletons Indiana Jones found in one of his lost tombs appeared in his mind for just a second.

"You okay, Doc?"

Richard nodded, and his teary eyes scanned the skeletons covered by clothes and stiff with dried blood. The panic those people lived in their last minutes of life was obvious. Some had uselessly tried to run for the exit, and others climbed on top of the pews only to fall on top of others who had already fallen.

He stooped down, took a plastic bag from his pocket and tweezers from his breast pocket, and picked up one of the ants.

"There's lots of those, Doc. Biggest damn ants I ever saw. And carnivorous to boot. It's like they surrounded the place."

"Exactly what they did," he said.

"I hear you're the expert. They have some kind of intelligence, Doc?"

"More than we want to give them credit for, Lawrence."

"Larry. Only my mother calls me Lawrence."

"Larry is easier for me. Know where the nest is?"

"Well, that's the funny thing, Doc. We searched all around the church, but we couldn't find anything."

"Is this the only incident?"

"No, there were a couple of others. They got several head of cattle about a week ago, according to the Byson Cattle Company."

"Where?"

"According to Roger Malenkite, the police chief, they got to an elderly couple too." He referred to a notepad. "Jeffrey Davidson and his wife Carol were in bed, and the cattle they literally devoured were in a field behind their house."

"Has anyone gone over there?"

"I just got here a couple of hours ago. Been pretty busy setting up a headquarters, and this church will take days. Don't want people just walking around out there."

"Good."

"You know how to kill these things, Doc? I don't think the commercial stuff will work."

"I have a colleague working on a toxin. May need your help to get its registration—or whatever it is they need to get—so I can use it."

"We have emergency procedures, Doc. I'll take care of it. Ralph will help. Just let me know when it's ready. What's this guy's name?"

"His name is Dr. Michael Morton, University of Kansas. He's the best. We really need to move on this. In the meantime, let's see if I can find the nest." *Or nests.*

"I'll send one of my men and a radio with you."

"Thanks. I'll start with the house."

"The house? Sure you're all right, Doc? You're trembling."

"Yeah. I'll be fine." Richard took a deep breath. "Takes some getting used to, you know?"

"Yeah. Unfortunately, I do. Oh, uh, Doc?"

"Yeah?"

"You have any idea what species these are? Dr. Mullen asked me, and I have never seen this one."

He sighed. There was no reason to string this part out.

"It looks like their sting affected the people by paralyzing them, and it was very strong. Most likely *Paraponera clavata*."

"This size? Here? In the US? Damn!"

He was better informed than Richard thought.

"Size of the giant ant—or maybe bigger," Larry continued. "And the quantity suggests the *Siafu*. Had to be millions here. Doc? We both know this is not possible unless this is a hybrid, right?"

Richard looked Larry in the eye and nodded.

"Someone made these, maybe? I mean, evolution just isn't that fast. Ralph and I both think so."

"Possibly, Larry. But nature does create its own hybrids, you know. Think someone really has the ability to play with the DNA to this degree?"

"Very few, Doc. Very few in this world have that kind of knowledge. I hear you're one of them."

Richard couldn't meet Larry's eyes. He nodded slowly and shrugged. "Maybe they came in on a ship like the fire ant."

"Could be. Actually, that is our guess too. We have extra security at all the ports as we speak. They are going to complain big time. And I highly doubt nature made a hybrid like this. Maybe a giant carpenter, or harvester, but nature changing such a small ant with characteristics of producing such small colonies to such a large one producing colonies in the millions? No, Doc. Some genius made these. Yep. Some genius has become a modern-day Frankenstein. And you know what the bottom line is to this, Doc?"

"No, Larry. What?" He began to tremble again.

"It's going to take that same genius to combat these things. My biggest fear is some kind of genius terrorist in Europe."

Richard nodded slowly and sighed again. "You may be right."

"What did you say, Doc?"

"You have a good point, Larry. Let me get to work and see if I can find the nest."

Larry's radio crackled. "71."

"Go ahead, 71."

"Dr. Denton will be stopping by in a few minutes. I want Saul to join him."

"Copy that, 71."

"Okay, Doc. I'm afraid I have to continue here for a while and then go back across the street. Saul will be your eyes while you work."

"Thanks," Richard said. *My eyes or my watchdog?*

"Oh, Doc?"

Richard turned to face Larry once again.

"I can't let you go anywhere alone. Understood? Procedures. And be careful. We don't want any more casualties."

Richard nodded and left. *I'm already a prisoner. God, I am so screwed. I should just tell them, but then there is Mary. At least their attention is diverted for the present. How long will that last?*

— — — — — —

Saul was one of those quiet, serious ones. He led Richard to the Davidsons' home and directly to the bedroom. "This is where they were. Unfortunately, that hillbilly police chief sent the bodies to Oklahoma City."

Richard waited for him to continue, but Saul went silent. He began to look around and found his way out the back door. He found another killer ant beside the step in the grass. He picked it up and bagged it. He could see how they broke off into five columns. He smiled and nodded in understanding. They had surrounded the house too.

"What is it?"

Richard looked at Saul and pointed to one of the trails. "They surrounded the house before they attacked."

"Can ants be that smart?" Saul asked.

Richard nodded and followed the trail to the field. "You know exactly where the cattle were, Saul?"

"Center of the field. There's a feeder out there. Dumb cattle company came and picked up the bones. Locals let them throw 'em away. Unbelievable!"

Richard nodded and started for the center of the field.

"I'll lead the way." Saul began walking with his head glued to the ground. When they arrived at the feeder, Saul stopped.

There were many more samples, and Richard bagged a handful, carefully marking the location. It would be too difficult to follow a trail through the high grass. He made a 360-degree turn. "Who lives in that house?"

Saul paged through a little notebook and kept looking at the ground. He seemed nervous.

"Simon Schneider. His field."

"Let's go to his place."

"Been there. Was the one who reported the cattle and the Davidsons."

Richard walked through the field until he came to a wire fence. He began to walk along the fence but stopped suddenly.

"What? See any of those damn ant things?" Saul looked all around.

Richard pointed ahead.

"What? Those piles of dirt?"

"Those 'piles of dirt' are their nests. Let's walk slowly and quietly. They can hear you by vibrations. If you see them coming out of the nest, run as fast as you can in the opposite direction."

He nodded. "You can bet on that."

They kept their eyes on the ground, occasionally looking up at the two-foot mounds of dirt.

"We're looking for a scout."

"A scout?"

"Yes. They send scouts to look for food. When they find some, they let the others know," Richard said, "Jesus. They even have their own spies. There!" Richard pointed at the ground. He took a piece of plastic from his breast pocket, peeled off the adhesive, and placed it in front of the ant.

Saul took a step back and looked around anxiously.

The ant detoured around the plastic, but Richard placed a small stick in front of the specimen. It climbed the stick, quickly heading for Richard's fingers. Richard put the stick on the black plastic and turned it quickly. The specimen stuck to it.

He pulled out a plastic bag, carefully removed the ant from the sticky surface, thrust it in the bag, and sealed it. He punched a couple of small holes in the bag.

"Looks like a rat trap."

"*Ant* trap. Let's go."

"Sounds like a good idea to me!"

CHAPTER 22

"71. COME IN."

"71."

"43. Found the nests. Doc has a live sample. On our way to headquarters."

"Great! That was fast."

"10-4. Out."

Larry looked at his watch when Richard and Saul entered the restaurant.

"Four hours? Fast work, Doc."

"Got to get her in a test tube. Where can I work?"

"Over in the corner where Dr. Mullen is. Give 'em space, everybody."

Richard sat down, pulled a large test tube from his pocket, and unscrewed the cap. It took a while, but he finally cornered the specimen and held it in his tweezers. He shook the ant's hold on the tweezers, grabbed the cap, and screwed it on top. Two tiny holes had been drilled in the cap.

"Very good, Richard. Your hands didn't even shake. Mine were from here," Dr. Mullen said with a smile.

Richard sat back in his chair, and his audience let out a sigh. Their sighs startled Richard, and he turned around to see them crowded around his back. He was glad he wasn't aware of their presence while he worked. " I've got to get this to my colleague."

"I have someone, Doc. I'll take care of it from here." Larry opened his hand for the test tube.

"What do you mean? I told you I have a colleague working on a toxin. He needs a live specimen."

"The United States Government has its own resources. I have to report this to Homeland Security. Now give me the test tube."

Richard reluctantly handed over his specimen. He had to get another one. How was he going to get away to do that?

"Saul, give me the coordinates of the nest."

"Nests, sir. There's like six of 'em. All in a row too. " He handed a piece of paper to Larry.

"Eight," Richard said. "There are eight of them. They are all in a row, quite possibly connected underground."

"Thanks, Doc. We'll keep an eye on them. Go back to Clinton. Your wife's waiting for you."

"My wife?"

"Yeah. She called a couple of hours ago, asking for you. Seems very nice … and very worried about you. You seem to have forgotten to bring her along." He smiled a knowing grin.

"Oh, Mary? My wife."

"Forgot about her, huh?" Ralph said.

"Just for a little while."

"Yeah. But they got ways to make sure we're reminded, don't they?" Dr. Mullen chuckled.

"Sure do. Sounds like you have experience."

"More than you know, Richard. More than you know."

"Well, thanks, Doc. Stay in your hotel. Motel 6, right? We'll call you if we need you. Meanwhile, enjoy the vacation. Room and meals will be on the US government. Baines, give Doc a format—a couple of them. They're self-explanatory, Doc. Fill them out, attach the receipts, and you'll get a check in the mail." Larry walked off and began giving orders to another of his crew.

Yeah, in maybe three months, Richard thought.

"How long do you think it'll take your man to come up with a toxin for these? They are going to propagate again," Richard asked when Larry was free.

"Don't worry, Doc. A helicopter's on its way to pick this up now. He'll have the specimen within three hours. They've already been notified."

"I guess you do work fast."

"Your government is as fast as it wants to be."

"Gotcha."

"Go get some rest, Doc."

Dr. Mullen was looking at the sample through an inverted microscope.

Richard's stomach began to churn.

— — — — — —

"Oh, thank goodness you're back." Mary threw her arms around him and hugged him tightly. "I was so worried. It's so late. And it's dark already."

"So my wife is worried, is she?"

"I'm sorry. They wouldn't let me talk to you. I told them a little white lie so they would at least give you the message."

"Well, it did catch me off guard a little."

"Just a little?"

"Yeah. Just a little." He gave her a lingering kiss.

"Hungry?"

"A little. And by the way, we're going to eat well. The government is picking up the tab for room and meals, by reimbursement."

"Figures. Exactly how long will we be here, dear?"

"That's why I wanted to come by myself—until they tell me I can go home. I'm kind of like a prisoner here it seems. I know you have the business and all."

"Oh my. I'll have to call Susan. You could have just told me."

"I did. But you didn't listen?"

She smiled and pulled her cell phone out of her purse.

Richard nodded and went to the bathroom to make a call.

"M?"

"Richard? Congratulations!"

"Congratulations?"

"Yes. You got a live specimen."

"How did you know?"

"I told you I have connections. You don't think Lawrence Trexler is there by chance, do you?"

"But he told me the government has their own research scientists. When I mentioned you, he didn't even seem to know you."

"Some things are kept low key, Richard."

"Jesus. You know he suspects this is a hybrid and that someone made it? I told him nature creates hybrids. Just how much have the two of you talked?"

"Enough. Richard. Admit it. Nature just doesn't work that fast. And there's only a handful of people in this entire world who could work with DNA like that. And you, my friend, are the best in the world."

"I'm getting to hate those words. He mentioned the possibility of it being some terrorist. So, now what?"

"That's good for you. Now I finish my compound. I believe I have the answer. Ann has come up with a good application method. After I receive the specimen, which should be here very shortly, I'll test the toxin on the specimen. Larry told me he was going to push this through."

"And then it's over?"

"Oh, this is just the beginning. And you know it. We'll be doing this for years—until you come up with another hybrid to change the characteristics of these killer ants. I told you, Richard. You are going to be famous, and we are going to be rich! You have years of work ahead of you now."

"That's why he said that. You've got this all figured out, don't you?"

"Sure do. I even got the sex goddess here. And I do mean she is fine!"

"Are you referring to Ann?"

"Who else?"

"Jesus, M. You're more than twice her age, for Christ's sake."

"Oh, how sweet it is!"

"You're sick. I hope she gives you a heart attack."

"I won't mind at all. By the way, the government's picking up the tab, aren't they?"

"Yeah. They'll send me a check. You know how long that takes. Your idea too?"

"Send the receipts and whatever report you have to fill out to me. I'll rush them through. Just the beginning of the bennies you're going to get, my friend. Enjoy! And don't be cheap with that lady of yours, what's her name?"

"Mary, M. Mary. As if you didn't know."

"Oh, yeah. Mary. I'll try to remember. Looking forward to meeting the woman who actually could get the great Dr. Denton out of the lab."

"Somehow I get the feeling she had help with that."

"I can't take credit on that one, Richard. Sorry."

"Are you okay in there?"

"Yeah! I'll be right out. Got to go, M."

"I can tell. Say hello to her for me.

"Bye."

"What were you doing in there for so long? I thought you were sick or something."

"No, no. Just talking to someone on the phone."

"Who was it?"

"Wow, do I have to tell you everything?"

"Sorry, darling. I was just interested is all. Susan says hello."

"Everything okay at the store? You need to go back?"

"Richard Denton, are you trying to get rid of me?"

"No, of course not. Just being interested."

"Oh, you!" She punched him on his chest.

"Let's go eat. What do you feel like? Steak and potato, Chinese, Italian, or just McDonalds."

"It's getting kind of late. Let's eat Chinese. It's lighter on the stomach."

"Chinese it is, my dear."

CHAPTER 23

MARY AND RICHARD CASUALLY STROLLED THROUGH downtown Clinton.

"Hungry, darling?"

He looked at his watch and nodded, puckering his lips. "For quite a while now, actually. My feet are tired, too."

"Look. There's a restaurant. Says 'home cooking.' Want to try it?"

"Sure, why not?"

Being in a hotel in downtown Clinton had its advantages; shopping, theaters, and restaurants were all within walking distance.

They found themselves a booth and eased into the wooden seats that reminded Richard of the wooden pews in a church. The bodies of all those people flashed back for a few seconds. It was a quaint place with an atmosphere of home, white linen tablecloths on wooden tables, farming pictures, and paraphernalia were displayed throughout the restaurant.

"Hi, folks. Whadjahave to drink?"

"Iced tea for me," answered Richard.

"Diet Coke."

"Gotcha. Be back to take your order in a second."

"She's so thin, isn't she?"

"Who?" Richard asked, looking around.

"The waitress, silly. And still young enough to have acne."

"Acne? Is there anything else the matter with her? Poor girl," he said, shaking his head and looking at the menu.

"No, that's all. She's cute, don't you think?" Mary said. "I think I'll have a club sandwich."

"Sounds good. Think I'll have the cheeseburger 'smothered with fried onions and mushrooms.' Comes with fries."

"You are hungry."

"The picture made me hungry." Richard nodded at a picture in an acrylic holder on the table.

"And the aroma. Smells good—whatever they're cooking back there."

"Ready to order, folks?"

Richard took a closer look at the young redhead. Lots of freckles and zits. "My lady will have your club sandwich, and I'll have your mushroom cheeseburger plate."

"Gotcha. Save some room for dessert. We got homemade pies and cheesecakes that are out of this world!"

Probably what gave her those zits, Richard thought.

"Oh, my God!" a customer exclaimed, bringing everyone's attention to the television in the corner.

"Alarming news just in! Man-eating ants have just attacked the town of Raymore, Missouri, killing an estimated eighty residents in their homes. This is the second report of these killer ants. Just last week, they killed 392 men, women, and children in Custer City, Oklahoma. The entire town was attending the Sunday service. The federal government is on site in Custer City now but is not available for comment. They're not letting anyone in or out of town. Our news team is on their way to Raymore, a town of eighteen thousand, located just twenty-three miles from Kansas City. We should have more for you on this terrible tragedy within the hour."

"Oh, my God, dear. Did you hear that?" whispered Mary.

Richard nodded and held a finger to his lips.

"Wow, did you hear that?" the waitress exclaimed as she set their orders on the table in front of them.

"Yes, that's terrible!"

"I'm really scared. Those killer ants are only twenty miles from here. You think they could be here in Clinton?"

"I don't think so. The authorities are keeping an eye out for them," Richard said softly. "No reason to panic. Just be careful is all."

"Yeah? Well, some people have already left town. If I had someplace to go, I would to."

"I'm sure they'll find a way to eradicate them real soon, hon," Mary said.

The waitress nodded and left, her jovial face replaced with a deep frown.

"Do you think they are the same ones?" Mary whispered.

Richard nodded. All of a sudden, he wasn't hungry anymore. "Mind if we bag our meals to go? Can't talk here."

Mary nodded and raised her arm to get the waitress's attention.

As soon as they closed the hotel room door, the phone rang.

"Hello?" Richard noticed the message light was on.

"Hear the news, Richard? Raymore, Missouri. Another eighty people."

"Yes. I heard. Got the remedy?"

"I got something that'll work—if Larry will approve it."

"Larry? Lawrence Trexler? Of the EPA, right?"

"Yes. The same. He's been trying to get ahold of you."

"Okay. I'll call him right away. That must be what the message is."

"No need. He wants you to go to Raymore to see if these are the same as the ones in Custer City. We both know they are."

"What about eradicating these?"

"His people are going to apply the pesticide."

"His people?"

"What? You think you're the only one who can do it?"

"The Ant Busters," Richard said softly, thinking of Bill and shaking his head.

"What?"

"Nothing. Talking to myself. Okay. On my way."

"Good. Call me when you get there—before you do anything, okay?"

"All right." He hung up the phone.

"Now you need to go to Raymore?"

"Yes. I really would feel more comfortable if you went home."

"I think you're right, dear. But let's eat first, okay? Maybe I can take your mind off these ants for a little while too."

How am I supposed to concentrate with all the pressure on me? How can women do that? But then, she had a clear conscience.

CHAPTER 25

"OKAY, M. I'M IN RAYMORE. THE HOLIDAY INN. ROOM 228. Got the toxin off to Custer City?"

"Yes. Larry's people are applying it as we speak."

"Let's hope they don't get themselves killed."

"Have you seen the news?"

"No. I just got here."

"Gardner, Kansas. Another forty-three people."

"Shit!" Richard sighed.

"I got Larry to okay your applying the toxin in Raymore. You up to it?"

Richard nodded.

"Richard?"

"Yes, M. I'm here. And yes, I'll do it. Got the antidote?"

"Not yet. You got to get a sample and send it to me. I know it'll be the same. It doesn't have to be a live one this time. We just need to verify that it's the same species."

"All right, M. How long will it take?"

"It's coming FedEx. You'll have it by daylight. I'm sending enough for Raymore and Gardner."

"So I'm going to Gardner after this?"

"They're your babies, my friend."

Richard had a sleepless night. He talked with Mary for over an hour, something he'd never done before with anyone—business or pleasure.

Everything was happening so fast and almost exactly the way he was afraid it would. His only surprise was the distance the queens could fly.

There were now four locations. He was missing one of the original queens, but he couldn't even imagine how many queens were out of nests and beginning new colonies by now, although they seemed to colonize close to the mother's location.

━ ━ ━ ━ ━ ━

His familiar green bottle of spirits was on the desk in front of him. He had broken down and bought a bottle after getting Mary off.

He opened the bottle, poured a half a glass, and added an ice cube. He held the glass in his right hand and watched the yellow mental painkiller swish around the glass. Its delicious aroma drifted to his nostrils. He raised his glass to the light to look at its color and body.

He raised the glass to his lips, but when the liquid just touched his lips, he stopped. He licked his lips, placed the glass on the desk, and stared at it.

He wanted to erase what was happening, rinse it all away. What had happened? Why did he create this killer ant? He wanted to escape, to disappear. The yellow elixir in front of him had been his answer for a long time, and it was beckoning to him.

A gun would be faster and more permanent, my friend. All the people in the world could hate you and talk bad about you, the government could try to arrest you, but no one could touch you. You could cheat them all, yessiree, bub!

And Mary? Huh, bub? What about Mary? Just chalk her off, is that it, bub? I mean, you did that to the other one, didn't you? Why not Mary? Huh, bub? Why should you worry about her—or anybody else for that matter? Who worries about you? Well, yeah. Mary. Right, bub. But she's only one person. Who cares, right? Go ahead. Take a long swallow of that smooth single-malt scotch. It's just the courage you need. Then go out and buy a nine millimeter and finish it. End it. Go ahead, bub! Do it!

"Mary," he croaked, the tears rolling down his cheek. "I need you, Mary. Oh, God, how I need you." He sobbed quietly, and his body trembled.

He gathered himself after a few moments, took a deep breath through puckered lips, and slowly exhaled.

Okay, Dr. Richard Denton. You made this. You stop it. I'm going to need more live specimens—and a queen. If you can make them, Doc, you can unmake them, too.

He picked up the glass of scotch and threw it down the bathroom sink—and then he threw the bottle in the trash.

He looked at himself in the mirror. *You're not going to lose this one. Mary's the best thing that ever happened to you. You're going to eradicate those ants in Raymore and Gardner—and then you're going to create a docile* Paraponera *with a much-weakened venom and cross-breed it with that creation of yours. Even if it takes the rest of your life.*

— — — — — —

"Hello?" Mary said sleepily.

"Hi, Mary. Did I wake you?"

Mary looked at the red digital numbers on her clock. *2:58.* "Richard? It's three in the morning. What's wrong?"

"Oh, nothing. Wrong? Nothing at all."

"Then what it is, dear?"

"Oh. Uh. I just … uh … I …"

"What is it, darling?"

Richard took a deep breath and sighed. "I miss you."

"How sweet," Mary said. "I miss you, too, darling."

"I just wanted to tell you something before I went to sleep."

"Which is?"

"Oh. Yeah. I … uh. Oh, hell. I love you, Mary. You are the only woman I can truly love for the rest of my miserable life—what there is left of it."

"Oh, my God. Oh, darling. I love you, too. With all my heart."

"Okay, then. Good night. Sorry I woke you up. Go back to sleep. Bye."

"Hello? Richard?" She smiled as she softly hung up the phone. "Finally. Go back to sleep. Sure, darling. Ha, ha, ha. What a crazy brilliant man."

Richard felt relieved. *When I get home, we'll make plans— permanent plans.*

━━ ━━ ━ ━ ━ ━

"Dr. Denton?"

"Yes?"

"There's a guy from FedEx with some packages for you. You'll need to come down to the lobby to sign for them."

"Ah, yes. On my way."

━━ ━━ ━ ━ ━ ━

"Dr. Richard Denton?" A tall, well-built young man in a FedEx uniform asked.

"Yes, that's me."

"I need to see some ID, sir."

"Of course."

"Thank you. Please sign here." He placed an x where Richard was to sign on a paper with a clipboard.

"Okay. That's it, sir. Have a nice day."

Richard looked over at the desk clerk. She was a large blonde with blue eyes. She had been watching him with curiosity.

"Excuse me, miss?"

"Yes, Dr. Denton. Can I help you?"

Richard nodded and patted the packages with his left hand. "Is there someone who can take these to my room?"

"Certainly. I'll call someone right away, sir."

"Thank you." He stood by the packages and waited.

"You don't have to wait, sir. I'll take care of it."

"That's all right, miss. I'll wait."

A busboy came with a luggage cart and loaded the boxes. When he got to the room and the boy left, he unpacked the boxes. There were four large plastic cylinders about two feet high. He had a black harness on the desk with the various bottles of chemicals. He grabbed his cell phone. "M?"

"Hi, Richard. Got the equipment, I presume?"

"Sure did. Be nice if it included instructions though."

"Ha. I was waiting for your call. You wouldn't want those chemicals getting in some stranger's hands with instructions on how to use it, would you? And your antidote is included."

Richard wrote M's instructions down to not leave anything to chance. "Hey, M?"

"Yes, my friend?"

"Tell me something. Exactly what is your relationship with the feds?"

"Larry and I knew each other in college. Made a few trips together. Chicago, New York, Fort Lauderdale. You know, wild parties with the broads."

"Naturally. Funny. We went to the same college. Never saw him."

"Different classes, different major, and graduated after us. Besides, who did you notice? You always had your nose in the books."

"Touché. Come to think of it, I didn't actually know you either. I mean, I saw you, but I don't think we ever spoke, did we?"

"Like I said. Different majors. Different interests."

"You got some kind of deal with him?"

"What do you mean by *deal*?"

"You know. You in cahoots with him about your pesticide? Going to make him rich too?"

"Better you don't know all the details, my friend."

"Thanks for the warning."

"You've got enough problems as it is, my friend."

"Got that right. But I'm going to fix them, my friend."

"What do you mean by that?"

"Just that. I'm going to right a wrong."

"I'd be careful if I were you. Your Mary wouldn't want to have to visit you behind bars."

"Mary? As soon as I finish this, I'm going home to marry that girl."

"Marry? Whoa! That's rather quick, isn't it? And totally drastic for the great Dr. Richard Denton!"

"Should've done it a long time ago. Like you said, had my nose so deep in my work, I couldn't see."

"Ha, ha. Definitely have to meet this girl. Good luck. Might be good enough to steal from you."

"Never happen. Now who do I see here in Raymore?"

"Saul will be there to help you shortly. Probably within the hour. He volunteered. He's got all the data. The local police chief is a woman by the name of Kristen. Here it is … Kristen Weathersby."

"If you're so busy with all these logistics, obviously administrating everything, how do you find the time to work on your toxin? I mean, you certainly can't market your method you sent me."

"Actually, Ann is doing that part. My part is done. I believe she seems to have it solved. Impressive young lady in every way. Still thinks your God, by the way."

"And, of course, you're going to make her rich too."

"That's right. There will be plenty for all of us."

"So, I wait for Saul now?"

"Yes. You'll meet with Kristen tomorrow. The two of you will find the nest. So far as I know, they still haven't found it. I don't really think the people looking are trying real hard … if you know what I mean."

"Kristen and me? Is that a good idea?"

"No! Saul and you."

"Oh. Can't blame the people, can you? I mean, for not trying hard. The people?"

"Nope. Fear does that. That's why you'll be there."

"And Saul. Thanks. I'll find them. That's a sure thing, M."

"I have all the confidence in the world in you, my friend."

"I'll let you know when I find them."

"Please. And by the way, Richard."

"What?"

"Be careful."

"Right!"

"This is a map of the area, gentlemen. I highlighted the homes involved. It's a large area."

Richard nodded. *Multiple nests.*

"So, no one has found anything yet?" Saul asked.

"To be frank with you, my people are scared to even get close. We were all waiting for you," Kristen said.

"Understandable … and intelligent," Richard said.

"Don't worry, Chief. We'll find and destroy them," Saul assured her.

"You'll be heroes."

"Ant Busters," Richard whispered.

"What?" Kristen and Saul both said.

"Oh, nothing. Talking to myself. Sorry."

She took a deep breath and exhaled. "Gentlemen, do I need to evacuate?"

Saul drew a red line on the map, turned to Richard, and handed him the pen. "To where, Doc?"

Richard took the pen and marked the area. "Just till we eradicate them. I don't think they are ready to forage yet."

"Forage?" Kristen asked.

"Look for food," Richard said.

"Oh, God. How can you guys just stand there and be so calm about all this?"

"We have to be, Chief," Saul said. "We're the ones who are going to eliminate them."

Saul's cellphone rang. "Yes, sir? Great! Congratulations! Will do, sir."

"Larry?"

Saul nodded. "Boss said it worked like a charm. Mound's dead."

"Casualties?"

"Only two ... and one hospitalized."

Richard nodded, clenching his jaws. "Only two?"

"Are you guys talking 'bout Custer City?"

"Yes," Saul answered. "It's safe now."

"For whom?" Kristen fired back. "There's no one left!"

Richard winced.

"We'll take care of these, Chief. Won't be long, right, Doc?"

Richard nodded.

"I hope so, boys. I really hope so. Whatever you need, you let me know."

"Really? An open jeep would help." Richard looked at Saul. "Better than my old pickup."

Saul nodded.

Kristen was on the phone, and fifteen minutes later, a jeep pulled into the police station.

"Mind if I leave my pickup here, Chief?"

"Course not."

"There! Richard pointed.

"Let's go!" Saul turned in the direction Richard had pointed.

"Wait. Not so fast, Saul. Stop."

"What are we waiting for, Doc?"

"There's more than one nest, Saul. Let's find and mark all of them first. Then we'll eliminate them one after another."

"Why not eliminate this one now and then find the next ... and so on?"

"Don't want to gamble on alerting the others. What if they get to us while we are occupied getting their buddies?"

"You really think they have that kind of intelligence? Communication skills, Doc?"

"They've been smart enough to build nests that are hard to find and could surround a church, a house, and a small herd of cattle in Custer City. And I believe we will find they did the same here."

"Yeah. I guess you're right. Okay, Doc. You're the expert. Where to then?"

"South would be logical." Richard marked the location on the map and nodded toward the south.

It took all day to locate and map all seven nests. One nest was built around a tree and four feet up the trunk. Richard explained it was an adaptation because of the rocky terrain.

"So we get 'em first thing in the morning, right, Doc?"

"Tonight."

"Tonight? Are you crazy, Doc? It'll be dark!"

"Exactly. When do you spray a wasp nest?"

"After dark. But these are ants—not wasps."

"Same family. I guess you could say wasps are simply ants with wings."

"Jesus. Can you imagine if these had wings?"

"Already exist. Not here, though."

"You're shittin' me."

"Nope. Our friends will be a lot calmer at night. They're resting. They'll be real busy with the queen. They *normally* don't come out at night unless disturbed. We need floodlights. The jeeps will help. Let's go eat our last supper."

"Very funny, Doc. Who's hungry now?"

"I'm starving. Call Kristen. See if she'd like to join us. She can get us the floodlights and take us to a good Chinese place. I feel like Pad Thai."

"You're sure in good spirits for a man who's about to put his life in danger of being eaten by ants."

"Eaten alive."

"What?"

"Yes. Their venom paralyzes your legs and arms, and then it begins to feed before you die. Maybe as much as five minutes."

"Why the hell did you have to tell me that, Doc?"

"Just kidding."

"The hell you are. You're too serious."

"Thought it only fair you should know. Well, we'll just keep it between you and me."

"Yeah. The public is panicked enough as it is."

■ ■ ■ ■ ■ ■

When they pulled up to the first location that evening, Kristen turned on the jeep's spots. The mound was only ten yards in front of them. Richard had asked her to get someone to accompany them at dinner so they would never have to leave the jeep.

"Married, Saul?" Kristen asked.

"Yes. Two children—eighteen and sixteen. Both girls. You?" Saul pulled the harness with two tanks out of the back of the jeep and helped put it on Richard's back.

"Divorced. My boy's at MIT. You, Doc?"

"Single."

"Shame."

"Thanks for helping us out, Kristen. You could've sent one of your men."

"Couldn't find any volunteers. I wasn't one either."

Saul and Richard looked at each other and nodded.

"Okay, Doc. Ready?"

Richard pressed the trigger on the pistol and a spray shot out a good five yards.

"Yep." *Who ya gonna call? The Ant Busters!*

"This is for you, Bill."

"Who's Bill?" Saul asked.

"Long story. We start on the other side, okay?"

"Right behind you, Doc."

"I prefer right beside me."

They cautiously moved to the left of the mound, which was three feet in diameter and two feet high.

Saul's light began to quiver.

"Easy, Saul. They can feel vibrations," he whispered.

Saul held the lamp with both hands, but it still shook. Richard started the starting at the base like he was painting a wall. He walked the mound's circumference, and Saul kept the floodlight directed on the base.

Richard finished saturating the mound, and they climbed into the jeep.

"Okay, Kristen. Next one," Richard said.

They finished the seven mounds without mishap and pulled up to the police station.

"Is that it?" Kristen asked.

"I guess you were right, Doc. It was almost like no one was home."

"We find out tomorrow afternoon. I want to give the gas time to penetrate as deep as possible. It'll take a couple of days to be sure, but I believe your emergency is over, Chief."

"Kristen. Please."

Richard nodded.

"I feel like celebrating, gentlemen."

"Not just yet, Kristen. Patience."

"Yes," Saul said. "Please don't make any public announcements yet. Maybe by tomorrow afternoon, Doc?"

"Tomorrow evening."

"Okay, Doc. But I'm still going to have a stiff drink right now. Care to join me?"

"Why not?" Saul said and followed Kristen inside.

"All right, but I've got to make a phone call first. Join you in a few minutes."

CHAPTER 26

"PITY THIS TOWN," SAUL SAID AS THEY CLIMBED INTO THE jeep and headed toward their room to prepare their equipment.

Richard nodded.

"Same plan as last time?"

"Mean you don't want to start now?"

"I'm a believer, Doc. 100 percent. You call the shots."

"Let's hope it goes as smoothly as the last one," Richard said with a sigh.

"You have doubts?"

Richard shrugged.

"Out with it, Doc. C'mon. What can go wrong? I have a right to know, don't you think?"

"Yeah. You are absolutely right, Saul. Lots of things can go wrong. There are always variables in science."

"Variables? What the hell are you talking about?"

"I guess you could say this is like an experiment."

"Experiment? We're not in a damn lab, Doc. Talk English, will ya?"

"In a sense we are, Saul. This town has become our lab, at least temporarily."

"Aw, c'mon, Doc, you're starting to scare me ... more. What can go wrong? Seriously."

They entered the room, and Richard saw the message light flashing, but he sat down on the bed to explain. "Well, let's see. First, we have a bunch of volunteers supposedly manning the blockades."

"Yeah. I can see why that could be a problem—in more ways than one. Second?"

"Two, we could make a mistake and run into a nest—or even trip and fall into one."

"Thanks. I needed that. I'll be sure that doesn't happen, believe me. And?"

"Three, we don't know for sure if the chemicals will work the same way this time."

"What do you mean? They're the same chemicals and the same ants."

"Yes, they are. But we don't know the shelf life of the chemicals. Now that we used them, will the time have diluted their effect?"

"In just days?"

"I didn't mix the chemicals, Saul. I really don't know. It's a variable."

"Shit. Maybe we should shake up the tanks or something. What else?"

"Fourth? The worst."

"C'mon, Doc."

"Okay. We don't know what their adaptations are. Maybe they won't react the same to the chemicals, or ..."

"Or what, Doc?"

"Or just maybe they'll come out at night to forage."

"Aw, shit. Now I'm more nervous than I was in Raymore."

"You asked."

"I'll know better next time."

"Your boss hear of any other hot spots?"

"No. Hopefully this is the last."

"Maybe for a while."

"Yeah. I don't think I want to do this for a living."

Richard picked up the phone and listened to his message. Bill had called. He dialed.

"Hi, Doc!"

Richard winced and held the receiver away from his ear. "I can hear just fine, Bill."

"Oh, sorry. So now you really are the Ant Busters, huh? Why didn't you include me?"

"It sure seems that way, but hopefully not for long. How did you find me?"

"I'm the long arm of the law, remember? I called Mary. She gave me the lowdown and your number. Getting close to home, aren't we?"

"Home? Oh, yeah. I guess I am."

"They're surrounding Kansas City, aren't they?"

"You noticed? Let's keep that under our hats."

"Kansas City has a population of around two hundred thousand, Doc."

"Yes. I am well aware of its population."

"Good. How are you holding up?"

"Okay. Kind of nervous, you know."

"Kind of? Most guys would be basket cases by now. You're a tough cookie to be such a nerd. I gotta admit."

"Only on the outside."

"Did you take care of them in Gardner yet? Your success in Raymore is all over the news."

"Tonight. Maybe I'll get lucky, and it'll start drizzling."

"Since when don't you work in the rain?"

"No. No. It'll just make the *Paraponera* go deeper, give me a little more time."

"Oh, I get it. Yeah."

"How's your better half?"

"Fine. She says hello."

"Tell her I miss her cooking."

"Well, all you got to do is come down and see us. She'll fatten you up some more."

"Oh, that's for sure!"

"And she's really eager to meet Mary. So am I. The woman who got through to Richard. Wow. She has to be some kind of special. Okay, Doc. I'll let you prepare for tonight. Good luck, and hurray for the Ant Busters! Be careful, Doc."

"Will do, Bill. Will do. Thanks." He cradled the phone and a smile crept across his face.

"Just a very close friend, Saul. He was with me on the first incident."

"Ant Busters?"

"You heard that? Of course you did. Yeah. His doing."

"Appropriate." Saul smiled.

— — — — — —

Finding the nests was much more difficult this time. There was no straight line. The streets of the community curved and twisted, and the wooded areas were erratic.

"It's three in the morning, Doc," Saul said. "Think we got 'em all?"

"Two nests?" Richard shook his head. "Nah. Impossible."

"We've circled the town twice."

"Yes, I know," Richard said softly. "I'm afraid we're going to have to use daylight to locate them."

"Good. I'm bushed. I don't mind telling you."

"You didn't have to," Richard said with a chuckle. "Let's get some shut-eye and start after a good breakfast."

"I can handle that."

"Me too."

— — — — — —

"County Courthouse first, Saul," Richard said as they started out after breakfast at Denny's.

Saul gave Richard a quizzical look.

"Our maps obviously aren't good enough."

Saul nodded acknowledgement and headed downtown.

"I should have thought of this. Sorry, Doc."

"For not thinking of everything? Please!"

"Well. It's my job."

"Wish I could say I never overlooked anything," Richard said softly.

"There!" Saul pointed to a tree and pulled off the road to within twenty yards.

"Do me a favor, Saul. Turn the jeep around and back off about ten more yards. Slowly."

Richard slid out of the jeep and fished some things from the back. "Stay put, Saul. Keep the engine running." He cautiously approached the mound and took a GPS reading. He saw a few ants emerging and quickened his pace back to the jeep and climbed in.

"We good to go, Doc?"

"Not quite yet." He pulled out his notepad, noted the GPS reading, and took a thin piece of wood about two inches in diameter and tied a long string to it. Then he coated the stick with a sticky gel.

"What are you going to do, Doc?"

"Something I've got to do."

"I don't like the way that sounds."

"Just keep the motor running and the jeep in gear, Saul." He slid out of the car.

"Aw, shit!"

Richard slowly made his way to the mound. More scouts had come out, and Richard tried to keep a close eye on the ground surrounding him.

When he got within three feet, he threw the stick on the mound and made his way back to the jeep, letting out the string as he went.

Several ants flowed out of the nest and swarmed the stick, seemingly to attack it, but they got stuck in the gel.

Richard stopped by the jeep and began to pull the stick toward him. When it was a good ten feet from the mound he stopped. He watched the ants discover the stick was a false alarm and observed them trying to return to the nest.

When they had completely exhausted themselves on the stick, he pulled it toward him. He pulled out a test tube and a tweezers from his breast pocket. He bent down, pulled several ants from the sticky gel, and carefully placed them in three test tubes.

He threw the stick away, climbed in the jeep, and placed the test tube in his pocket.

"You are a lunatic, Doc!" Saul stepped on the gas slowly.

"Stop over there, Saul."

"How can you put those things in your pocket?"

"It's a screw-on cap. It's safe." Richard reached for his notepad and began to write. He had just finished putting his notepad away when he felt a sting. "Ouch!" He slapped at his left forearm.

Saul saw the ant fall to the floorboard, slammed on the brakes, threw the jeep in neutral, pulled the emergency brake, and jumped out of the jeep. He began to frantically slap all over his body.

Richard was slumped motionless in his seat.

"Oh, shit! Doc? You all right?" He looked around Doc's seat. Only the one dead ant on the floor could be seen. He brushed it out on the ground and made sure Richard was strapped against the seat. He ran around the jeep, jumped into the driver's seat, and sped off toward their hotel room.

Saul ran up to the room, returned to the jeep, slapped a tiny tube with a needle on it into Doc's leg, squeezed the tube, removed it, and threw it on the ground. "Doc? You all right?"

"Huh?" Richard felt numb.

Saul began rubbing his arms and legs again.

"C'mon, Doc. Snap out of it."

"All right, Saul. You're going to rub my skin right off." Richard began to slowly move his arms and legs.

"God, it feels like I've been sleeping in a cramped position for hours. Worse than last time."

"Worse than last time? What do you mean—worse than last time?"

Richard shook his head.

"That was in Smithtown."

"With your friend? Bill?"

Richard nodded once.

Saul raised his arms in exasperation.

Richard reached into a pocket, pulled out the test tube, and rolled it in his fingers. "These have a more potent venom," Richard said. "I better let M know. You gave me the antidote, right?"

"Yeah. Thank God I remembered. But I had to bring you here first. We forgot to take it with us."

"See? I forget things too."

Saul nodded.

"Maybe that's why. How long from the time I was bitten till you applied the injection?"

"Oh, I don't know, Doc! I wasn't exactly looking at the damn clock!"

"Take a careful guess, Saul. It's important."

Saul shrugged. "Oh, let's see. Probably between twenty-five and thirty minutes."

"Okay. Where did you apply the injection?"

"I told you. In the jeep."

"No, no. Where on my body?"

"Oh. Right leg."

"My right or yours?"

"God, Doc. Uh, yours."

"Okay, Saul. Thanks."

Richard went to the desk and spread out the map. Then he took out his notepad, started writing, and picked up the phone. "Do me a favor, Saul. Plot the coordinates of the mounds we killed in red and the one we just found in green."

"You got it."

"M?"

"So. How's your all-expense-paid vacation in Gardner, my friend?"

"I'm sending you live samples."

"Fantastic! No, wait. I'll send you a courier. I don't want to take any chances. Leave it at the front desk with my name on it. Well packed, of course."

"Of course. Listen. I want you to check the level of potency of the venom of these."

"What is it? Think they are more potent or less?"

"More. Quite a bit more, but I could be wrong."

"You are never wrong when it comes to ants, my friend. I'll get Ann on that immediately. What else?"

"The antidote. It works, but it's slow. Maybe you could fix that."

"I'll work on that too, but tell me how you know that, my friend. You got bit again?"

"Good guess."

"Oh, Jesus, Richard! You can't put yourself in danger like that! That's why Larry and I have Saul there with you!"

"Saul saved my ass, M. He deserves a medal. He didn't panic and run."

"The hell I didn't," Saul said.

"Okay, my friend, okay. But let's be more careful next time."

"These were more hidden, M. I haven't figured out their strategy yet."

"Strategy? Aw, c'mon, Richard. You still believe they are more intelligent?"

"Maybe we're just dumber."

"How many nests have you found in Gardner?"

"Killed two, found another."

"Just three? Think there's more?"

"No doubt. Estimate between seven and ten."

"That many?"

"I'm afraid so. And it'll take a while. I have to hunt them down during the day and eliminate them at night. Unless, of course, you have come up with a really long-distance application."

"No. I haven't. But I have come up—well, Ann has come up with a granular application."

"I guess your friend has already approved the patent?"

"License? Yes. Larry took care of it. By the way, he wanted to come up to Gardner with you and Saul, but I convinced him it was more important to work on my end since we had such a great team already there."

"Larry, right? No room for more here."

"Yes. You do remember him, right?"

"Oh, yes. Well, that was good. I certainly don't need any more interference."

"Exactly what I thought," Dr. Morton said.

"Yeah. Well, if there's nothing else, I'll send a written report with the samples and plan our next move."

"Great! I'll let you get to it then."

"Yeah. Thanks, M."

Richard hung up the phone and stared at it for a couple of seconds.

"That son of a bitch!"

"Surprised, Saul? I'm not."

"Naw. Not really, but it still pisses me off."

"It's all about money, Saul. It's all about money."

"Got your coordinates plotted, Doc? And thanks for standing up for me."

Richard turned and looked Saul directly into the eye. "Thanks for saving my life."

"We do make a pretty good team, don't we?"

"That we do, Saul. That we do."

"The Ant Busters." Saul smiled. "Has a nice ring to it."

That reminded him of Mary, and he picked up the phone again.

CHAPTER 27

IT TOOK TWO MORE DAYS TO FIND THE OTHER EIGHT NESTS and three nights to dispense the necessary chemicals to eliminate the killer ants.

"You're positive you eliminated all the nests, Dr. Denton?"

"Quite sure, Mr. Hodges."

"You can lift the barricades and inform your people that Gardner is safe again," Saul said.

What barricades? Richard had rarely seen them attended. The people's fear of the ants was the only thing that kept them from getting close—except for a few crazy guys looking to make themselves heroes, armed with ant killer spray cans.

Laura Hodges sighed. "Thank God, but I still don't think I'll be able to sleep well."

"That'll pass, ma'am," Saul said. "What do you say we Ant Busters head on out, Doc?"

Laura Hodges laughed. "Ant Busters. Yeah."

"Don't pay any attention to Saul, young lady. He likes to kid around." He gave Saul an angry look.

"I like it," she said. "I think it'll be a while before the visitors want to return, however. It'll take long enough for the residents to return."

"Okay, Saul. I'll get you to the airport. Thanks for the jeep, Mr. Hodges. It really came in handy."

"You can say that again," Saul said.

"It came in really handy."

They all chuckled.

"Well. Thanks again, gentlemen. Have a safe trip back."

"Why don't you give the man a ride to the airport, dear?" Mrs. Hodges asked.

"Oh, it's okay, sir. The airport is not that far, ma'am. I'll get him there in my pickup," Richard said.

"Suit yourself, gentlemen," Mr. Hodges said.

Saul and Richard made their way to Richard's pickup, accompanied by the Hodges family.

They waved good-bye and pulled away.

"If every town's sheriff was like this one, we'd be in deep shit," Saul said.

"Ha, ha. Yeah. Talk about lack of control."

"You know, Doc. It's kind of scary seeing how our small-town governments govern."

"Are you sure the big-town governments are any different?" Richard lit up one of his Marlboros and cracked the window.

"I would tell you those things will kill you, but somehow, after what we've been through, it seems asinine."

Richard smiled and nodded.

"Never smoked, Saul?"

"In the military. Till I flunked requalification and had hell to pay to re-qualify."

"Mary wants me to stop. Maybe I will after all this is over."

"It is over, isn't it?"

"No, Saul," Richard said with a sigh. "I'm afraid not yet. More will pop up—and maybe more frequently."

"So we're going to do this the rest of our lives? The Ant Busters forever?"

"No. That's why your boss and M are very busy making a commercial ant killer for these particular ants."

"And to get rich. You know, Mr. Taylor has changed a lot these last couple of months. It's like he's lost the passion he used to have for the environment. Actually, he seems to work more with this

Morton guy from the university than the federal government. I don't mind telling you that it makes me feel a little uneasy."

"Betrayed maybe?"

"Yeah. That's exactly it. You know, Doc. You're an all right guy. I don't care what they say about you."

"Ha, ha. Thanks, Saul, but I am far from perfect, believe me."

"I didn't say you were perfect—just an all right guy."

Richard nodded and smiled.

"Maybe we should get us some kind of uniforms, you know? Like the Ghost Busters had?"

"Will you lay off of that Ant Busters' stuff? Jesus, if that gets out."

"Okay. Maybe we should get some kind of rubberized suits or something to protect us, you know? Gonna go see this Mary of yours?"

"Oh, yes."

"Serious?"

Richard nodded. "She's the reason I'm a little afraid now."

"Know what you mean. It's a lot easier being fearless when you have no one to take care of but yourself. Kind of like it was in combat."

"I bet your family will be glad to see you. I have a feeling you're a great dad and a good husband."

"Well. I'm hoping they feel that way about me."

"Giving you hell about your present job, I bet."

"The wife is. The kids think I'm a hero. They're popular in school now."

"A hero, huh? We're all heroes until we mess up, right?"

"Yeah. You got that right."

— — — — — —

Richard pulled into one of the five parking spaces allotted to Mary's Family Groceries and turned off the engine. He pulled out a cigarette and then changed his mind and put it back in the pack.

He pulled out a Tic-Tac instead and popped it into his mouth. He waited nervously for a couple of minutes before he stepped out of the truck and walked up to the store.

When he opened the door and stepped inside, Mary was taking a check from a customer. He froze in the doorway. His heart pounded as if he were seeing her for the first time.

The customer glanced up first, and then Mary did too. She dropped the check on the floor and almost ran into Richard's arms.

"Get a room," the customer called out in jest.

Mary glanced back and said, "We already have one, thank you. Why didn't you call? I was so worried. I called the hotel, and they said you had checked out."

Richard put his finger to her lips. "I wanted to surprise you."

"Well, you did, you—"

He planted a kiss full on her lips.

"Sally?" she yelled without taking her eyes off of Richard.

"I'm right behind you, Mary. I know. I'll take care of everything." She waved the check in the air.

"Good-bye," Mary said without turning around and walked out the door with her arm around her man.

━━　━━　━━　━━　━━　━━

Mary woke up and found herself alone. She slipped into her clothes, made the bed, and made her way down the stairs, feeling just a little bit stiff and pleasantly sore.

"Honey?"

The kitchen was untouched—and so was the rest of the house. She glanced outside and saw the pickup.

"Richard?"

She went to the cellar door, opened it wide, and saw the light was on.

"Richard? You down there?"

"Yes."

She slowly climbed down the stairs. A musty smell filled her nostrils. When she got to the last step, Richard was bent over one of the aquariums.

"What are you doing?"

"Working," he said.

"Oh!" She waved her hand in front of her nose. "I need to work down here too."

Richard looked around, sniffed, and glanced over at Mary. "Well, I know where everything is, but I guess this room could use a little attention."

"Little? Where do I start?"

"Well, maybe over there by my desk, but don't throw anything out. Uh, wait. Maybe you better start … no … maybe over here,"

"You don't know where to start either."

"No. I mean. I know where everything is … and I—"

"I know. You don't want me to touch anything. How about if I just pick up all the garbage and mop the floor for a start?"

"Yeah. That sounds good."

"You want to tell me what you're working on?" She stood beside him and looked into the aquarium.

"There's nothing in here right now. I'm preparing it."

"For what?"

"My research."

"You got a job? You didn't tell me. I told you you would."

"Well. Yes and no. It's kind of complicated."

"Try me."

"I … how do I explain?"

"Try just blurting it out, genius. I may be more intelligent than you think."

"I didn't mean you were. Oh, hell. Come sit on the lab stool." He led her over to one of two wooden lab stools close to his power scopes. He pulled another one closer.

"You are the first human being to step into this lab," he said. "Besides me, of course."

"Wow. I'm privileged. Thank you."

"I have never shared my research with anyone—ever."

"Keep talking, big boy, but don't take all day. Sounds interesting, and I'm all ears. Relax though. I can keep secrets—if that's what's bothering you."

Richard stared into her eyes. "I hope so, Mary. I really hope so."

"Wow. You sound really serious, darling. I promise. You can tell me whatever you want. I mean it. You don't ever have to keep everything to yourself anymore, poor darling. I'll help you in whatever you need. Cross my heart."

"I need to trust you—really trust you."

"Sounds like a deep, dark mysterious secret. You can, darling. I promise." She smiled.

"Not everything is all peaches and cream in science. I've made some mistakes."

"So has everyone else in the world, including yours truly. I love you, darling. I would never betray you."

Richard took a deep breath and sighed. If Mary betrayed his trust, he would go find that nine millimeter and use it. "And if you don't like a decision I made in the past?"

"And if *you* don't like a decision I made in the past?"

"Touché."

He wanted to tell her everything, but he couldn't. Not yet. He knew the day would come when she would have to know.

"Okay. A coworker from the university I used to work for— his name is Michael Morton—I call him M. He's a specialist in biochemistry. He's working on, and has found, a poison to kill these ants."

"You mean the killer ants? Yes, I heard. That's wonderful! But you already told me something about him."

"Yes. That's right. I guess it is. Anyway, I've been working with him. He's got connections and has gotten approval to market the poison."

"You mean, commercially, like the fire ant poison?"

"Exactly."

"So, that's great. But if he already has it, what do you have to do with it?"

"The poison doesn't really eradicate the species. For example, the fire ant came over as one queen from South America—and has spread to half the US."

"Oh, my God. And you think the same thing will happen with the killer ant?"

"Exactly."

"Oh, my God! The whole US will live in fear of their lives!"

"There's more. No one will want to receive any goods from the US."

"Oh, I see. That would just kill our economy, wouldn't it?"

"Right. I think you're getting the bigger picture now."

"Oh, Richard. You paint such a terrible picture. What are we to do?"

"Remember the killer bees?"

"Yes. Whatever happened to them? You don't hear about them anymore."

"They still exist, but through science, we have changed their characteristics."

"How?"

"We changed their DNA."

"Is that what you're going to do with the killer ants?"

"My specialty is DNA."

"And you're going to do that here?"

"Yes. I have everything I need here."

"But don't you need to have the killer ant to work with?"

"Yes. That's logical."

"But isn't that dangerous?"

"I have to take my precautions."

"Oh, Richard. I don't know about this. Can't someone else do this? Somewhere else? Why you?"

"I have my reasons. M wants me to—and the federal government wants me to—but I have my own reasons as well."

Mary studied his face and nodded.

"I don't like it. I don't like it one bit, but if you feel you need to do this, I'll be right here beside you."

He drew her into his arms and held her tightly. "I love you Mary," he whispered.

The phone rang, interrupting the romantic moment.

"Hello?"

"Richard!"

"What's up, M?" He glanced at Mary.

"Larry just went out to a town just east of Kansas City with Saul."

"Another one? Where?"

"Don't worry. They're going to take care of this one. It seems to be small. A single dwelling."

"Good. I could use the time."

"Richard, have you plotted the events?"

"Yes, I know. They're surrounding Kansas City."

"Is that really possible? Can they really have that kind of intelligence? Saul seems to be convinced. I think you are too."

"This species seems to have it, I'm afraid."

"Wow. If they have that kind of intel, how do we stop them?"

"Exactly what I'm working on."

"How, Richard?"

"DNA. We change their DNA."

"Yes. Just like the killer bees."

"Right."

"Oh, by the way, what's this Ant Busters thing Saul keeps talking about?"

"Ah, Jesus. Just something my friend Bill from Kentucky mentioned that Saul overheard."

"Well, my friend, believe it or not, it seems to be sticking. Have you read the papers lately?"

"Actually, I haven't had the time."

"Not surprised. You'll see. Probably be on the tube next anyway, but you don't watch TV, do you?"

"Not much."

"Here's the good news. The killer ant poison will hit the Walmart stores in Kansas, Kentucky, Ohio, Oklahoma, Missouri, and Texas within thirty days. Larry even gave me an extension on the discounted fee of $67,500 for the license so our proceeds will pay for that too."

"Convenient."

"Who you know, my friend."

"Obviously."

"Cheer up. Within six months, you'll be rolling in dough, Richard. You'll have plenty for your research. Maybe even build your own research institute."

"Yeah. At least something good would come of all of this."

"You don't sound happy, Richard."

"I'll be happy when people's lives are no longer in danger, M."

"Yeah. Being that these are your creation, I guess that really would eat at your guts, wouldn't it?"

Richard sat in silence behind his cluttered desk.

"Okay, my friend. Keep in touch."

"Yeah. You too. Tell Saul to give me a buzz."

"Will do. Bye."

"Who was that, dear?"

"That was M."

"What did he want?"

"Huh? Oh. Walmart's going to sell his killer ant poison in thirty days. And we're going to be 'rolling in dough' in six months."

"We?"

Richard nodded.

"He included me in his money-making scheme."

"Great! But you don't sound too happy about it, dear."

Richard shook his head.

"What is it? What's bothering you? Is it illegal? He's a friend of yours, right?"

"Not really. He's the kind who would stab you in the back if it would benefit him, yes."

"I'm not understanding."

"I just don't like how he is taking advantage of the general public to make himself rich."

"Because he came up with the poison to kill these ants? If he didn't, someone else would. You just may be in the right place at the right time, dear."

"Yeah. I guess you may be right, hon."

"I guess we better get back to business here."

Richard nodded and worked alongside of Mary, beginning with the lab area. "Aren't you tired?"

"I guess you're right, dear. It's eight thirty already. And I'm hungry. How about you?"

"*Starving* is a more accurate word. What do you feel like?"

"Chinese."

"Again? Whoa. That's a little drive. But okay. You certainly deserve it." He looked along the entire wall. The lab looked like it had just been installed.

"Hello?" Mary said into her phone.

"Mary. The camping gear came in this afternoon, and I just wanted to let you know I received, marked, and put everything out."

"I hope you're right on this, Sally."

"You'll see. I'm going to make a sign for the window tomorrow."

"Okay. Thanks."

"Camping gear?" Richard asked when she hung up her cell phone.

"Yeah. Sally's idea."

"Shall we go?"

"Yes. And you will treat me to desert when we get back, won't you?" She reached between his legs.

"Ouch! Easy lady. Most definitely. We could have an appetizer right now—if you like."

"Easy, stud. Feed me first."

"Thought I could get away cheap, but I guess not. You got it."

CHAPTER 28

"AW, C'MON, ANN. YOU KNOW I HAVE A HARD TIME KEEPING
it in my pants. Besides, she came after me, babe."

"Oh, I see. The great Dr. Morton has to 'spread' his wealth. And
I guess that means there will always be another babe."

"Hey, listen, babe. I'm going to make you rich! Don't go getting
on your high horse with me! I'll cut you off just like that!" He snapped
his fingers.

"Really?" She snapped her fingers. "Just like that, huh?"

"That's right. C'mon, babe. She meant nothing. You're my girl.
She was just an hour of diversion. No big deal."

"I'm sorry, Michael. I was looking for something a little more—"

"Committed? Did you forget I'm married? Don't tell me you
thought I was going to get a divorce!"

"Yeah. That's it."

"What? You want me to be like Dr. Richard Denton? You can't be
serious. Besides, he has a woman to be 'serious' with now."

Her face dropped.

"You didn't know? Oh yeah, babe. He's got this broad, Mary.
Owner of a grocery store in some small town—probably supports
him. He can't find any work. Ha, ha. He's a loser, babe. Face it. Sorry
to disillusion you."

"He's not any such thing. He's the most brilliant entomologist
probably in the world, and he's honest as the day is long."

"Honest? Oh, baby, has he ever fooled you? Who do you think

made these killer ants? They didn't just arrive on some boat from Africa or South America like the fire ant. They were made! And they didn't get planted here by some terrorist like those poor chumps think in Homeland Security, running around the world, spending our tax dollars, and investigating all the top entomologists in the world. It was your genius who cooked them up!"

"That's not true!"

"No? Than go ask him. Go ahead. Just go to him and ask him."

"He wouldn't do that. He wouldn't create such an insect."

"Aw. C'mon, babe. Use your head. Smell the coffee!"

"I will ask him. And I'm not your babe. You'll never see this body again." She turned and stormed out of the room.

I can't believe she's still in love with that guy. "You'll be back, babe," he called out after her. "I'll see that great bod—and do a lot more. Ha, ha, ha! Money talks, bullshit walks! Ha, ha, ha. Otherwise, you'll never get a dime from me, bitch. With my money, I can buy ten of you!"

"Mr. Morton? Call on line one."

He reached for the phone. "Hello?"

"Whoa! Is this a bad time?"

"Larry! Sorry, my friend. I just had to kick someone out of my office."

"Must've been tough. Female, I presume."

"You got it."

"Just called to touch base with you on our product."

"No problem. Should be on the shelves in less than thirty days now. You've leaked it out?"

"Yes. We should see headlines everywhere within a week. By the time it hits the shelves, it'll sell within twenty-four hours."

"Great job. You should have your first bank deposit within sixty days. You still going to retire?"

"Sure am. Get out while the gettin's good."

"I've been thinking. What if we have our good doctor find me a queen—and we drop it off in South America or Europe?"

"Whoa, Morton. Jumping on the bandwagon over spilt milk is

173

one thing, but what you're talking about will put us both in jail—or worse."

"Okay, my friend. Just tossing money-making ideas around."

"Do you really think Dr. Denton will be able to change the DNA on these things?"

"I believe he's the only one who can. But it'll take a while. And by the time he does, my friend, we'll be millionaires."

"And I'll be in Brazil."

"So that's why I'll be depositing it in a Brazilian bank. Who's going to take your place?"

"Don't know and could care less."

"Gotcha."

"And you, Michael? Going to take that sexy assistant to a deserted island somewhere? You're not going to continue at the university, are you?"

"Hell no. I'll give my resignation by the time you get your first piece of ass in Brazil."

"I'm married, remember?"

"Okay. By the time you screw your wife for the first time in Brazil—and do it on the beach for Christ's sake!"

"You're a sick man, Michael."

"Yeah. Isn't it great?"

"Unreal. Feel sorry for your wife, man. Okay. Got to go."

"All right. Start checking your bank balance in about six weeks."

"All right, Michael. Bye."

"Bye, Larry."

"What a wimp," Michael said as he hung up the phone. "Barbara! Get in here!"

"Yes, sir?"

"Close the door and lock it," he said with a smile.

She obeyed like a puppy—eager to please her master.

CHAPTER 29

"I THINK YOU BETTER INFORM THE PRESIDENT."

"He's got much more important things to deal with than ants."

"Okay! Your head. Would you prefer he calls you and asks about it?"

"What am I going to tell him? A bunch of ants are eating humans? That's plastered all over the headlines. He's going to want to know what's being done about it."

"So what's being done about it?"

"We're killing millions of ants. We even have the damn Ant Busters!"

"Oh, that'll go over well, I'm sure. Ha, ha, ha!"

"Exactly!"

"Mr. Wise? The president wants to see you, sir."

"Told you."

"Aw, shit."

"Good luck."

"Thanks … for nothing."

"Go right in. He's expecting you."

Kenneth Wise nodded and proceeded into the Oval Office. "You asked for me, Mr. President?"

"Yes, Ken. Sit down. I don't have a lot of time. What do you have on these killer ants?"

"Our man Taylor is on it. He's got Dr. Burton from the University of Kentucky advising him. Dr. Ralph Mullen, a top toxicologist, and

Dr. Morton of the University of Kansas have developed the poison to kill these ants. It will be in all the Walmart stores within thirty days, I understand."

"That doesn't tell me how these got here in the first place, Ken. Or how long it's going to take to get rid of them. The people are afraid to go outside."

"I'm afraid I don't have the answer to that one, sir. At least not yet, sir."

The president rose from his leather chair and looked out the window. "Roses don't look so good."

"Sir?"

"Can you imagine taking your family on a picnic in one of our state parks only to find ants eating you instead of the food you brought?"

"Terrible thought, sir."

"That's what the general public is thinking, Ken. What am I going to tell them? Buy some killer ant poison and throw it on the ant hill as if they were these bothersome fire ants?"

Ken remained silent.

After a couple of long minutes, the president said, "Who took care of the killer bees for us?"

"I don't remember, sir."

"Find the best entomologist we got and put him on doing the same with the killer ants as we did with the killer bees. ASAP!" He turned toward Ken and supported himself with his extended arms on his desk. "And let me know who he is and every damn thing about him! And you keep me informed, damn it!"

"Yes, sir!" Ken rose and almost ran out of the president's office. He heard him yelling for Silvia Busby, one of the public relations advisors, and saw her bolting down the hall just seconds later. He could feel the wind as she passed him.

"Get Sam on the phone," the president ordered.

"Sam? Killer ants."

"Yes, sir. Know all about it. Got Dr. Ralph Mullen investigating.

It's a hybrid, sir. Someone played with its DNA. Suspicion is overseas origin, Africa in particular."

"Are we talking terrorism here, Sam?"

"There is that possibility, sir. Homeland Security is on it, but Ralph is leaning against it."

"His opinion?"

"Experiment that went sour, sir."

"Jesus!"

"He'll find out, sir. He's the best. We have the leading entomologist working on changing its DNA. Dr. Richard Denton."

"Good job, Sam. Glad someone is on the ball, here. Denton? Isn't he the one they are calling the Ant Buster?"

"Yeah. That's him."

"Tell him to hurry, Sam. And keep me posted."

"Yes, sir."

"Get Ed in here," Ken told the box on his desk.

"So? What did he say?"

"We have a lot of work to do … top priority."

"Yeah. I knew you were going to say *we*. I made some calls. Dr. Taylor has his man Saul and one of the top international entomologists, Dr. Richard Denton, working together to kill the ants at the sites as they're found."

"The Ant Busters?"

"Yeah. Really catching on, isn't it? Anyway, Dr. Morton came up with the poison. He and Taylor got it rushed through the EPA to get it on the market. Denton is a specialist on DNA and can do whatever they do to change the aggressiveness of these killer ants so they don't eat humans—or something like that."

"Great! Good work! I'll inform the boss. What kind of time table do we have here?"

"I haven't the slightest. I haven't even talked to Dr. Denton yet to see if he'll do it—or anything else for that matter."

"I think we better bring Dr. Denton to the White House. We won't give him a choice. I can't go back into the president without better info."

"Right. I'll get right on it."

CHAPTER 30

"WHERE ARE YOU GOING?" MARY ASKED.

"Washington." Richard continued to pack his small travel bag.

"Washington? You mean DC?"

Richard nodded.

"Why? What do they want? They don't have ants there, do they?" Mary asked.

"I really don't know. I'm sure they have ants—hundreds of millions of them—but not the carnivorous species, dear." Richard shrugged. "Edward Hamilton just called and told me I had to go to Washington to meet with Ken Wise—right away. He's one of the president's advisors."

"I see. How long will you be gone?"

"He didn't say."

"Are you in trouble?"

How does she do that? He swallowed hard. "Why would I be in trouble?"

Mary walked over to him, grabbed his arms, and sat him on the bed. "You look like someone who's about to be sentenced to death row." She placed her hand on his chest. "Your heart's beating a mile a minute. What's going on?"

Richard wanted to tell her something, but he remained silent.

"What is it, dear?" she said softly. "Something is really wrong, isn't it? You're afraid of something."

He shook his head and looked at the floor.

"You can tell me. I will never rat on you, but I can't help you if you don't tell me what's wrong."

Richard took a deep breath and sighed heavily. "I ... I did something really stupid—and wrong."

"We all have done that, dear. We don't live as many years as we have without having some skeletons in our closets."

He looked at her with watering eyes, and she waited patiently. He remembered the church and all those skeletons. "I ... I did it."

"Did what, dear?"

"I'm responsible for the killer ants."

"What?"

"It was an accident. Someone threw a baseball through the cellar window and broke the glass cover on my ant farm. The queens and males had just surfaced to mate. They escaped through the window."

Mary slowly stood, staring at him. "*You* created those things? You *made* those things?" She shook her head and took small retreating steps. "You *killed* all those people!" She turned and ran out of the bedroom.

It took a few moments to recover, and then Richard finished packing and made his way to his truck.

Why did you have to open your big mouth? She's right, you know. You're a killer—a no-good murderer. And now you have to face Uncle Sam, don't you? How are you going to fix this shit, Doc? You finally met the woman to share your life with—and you blew it again, didn't you? So much for the peaches and cream, huh, Doc? Where's the nine millimeter? He took a deep breath and sighed. *Time to face the music, Doc.*

As he passed Mary's Family Groceries on the way out of town, he reduced his speed to a crawl. He changed his mind and sped on to the airport to catch his flight. *Maybe I should pick up a bottle of courage.*

— — — — — —

After he landed, he walked toward a man with a piece of poster board with his name on it.

"Dr. Denton? Good to meet you, sir. I'm Edward Hamilton. I have our transportation ready. Do you have baggage to pick up?"

"No. Just this." He raised his small travel bag. "I'm sure I'll be provided with more appropriate clothes."

Edward glanced at him with bewilderment. "This way, Dr. Denton."

They walked in silence, and Richard climbed into the back of a black sedan with Ed.

"Ready," Ed said to the driver, and the car took off with a jerk.

"Do you mind if we go to the office, first, Dr. Denton. We have you in a good hotel close by, but we're anxious to talk to you."

"Of course not. And please call me Richard. I feel bad enough as it is."

Edward gave him another look of perplexity, but didn't question him about his comment.

"I hear you are the best there is in entomology—internationally renowned."

"Really? I don't really pay much attention to what my peers say. Besides, you shouldn't believe everything you hear."

"Oh, believe me. You were checked out like a fine-tooth comb. We know all about you, including your problems that got you dismissed from the university."

"You gotta be shittin' me."

Ed chuckled. "The government knows everything about everybody—or at least can find out whenever they want. You still on the juice?"

"I do now. And no." *I'd like to be though.*

"We know every place you worked, how long, how much you made, how much in taxes you paid … everything."

The car pulled to a stop inside the White House grounds.

"We're here, Richard. Follow me please."

"Well, they certainly are polite when they're going to throw you in the slammer."

They walked through some corridors, made some turns, and stopped in front of an unmarked door.

"Here we are, Richard. Please come in."

They stepped into a small office with two wooden chairs in front of a highly polished wooden desk.

"This is Dr. Richard Denton. Richard, this is Kenneth Wise, one of the advisors to the president."

"Pleasure to meet you, Dr. Denton. Please have a seat. Can I get you something to drink? Coffee, beverage, water?"

"No, thank you, sir. I'm fine."

The man behind the desk wore a gray, obviously expensive suit, but Richard thought the pink dress shirt and choice of tie were a little tacky.

"I appreciate you coming in to talk with us on such short notice, but we have an emergency that needs the talents of a man of your qualifications, Dr. Denton."

"He likes to be called Richard," Edward interjected.

"Great. Richard. Please call me Ken. I really hope we are going to know each other for a little while."

"I'm sorry. You have me at a disadvantage here."

"Sorry. Of course. We haven't told you why we asked you here. You have heard of the killer ants. We know that because I hear you are one of the so-called Ant Busters." Ken's thin mouth opened, showing large, yellowed teeth. The ashtray filled with cigarette butts gave away the reason.

"Oh, yes. That … uh … wasn't my doing."

"Well. It's made you famous. Anyway, we are more interested in your talent working in insect DNA. Your specialty, right?"

Richard nodded.

"I'll come right to the point. Don't want to waste your valuable time. We need your help. The American people need your help, Richard. Do you know how we can stop these killer ants?"

They don't know I created them yet. I should never have told Mary.

"I only see one way, sir—Ken. You need to make them less aggressive."

"You can do that? How?"

"Change their DNA. Crossbreed them with males of docile species."

"You can't just eliminate them?"

"No more than we have been able to eliminate the fire ant."

"Wow. If these killer ants spread like the fire ants, this whole country will be at war."

"It'll kill the economy too."

"Excuse me?"

"The fire ant was introduced into the US by boat. I don't think other countries will want to receive anything from the US if they fear these particular ants will spread to their countries."

Ed and Ken looked at each other. Ken looked down at the papers in front of him for a few seconds before he locked his eyes on Richard. "Can you help us, Richard?"

"As a matter of fact, I've already started on my own."

"What do you mean?"

"I made myself a lab in my basement and began the research to come up with a way to change their DNA."

"Fantastic! Naturally, we can set you up in a state-of-the-art lab—and we'll supply you with whatever you need to work."

"I already have everything I need, and I prefer to work in my own lab. I will need some funding, of course. Travel expenses for field research, mostly."

"And a salary for your work, of course. I'll take care of it."

I stepped in shit and came out smelling like a rose? "Do you need my checking account number to electronically deposit the funds?"

"We already have that, Richard," Ed said with a smile.

Richard nodded. "Of course you do."

"Are you sure we can't convince you to work here? There are great labs at the universities in the area."

"Please, Ken. I would feel much more comfortable in my own lab."

"I guess I know what you mean. All you scientists are like that.

Ed, get Richard a government credit card. You won't need to carry much cash this way. Makes excellent accounting for us too."

"Of course."

"You'll need some help. We have been in touch with our man, Taylor, in EPA, and he has been working with Dr. Michael Morton. He came up with a poison to kill these ants."

"Yes. I am quite familiar with Dr. Morton. He sent me the poison to apply at the three sites I was at."

"Right. Good. That will make things easier. We have asked his assistant—highly recommended by him and the University of Kansas—to assist you. I believe Ann Kreindler was a student of yours?"

"Yes, she was. But I really don't need an assistant."

"I'm afraid I must insist on that detail, Richard. In fact, if you need more assistants, let me know. We need to solve this problem ASAP. I'm sure you understand."

"Of course."

Ken stood up and extended his hand to Richard, and Ed followed. "Great. Then we have an understanding. Your government and the American people appreciate your loyal cooperation, Richard. Ed will be your liaison. He'll give you a direct line so you can call him anytime. He'll get you whatever you need. I'll also give you a direct e-mail to me so we can communicate more easily. You should receive your credit card by special delivery within forty-eight hours—and you will find some funds in your account by the time you get home. Is there anything else you need at the moment, Richard?"

"No. Wait. When is Ann supposed to report to me?"

"She'll be there within forty-eight hours. She has instructions to do all the paperwork for you so you don't have to worry about that either—accounting for the expenses and all that. We'll be in touch with the details. Please keep your new cell phone charged and on 24/7."

Richard nodded.

"Have a nice flight home, Richard." Ken sat down and began to work as if Richard had already left.

"Come with me, Richard," Ed said.

Richard followed Ed down the hallways in a fog. *Talk about short and sweet.*

— — — — — —

Ed returned to Ken's office after having Richard taken to the airport. The hotel wasn't necessary.

"Well, he's off. Have you informed the president?"

"Yes, but I didn't tell him the possible economic ramifications. Jesus Christ. I never even thought about that. This could be disastrous. We need to push Richard, Ed. Push him hard."

"Got it."

"You concentrate on Richard and the killer ants. Put off as much of the rest as you can until we end this. This is priority one."

"Understood."

— — — — — —

On the flight home, Richard's mind wouldn't stop racing.

You had to tell her, didn't you. You screwed it up big time. She'll never talk to you again. You know that, genius, don't you? Tossed some more memories into the fire, didn't you? Just you and your great creation now, isn't it? All those years of creating them, and now you have to destroy them. What a loser you are, genius.

CHAPTER 31

"I TOLD YOU TO GET THOSE BOXES OUT OF THE WAY!"

"Well, aren't we in a bad mood?" Sally said with a frown. "What's the matter? Have a fight with Richard?"

Mary gave her a stare that would kill a brown bear.

"Oh, my God! You did, didn't you?"

Mary grimaced, and a couple of tears escaped the corners of her eyes.

Sally grabbed her arm and led her over to the stool behind the counter. "Sit down, Mary. Tell me what happened."

Mary shook her head. "He isn't the man I thought he was. That's all."

"Maybe it's because you put so much shining armor on him and sat him on a tall, white horse. What did you find out about him that knocked your knight out of his saddle?"

"I didn't make him a knight in shining armor."

"Sure you did. You just weren't paying attention to yourself. You told me he was Mr. Perfect."

"I did? Well, I shouldn't have. He did something he shouldn't have. Something serious."

"Are you going to make me guess—or are you going to make it easy for me and tell me?"

"I can't tell you. I gave my word."

"Oh. One of those things? What? Does he have a police record?

185

Was he married? *Is* he married? Does he have six kids? Did he do drugs—like you did?"

"Sally!" Mary looked around the store.

"Don't worry. No one's here. And I would never tell anyone either. My word to you, remember?"

Mary took a deep breath and sighed heavily.

"You love this guy, don't you?"

"I don't want to, but I do."

"Right now, you don't want to. Whatever it is, you'll get over it. Of course, you can continue to be angry with him, end your relationship, and return to being the unhappy, lonely woman you were before he came along. All I know is that I haven't seen you so happy for as long as I've known you."

"I don't know if I can forgive him."

"Forgive him? He cheated on you?"

"No, no. Nothing like that."

"Look. You gave your word. I can respect that, but you have to think this out, Mary. You've got to deal with the problem. Are you going to end your relationship over it—or are you going to help him solve the problem? I remember a couple of people who did some real bad stuff that helped each other out, don't you?"

Mary looked at her as if she just uncovered a big discovery.

"What? Listen, girl. You're starting to scare me. You saved my ass and gave me a new life. I owe you mine. If you need me to do anything for you, even if it's a little illegal, count on me."

Mary threw her arms around Sally and gave her a hard hug.

"What was that for?"

"You just opened my eyes. I was being so selfish. Oh, Sally?"

"Yeah?"

"I thought you didn't like Richard."

"I didn't. At least not at first. But after I saw how happy you were with him, I guess I kind of accepted him."

Mary nodded. "Thank you."

"For what? What did I do? What are you going to do?"

"I don't know. I'm going to think about it first, but I really don't know. Not yet. It's so hard."

"Well, while you think it through, I guess I better get rid of those boxes before you huff and puff again."

"And I guess I better get on the paperwork. Otherwise, I'll be burning the midnight oil. Again."

"Yeah. That's one advantage of you being angry with Richard."

"What do you mean?"

"I don't have to do the paperwork."

"Hmm! I really have dumped on you lately, haven't I?"

"That's okay, Mary. You can dump on me all you want. And I'm really happy to do it for you."

"I don't know what I'd do without you, Sally. You've been a great friend—and employee."

"And you've been a great friend—and boss."

"Well. I'm glad we got all that sorted out. Let's get to work, shall we?"

"Yeah."

They both went about their chores, secretly wiping the tears from their cheeks.

— — — — — —

"Good afternoon," an attractive young lady said as she entered Mary's Family Groceries. "I wonder if you could help me. I'm looking for the residence of Dr. Richard Denton."

"And who are you?"

"Oh, forgive me, ma'am. My name is Ann Kreindler … from the University of Kansas."

"What do you want with Rich—Dr. Denton?"

"I'm his research assistant."

Mary took a step back and sucked in her breath. "And you don't know where he lives?"

"I'm just starting. Do you know where he lives?"

"Yes. It's a small town. Everyone knows everyone. Go right about a mile and a half. It's a two-story brick on the left. Should be a white pickup in the driveway."

"Thanks. Appreciate it." Ann took a couple of steps toward the door.

"I imagine you'll be looking for a place to stay," Mary said.

"Well, I don't know. I expect I'll be staying at Dr. Denton's place while I'm working on this project. Research is long hours."

"I see." Mary watched her glide out the door and slip her voluptuous body into a red Mustang.

"Quite a fox, eh?" Sally said as they watched Ann take off.

"Yeah, she's a looker all right," Mary tried to say with indifference.

"He may forget all about you working with that. Unless, of course, you do something about it."

"And what, exactly, are you suggesting? Go up to his place and tell him I don't want him to mess with that young skirt?"

"Well, not in exactly those words, maybe, but something like that." Sally smiled.

"I don't know. I don't know! This is getting too complicated."

"But you're thinking about it real hard, right?"

"Just thinking about it."

"Yeah, sure. Mary, you've always been good at making judgment calls on people's character. If you don't do something, you may let him slip away."

"He may do that even if I do something," Mary said in a very low voice.

"What?"

"Nothing. Nothing, Sally."

The store began to fill up with the afternoon rush, and Mary didn't get much of an opportunity to "think" about what she was going to do until that evening in bed.

CHAPTER 32

RICHARD WAS UP BY SEVEN. FIFTEEN MINUTES LATER, HE was in his lab. He went to his safe and pulled out a large test tube that was sealed with four holes drilled through the stopper. He walked over to the aquarium he had prepared and slowly opened the test tube. One ant climbed out onto the soil. He put the cover on the aquarium and looked inside the test tube. Only pieces remained of the other ant he had placed inside. He smiled and looked down at the ant that was still walking around like a dog sniffing for a place to take a dump.

"Just as I thought, my lady. But this time, there won't be any accidents. I'm afraid you'll have to feed on some insects until tomorrow. But then, you'll be quite busy constructing, won't you? While you're working, I have to figure out who I'm going to mate you with. *Monomorium pharaonis? Iridomyrmex humilis*? Maybe. Let me drive over to Lawrence for supplies first."

Ann rang the doorbell three times, but there was no answer. She tried the door, and it was open. She warily stepped inside and closed the door gently behind her.

"Dr. Denton? Dr. Denton?"

"Down here! It's open!"

Ann walked toward the sound of Richard's voice, which led her to the kitchen.

"Dr. Denton?"

"I said I'm down here!"

She noticed the door and peered down the stairs. She saw there was light, and she cautiously walked down the stairs.

Richard was concentrating on the screen of his PC.

"Hi, Dr. Denton."

"Hi," he said without looking up. "Who are you?"

"Ann Kreindler, sir."

Richard looked up for a moment, and then he walked across the room to greet his ex-student. "Welcome to my humble lab."

"Thank you, sir." She let her eyes roam the premises. "It looks real."

"It functions."

"Oh, I wasn't criticizing, sir. I just want to tell you it's such an honor to be working with you, sir."

"I heard you and M did a good job together on the special poison I needed. And I'm betting it was mostly you."

Ann's face turned red, adding to her attractiveness. Her tight red sweater accentuated the right parts.

"Thank you, sir. It means a lot to me for you to acknowledge my work."

"Work. Yes. We have a real challenge here." He walked over to the aquarium with his new queen and patted the clear acrylic tank cover. "She's busy starting a new colony. We should see the first results in about forty days." He turned to Ann. "That means we have that much time to find ourselves some male domestic species for the queens to mate with. I was thinking either the *Monomorium pharaonis* or the *Iridomyrmex humilis*."

I think the *Iridomyrmex humilis* would be a better choice, Dr. Denton. They're useful as termite exterminators and deterrents of paper wasps too."

"Good points. They're also easier to find—at least we can find them in closer proximity to our location."

"Are we going to just mate and wait—or are you going to extract their DNA and transport it to the killer ant queen? I really would like to learn how to do the latter."

"Ah. Both actually. I plan on extracting some DNA from the more docile species, but I'd like to experiment with the natural mixing of the DNAs before transplanting. My theory is that it will dilute the aggressiveness much more on the first generation."

"Wow. That sounds exciting, Dr. Denton."

"Ann, if we are going to work together, please call me Richard or Doc."

Ann chuckled softly. "Okay, Doc."

"Time for you to see what this baby can do." He placed a large roach in the tank, and they watched. In less than a minute, the queen ant emerged, waved her antennae, and went straight toward the roach. The roach moved, but it was too late. The ant grabbed a leg with its mandible and injected its venom into its victim. In a single second, the roach froze—and the ant began to tear at its underside."

"Oh my God, Doc. That's the most aggressive species I have ever seen. And look at the size of it! I hear it paralyzes its victim, right?"

"Yes. *Paraponera* trait. *Siafu* colony size."

"And giant ant body size. Impressive species!" She looked at Richard and studied his face. "Michael, I mean Dr. Morton told me you created this species. I told him he was wrong."

He looked at Ann, and they both studied each other's faces for a good thirty seconds.

Do you tell her? M told her. She just wants you to confirm. Mary knows. The government doesn't know, but that won't take long now. M hasn't said anything because it's not convenient for him yet. Once it's over, he's going to burn you. You know that. You might as well tell her. She's too intelligent not to figure it out from your notes. And you can't hide that from her for months.

He took a deep breath and sighed heavily. "It was a very successful experiment—years in the making."

"What you accomplished is incredible, Doc, but why those traits? Didn't you realize how dangerous a species you were creating?"

"Exactly for the traits you described. The notable traits made it obvious that I had succeeded in combining not one, but multiple

DNA characteristics. By being extreme traits, it proved beyond a doubt it was possible."

"Yes, I see. Now I understand why you picked the traits. They were so different."

"Exactly."

"But how did it get out of hand?"

Richard nodded at the boarded-up cellar window. "The neighborhood kids play baseball in the empty field on the weekends. I wasn't here. That one time … I just took …" Richard hung his head. "I took a weekend off—the first one in many, many months—with a very good friend who convinced me to take the time off. That weekend, a baseball came through that window and shattered this tank cover. They were made of glass to see the specimens better."

"They crawled out of the aquarium and out the window?"

"Oh, no. They can't scale the glass. I coated it with liquid graphite so they couldn't take hold."

"So how did they get out?"

"It just happened that the queens and males had surfaced to mate at that precise moment."

"No! Do you know the odds of something like that happening?"

"Ha, ha. Oh, yes."

"Well, it wasn't your fault then. I mean, you did create them, but you didn't … how many queens were there?"

"Five."

"Oh my. You mean they traveled all the way to Oklahoma? Custer City, wasn't it?"

"Yes. Incredible, isn't it? Flew south."

"Yes. Warmer weather. They would do that, wouldn't they?"

"Now I must undo what I did. The government doesn't know. I'd like to keep it that way until we finish. Then you can inform them. It won't matter."

"I won't be the one to rat on you, Doc, but I know who will."

"M. Dr. Morton."

"Right. You call him M?"

"Yeah. Long time ago. I heard rumor you and he are—you know—close?"

"We were, I am sorry to say. I was so foolish. I discovered the real Michael just recently. He'll probably try to cheat me out of my part of the business venture, but I really don't care. Seriously. Working with you is worth it."

"Oh, don't be like me, Ann. You'll have nothing to live for in the end. And no one to share it with."

"What about this Mary I heard about. Michael told me."

"Mary? I love her, you know, but I made the mistake of telling her I was responsible for the killer ants. She thinks I'm a murderer and wants nothing to do with me now. Honesty got me nowhere. And I don't blame her."

"Maybe she really didn't love you so much then. If she did, she would help you solve your problem—or at least give you emotional support. Anyway, it's better to find out before you do something more permanent—like getting married, right? Like I did about Dr. Morton."

"I guess you're probably right," he said.

"What you need, Doc, is a woman who understands you and your work—someone who can share your interests. You told her the details, right? I mean, how it happened and all."

"Never got the chance, actually."

"You'll find another woman to take care of you. I'm sure of it."

"Oh, that'll be easy."

"Maybe it will be. So where do we start?"

"Well. I got step one done. I've got my hybrid's DNA on deep freeze. Time to get our *Iridomyrmex humilis* specimens."

"Let me find the closest location. Should be some fairly close."

She set up her laptop on the counter and plugged the power cord into the wall, displaying a very nicely shaped buttocks.

If I didn't know better, I'd think she's doing that on purpose, Richard thought.

"All right. I'll do the same for the *Monomorium pharoanis*—just in case they're closer."

193

"I doubt that very much."

"So do I. But being thorough must be our motto on this project."

"That's always been your motto, Doc. Oh, by the way. Where do I put my things?"

"What things?"

"Eventually, I'm going to get tired, Doc. I see a couch over there. Is that where I can crash? I can bring my suitcase in. I would prefer going to the bathroom in a little more private area though." She giggled.

"Yeah. You'll need a place to sleep. And shower." He looked around the room as if he were searching for something.

"Let's see. Oh, hell. Uh, you take my room. It's upstairs. I'll sleep on the couch. I spent more time here than in my bedroom anyway."

"I believe you," Ann said.

CHAPTER 33

THE DOORBELL RANG, BUT RICHARD DIDN'T HEAR IT. ANN was about to go answer it when she stopped and walked over to the cellar window instead.

She peered out and saw a white van in front of the house with black letters painted on its side: Mary's Family Groceries.

She looked at Richard, sat back down, and continued working on her laptop.

Mary tried the door. Locked. She stepped back, a little surprised. She set the stack of three Tupperware bowls on the ground, reached into her purse, and pulled out her key chain. She had put Richard's house key next to her store key. She put the key in the door and opened it, picked up the bowls, and made her way into the kitchen. She set them on the kitchen table.

She didn't yell out. Instead, she went to the open cellar door and peered down, noticing the lights were on. Of course, he'd be working.

As she reached the bottom step, she saw Ann crouched over her laptop on the black countertop. To her left, Richard was engrossed in his PC.

"Hello," Mary announced tentatively.

Ann turned and sighed disappointedly.

"Hello. Mary, isn't it? From the store?"

"Yes. How good of you to remember. I see you have already begun to work with Richard."

"Oh, we've know each other for years. We know each other well."

"I see." Mary looked over at Richard as he scribbled on a yellow pad while looking intently at the computer screen.

She walked over and stood in front of his desk. "Hi, Richard." She put her hand in front of the monitor.

"Huh? Oh, Mary? I'm sorry. I didn't hear you come in."

"I'm not surprised. I see the two of you are quite engaged in your work."

"Yes. We're trying to work as fast as we can."

Mary looked at Ann, scanning her figure and smooth complexion with care. She turned to Richard, her stomach knotting up. "Can we talk?"

"Sure."

"I brought some food. Thought you would be hungry and knew you would never take the time to cook anything for yourself." She looked over at Ann and sighed lightly. "There's enough for everyone, young lady."

Richard explained his strategy over dinner. Ann said very little, but Mary noticed how closely she looked at her.

Mary washed the bowls, and Richard dried them. Ann excused herself and returned to the basement; however, she strained her ears to catch as much of their conversation as she could from the bottom of the stairs.

"Can I get you a beer? Scotch? I don't have any coffee made."

"No. I'm fine. Really. I really came to apologize, Richard."

"Apologize? For what? Telling me the truth?"

"I'm not proud of everything I've done in my past either. I shouldn't have jumped on you. I promised I would help you—no matter what—and the very first time you really needed me, I abandoned you. I'm really sorry, Richard."

"I can't blame you, Mary. I realize what I did turned out to be a terrible thing."

"Agreed, but I should be helping you—not making it more

difficult for you. Tell me what I can do to help, but tell me how it happened first."

"You mean we're still—"

"Whatever you want us to be, darling."

"That is so great! I thought I had lost you."

They embraced tenderly.

"I guess, maybe, there really is a God," he said softly.

Mary wiggled her finger at him and smiled. "I'll take that scotch now. I'll pour you one too. On the rocks with a splash of natural water, right?"

"Very good."

Mary prepared his drink and said, "I think I should tell you a big secret of mine too."

"That sounds ominous."

She sighed deeply. "Only one person knows about this. And that's only because I helped her through similar circumstances. I haven't been totally open with you. I … uh …"

"Just spit it out—as you would tell me."

"I guess you're right. Well, here goes. I spent some time in rehab."

"Rehab? Rehab for what? Drugs? Alcohol?"

"Well, you see, my husband was an alcoholic. He made my life, and my children's lives, miserable."

"I can understand that," Richard said.

"Well, the pressure was really heavy. He spent all his income on booze and cigarettes. I had to support us on my income. It wasn't enough, so I had to get a second job at night, which made it more difficult because he would come home—and the children had no one to protect them from him."

"Quite a dilemma."

"Yeah. My answer to deal with the pressure was marijuana, at least the first answer."

"I see. I know a lot of people who smoke pot. They seem okay. I tried it once. I was about twenty-four. Tasted terrible. Never tried it again."

"Unfortunately, it didn't stop there. The weed wasn't enough. It was at first, but then it wasn't."

"So you turned to the hard stuff."

"Yeah. It was easy at first. I got it cheap. But then they started charging higher prices."

"How did you pay for it? You needed two jobs to pay for a living."

She took a deep breath and sighed slowly. "I ... uh ... I fell to my lowest point in my life. I traded sex for the coke."

Richard sat silently for a moment, staring at the table and his drink. "Is that it? Is there more?"

"Oh, that's it. Rock bottom. My husband left me for some floozy who really took him for a ride. He died in a car accident."

"Sorry. You're not taking dope now—or hooking, right?"

"Of course not."

"How did you stop?"

"My son discovered me."

"Ouch."

"I saw his face and never hooked again. Stopped taking the dope too. Cold turkey all the way. It was some of the most miserable years of my life."

"I can relate somewhat to that part. And Sally?"

"Her husband beat her, and then he left her. She turned to booze for her solution. I got her off of it and gave her a job. Gave her food for a while to get her back on her feet. I didn't want her to be a hooker too."

"Good for you."

"Sally and I have kept each other company ever since. We look after each other."

"Now I understand her better. It wasn't so much that she didn't like me. She was protecting you, wasn't she?"

"Yes. Neither of us has had any relationships since our own personal disasters."

"Wow. How many years has it been?"

"A few."

Richard swirled the little scotch that remained in his glass, the small ice cubes clinking on the lead crystal. "Life is some kind of soap opera, isn't it?"

"Yeah. It sure is."

"I don't know why women watch those programs. We live our own soap operas every day."

"I think we watch them to help us feel more normal."

"Never thought about it that way. You know, this is the first time I have ever had a one-on-one conversation with anyone about their personal life. I feel so much closer to you. And I'd really like to be a permanent part of your life. I'm really not good at this romance stuff. Well, you already know that. The absentminded professor, you know? I really can't even remember being romantic with anyone, so maybe I don't even know how. All I know now is that I'd like to share the rest of my life with you. I'd like to tell you all my problems and listen to all of yours. I'd like to keep on making love to you—anytime and anywhere you want. I don't know what is going to happen to me when the government finds out I was responsible for all these people dying, but I will survive this. If I'm not thrown in jail for the rest of my life, I would like to put matching rings on our fingers."

"Matching rings?" Mary looked at Richard. "You mean you still want to—"

"Marry you. I want to marry you. Will you?"

"I thought you said you weren't romantic? That would make me the happiest woman in the world." She sat on his lap, wrapped her arms around his neck, and placed a lingering kiss on his lips.

"Careful, lady. You're stirring up the manliness in me."

"Well. Why don't we go upstairs so I can pay more attention to your *manliness*."

"Say no more."

As Richard and Mary's conversation went along, Ann had inched her way, little by little, to the third step from the bottom, leaning against the wall.

She retrieved her suitcase from her car, returned to the basement, and put her bag on the worn cushion. She returned to her laptop and began working, not able to deter the tears of disappointment that slowly trickled down her cheeks.

CHAPTER 34

"DO YOU THINK THIS WILL REALLY WORK, ANN?" ASKED Mary.

"If Richard says it will, it will."

"How does this work? I really don't understand what you all are doing."

"Basically, we will take the DNA of the *Iridomymrmex humilis* and mix it with the … sorry. We mix the DNA of the Argentine ant, or the common sugar ant, and mix it with the killer ant. The next generation of the killer ant should be a lot less aggressive and smaller. And we are hoping they even change their diets and become omnivorous. Then, the common pesticides we use will be sufficient to control them. If we succeed, we eliminate the danger. That's a really basic explanation, though."

"I'm sure."

"Well. Richard's also working on another property at the same time."

"Property?"

"Yes. If we can make the males sterile, we could reduce the population very quickly."

"You mean eliminate them?"

"We don't want to eliminate the ant. They actually are needed as part of the balance of the insect world."

"We need ants?"

"Oh, yes. They are a food source for insects that eat other

insects. The ants themselves eat insects too. Without this *balance*, we couldn't control the insects that eat our crops. It gets quite complex."

"Sounds like it, but I get the general idea. Thanks. I see you are working on more aquariums."

"Yes. These are where we will experiment to see if we are successful."

"You're actually going to grow them right here? That's scary. Aren't you afraid? Isn't all this dangerous?"

"Actually, it is a little dangerous. Comes with the territory, as they say. Makes it more exciting, though, don't you think?"

"Gives me the goose bumps just seeing them. In fact, I get goose bumps just coming down here."

Richard came over and put his arm around Mary's shoulder.

"Gives you a whole new outlook on ants, doesn't' it? We have good control down here. Don't worry. It's also why I insist on not having anyone else down here. The more people, the bigger the possibility of an accident."

Mary shuddered at the thought and snuggled even closer to Richard, putting her arms around his waist.

"Oh, by the way. Dinner's on the table. Pork chops and fried onions, buttered string beans with bacon, and a macaroni and cheese with tomato casserole."

"Oh my. Sounds delicious," Ann said. "I'm starving!"

"Macaroni and cheese casserole is one of my favorites," Richard said.

"I know," Mary said with a smile.

"How will you mix these sugar ants with the killer ants?" Mary asked while they sipped on post-dinner coffees.

"We'll need to take the males to the killer ant colonies. This particular species has the ability to coexist with other species."

"You have to go where the killer ants are? You? You can't send someone?"

"Don't worry, Mary. I'll see that he doesn't get himself in trouble."

"You're going too? Oh, no. You're so young. You have so much life ahead of you."

"We really need to be the ones to do this, hon."

"Yeah. It's our baby. We need to make sure it's done right. We don't want to do all this work just for someone else to screw it up for us."

"Oh my God. And just how soon do you have to do this?"

"We're pretty close. Maybe a week."

"Yes," Ann said. "They're looking for some killer ant nests as we speak."

"They?"

"Saul. There doesn't seem to be any more reports from Bill's area, but there will be some from around the Kansas City area. Logic."

"Saul's the one you were with in Raymore and Gardner, right?"

"Correct, dear."

"At least it's someone you know, I guess."

"Cheer up, Mary. It's the last step, really—for us. And when this is over, you and Richard can take off on your honeymoon—for a month!"

"From your mouth to God's ears," Mary said.

"Ha, ha, ha."

"What?" Ann and Mary said in unison.

"I just had a funny thought."

"You want to share it with us?" Ann asked.

"The killer ant poison is selling like there's no tomorrow, right?"

"Yes. Supposedly we're going to be rich," Ann said.

"Yeah. Sure. I have to see it to believe it," Richard said.

"So what's so funny, dear?"

"If we're successful, what are they going to do with all that poison? The people won't need to buy it anymore."

"Yes!" Ann said. "And that pompous son of a bitch will have his rug pulled out right from under him. And deservedly so!"

"I'm sorry. I'm not following you two," Mary said.

"Don't you see? Right now, Dr. Michael, the turd, is living high on the hog, taking in tons of money, but his gold mine will run dry," Ann explained.

"And knowing M," Richard said, "he'll have bought a multimillion-dollar house, expensive cars, and Lord knows what else."

"Expensive women," Ann added. "And when the well runs dry much before he expects, he won't have the money to pay for all his new toys."

"It'll be like a helium balloon rising. His balloon will burst when it gets so high," Richard added.

"But aren't the two of you supposed to get some share of all that money?"

Richard and Ann looked at each other and smiled.

"Mary, neither of us has ever received—or expected—a dime. Dr. Michael Morton is a cad. He and that guy from the government, what's his name, Doc?"

"Larry. Lawrence Trexler."

"Yeah. He and this other turd, Larry, have no plans on sharing any of that money with anyone."

"But the two of you have a deal, don't you?"

"Did you sign some kind of contract with any of them, Ann?"

"Nope. Did you, Doc?"

"Nope."

"That's not right!"

"Life sucks and then you die," Richard said.

"It's okay, Mary. Richard and I really never expected any money from him anyway. Well, I did in the beginning, but I learned better. Besides, our salaries from the government are sufficient, right, Doc?"

"More than the university paid me."

"Besides, Mary, the scientific recognition we will get from this will be much more valuable than the money he promised."

"So you really don't care about the money?"

"Nope," Richard and Ann said.

Mary looked at them both and sat back in her chair. "I'm envious—and humbled. And you're both right. We do have everything we need right here."

"Everyone has their own priorities. Fancy homes and cars are not mine. That's all," Richard shrugged.

"And that's why I love you so much, darling."

"You two make a really nice couple," Ann said.

"I hate to break up a tender moment, but we got to get back to work, Doc."

"Yeah," Richard said. "I guess you're right. Let's go."

"You two go ahead. I'll clean up and get back to the store. See you tonight, dear?"

"You bet."

CHAPTER 35

THE CELL PHONE CLIPPED TO RICHARD'S RIGHT HIP sounded like a phone from the sixties. He was peering into the aquarium of the Argentine ants.

Ann turned away from her microscopic study and chuckled. She shook her head, went over to Richard, and pulled out his cell phone. "Hello?"

"Hello?"

"Who are you looking for?"

"Dr. Richard Denton."

"Who's calling?"

"Saul."

"Saul who?"

"Just tell him it's Saul. He'll know. It's important."

"Doc?"

"Um." Richard had his large magnifying glass about three inches from his face.

"Saul is on the phone. Can you answer?"

"Who?"

"Saul."

"Saul? Why didn't you tell me?" He snatched the phone from Ann's hand.

"I did," she said almost to herself and returned to her work.

"Saul? Is that you?"

"Yes. Don't you answer your own cell phone?"

Richard looked at the phone in his hand. "It is mine. How are you? What've you been doing? It's been a couple of months now, hasn't it?"

"As a matter of fact, it has been four. And our friends have been busy."

"How many more? Where? Wait. Let me get a map."

"No need. Just listen, Doc. We've had a couple of sparse cases north and east of Kansas City."

"And you took care of them?"

"You don't watch the news? Never mind. I know the answer to that. Yes. I took care of those cases."

"Great."

"Uh. We got a situation that I need your help with, Doc."

"I'm listening."

"Good. Remember what you said about your prediction for Kansas City?"

"Don't tell me."

"Yep. Now. Got a map of Kansas City?"

"No, I'm afraid not."

"No matter. I need you to come join me. I'll send you an e-mail about where I am. I'll show you the details when you get here. I already called Dr. Morton, and I'll be receiving sufficient poison. I asked for ten tanks."

"Ten! How many nests are there!"

"Got no idea yet. A lot though. We know that. They have hit suburbs that totally surround Kansas City. If your theory is correct, they'll be merging toward the center of town."

"They've been laying low, Saul. Let me throw some things together. I'll be on my way within a couple of hours."

"Larry's not with the EPA anymore."

"What? Really? Well. No surprise, really. And no loss, I believe."

"Yeah. I guess it's better. He was really losing it. He seemed to be nervous as hell. It's more like he ran away."

"So who's in his place?"

"I am, temporarily of course."

"Maybe they'll see the light and keep you there."

"Ha. I'm not political enough. I'm one of the workers, remember?"

"And a damn good one. Just the kind of guy the government needs."

"Thanks. Anyway, it's big news—and the mayor of Kansas City is desperate for the Ant Busters to get started."

"Geez. Not that again. Okay. On my way."

"By the way, I heard a rumor through Larry that Dr. Morton left the university a couple of months ago too. Just thought you'd like to know."

"Yeah? Figures. Two plus two makes four. See you in a couple of hours, Saul."

"I'll have everything ready for ya, Doc. It'll be good to see you."

"Likewise."

"Who are you gonna call?"

"Don't start, Saul!"

Ann began to clean up her area. "Was that the guy you took care of the nests with?"

"What are you doing?"

"I'm getting ready to go to Kansas City. What else?"

"I'm afraid you can't go."

"What? What do you mean?"

"I can't spare you here. You need to finish the research."

"You want me to do the DNA experiments?"

"Yes. You can. You're ready. You have to. This has to be finished."

"Wow. That's ... quite an honor."

"Be very careful. No accidents. Understand?"

"Me! What about you? You'll be in the midst of millions of them! You're the one who needs to be careful!"

"Okay. So we should both be careful, right?"

"Right. Let me help you get your stuff together. Better stop by and see Mary on your way out."

"Oh, yeah. I guess that would be a good idea. Poor girl."

━━   ━━   ━━   ━━   ━━   ━━

An hour later, Richard pulled into one of the empty spaces in front of Mary's Family Groceries.

"Well, this is a switch," Sally exclaimed when Richard walked in.

"Hi, Sally. Mary in?"

"Back here, dear."

"Back there, dear," Sally said, following Richard's footsteps as he toward the back of the store.

Mary was putting price tags on some new sleeping bags. "Hi, darling." She put her arms around his neck and gave him a peck on the cheek. "I can't believe how fast our camping equipment is selling. It is just flying out of here. And I have Sally to thank for it. It was her idea. What's the matter?"

"Nothing's the matter. I just need to leave town for a little bit. I didn't want to leave without telling you."

"You better not. Where are you going?"

"Kansas City."

"Kansas City?".

"Yes. Saul called. Needs some advice is all. Ann's going to stay and continue. Can you, you know, look after her a little?"

"Of course. I'll just make dinner for two. We seem to get along well."

"Yes, you do. I'm glad. She's a sweet girl. Brilliant too. I've got to get going."

"How long will you be gone?"

"I don't know exactly. I expect just three or four days."

"Okay. Drive careful, dear."

"Will do." He made a quick exit.

Sally finished with her customer and said, "Where's he going now?"

"Kansas City."

"You're kidding!"

"No. Why?"

"You haven't seen the news?"

"What news?"

"I better show you." She turned on the news. "The death toll is up to 384 since the beginning of this week. After some months of quiet, the killer ants have emerged once again. There are now sixteen cases cited where the killer ants have attacked. They seem to be totally surrounding the city. Mayor Alan Simpson has called in the Ant Busters to deal with them. In the meantime, he has asked the citizens of Kansas City to try to stay calm and surround their properties with the killer ant poison. Walmart has already informed us that they are bringing as much as they can as fast as they can from their other stores. They should be able to handle the demand with no problem by tomorrow."

"Oh, my God! He didn't tell me that!"

"He obviously didn't want to worry you."

"I've got to go to Kansas City."

"Mary, think! If he didn't tell you and didn't ask you, don't you think he prefers that you stay here? He doesn't need to worry about you while he's fighting these killer ants. He needs to concentrate on what he's doing."

Mary stared at Sally. "I am so scared," she whispered.

"I know." Sally gave her a comforting hug. "He knows what he's doing, Mary."

"Yes," she said. "And he feels like he has to be the one to save the world."

"And that's exactly why you love him."

Mary nodded, and they embraced again. Sally patted her on the back like a mother comforting her baby. "We'll keep the news on. They'll keep us informed better than he will. He'll be too busy."

"Thanks, Sally. I think I'll try to keep myself busy. Let's see. What time is it? Three? I better start preparing dinner for Ann. He asked me to look after her."

"Good idea."

Mary walked up the stairs as if her legs were made of lead.

"Poor girl," Sally whispered.

CHAPTER 36

RICHARD TOOK I-70 TO 670, BUT HE HAD TO PULL OVER TO read his instructions again.

> Exit 2M/US71, go south, then exit Twenty-Second Street/Paseo, Twenty-Second Street bears to the right, go half a mile, then left on McGee Street.

He had no problem finding the exit. When he turned on McGee Street, the Hyatt Regency Crown Hotel loomed into the sky.

The government's paying for this? Unbelievable!

He walked through the luxurious lobby and took the elevator to the ninth floor. *9321.* He knocked on the door.

"Doc! Glad you could make it." Saul opened the door wide and motioned for Richard to enter while he continued to speak on the phone.

"Yeah. Dr. Denton just arrived. Sure. Breakfast at nine. Got it, Mayor Simpson," Saul said. "That was the mayor of Kansas City."

"Gathered that. We have a breakfast meeting at 0900. Here at the hotel?"

"Right."

"Then you better show me what we've got. Good to see you, by the way." He extended his hand. "How are the wife and kids?"

"Fine. Thanks for asking."

"Hotel looks deserted."

"Yeah. Nobody wants to be near here right now. As a matter of fact, let me show you the map and tell you the sightings so far first."

On the map, small dots of green marked the locations.

"Wow. There are a lot of them."

"Right. But even worse, wait till you see where they are. There are thirteen nests to find … so far. On the east side of town, we've got Children's Mercy Hospital, Lincoln High School, Barker Temple, and Holmes Square. To the north, we've got the Hotel Savoy, the Federal Courthouse, and a spot at Eighth and Main streets. On the west side, we've got the convention center and two other locations at the corners of Seventeenth and Summit and Sixteenth and Jefferson. Finally, on the south side, we've got the Amtrak station, Union Station, a swanky theater spot with a five-story cinema screen, a 360-degree screen, and a live theatre. Finally, there's the Crown Center—where we are."

"Here? They certainly didn't discriminate, did they?"

"Oh, aren't we funny? How's Mary, by the way?"

"Just great. In every way. When all this is over, we're going to get married."

"And when do you think all this will be over?"

"I'm close to finding the solution, Saul. A permanent one."

"Thank God."

"I'm afraid your ex-boss and Dr. Morton won't agree."

"What?"

"When my solution goes into effect, nobody will be buying the killer ant poison."

"Son of a bitch! That will be so damn great! It's just what they deserve. I hope they go head over heels into debt, thinking they will have millions of dollars coming in. Make my ever-loving day!"

"Wow. I didn't think you were that bitter, Saul."

"I've got my reasons."

"Yeah. I guess they both stepped on a lot of toes recently."

"Only the university, you, Ann, me, and a handful of others I don't know of, I'm sure. Money sure destroys people, doesn't it? What do you think, Doc? Where do we start?"

"I can't believe the government paid for such a swanky hotel for us."

"They didn't."

"And?"

"The mayor arranged it. The hotel management agreed to let us stay as guests. All our meals are on the house too."

"Probably because there are no customers anyway. Speaking of which, can we order something to be sent up? And why did we get a room so high up?"

"Here's the menu. I don't know. I didn't argue—not when it's free. Maybe they want the lower rooms in case they get clients."

"Yeah. Or maybe they think the ants won't come up to this floor." Richard picked up the phone and pressed the button that said room service. "Can I have a cheeseburger with fries and a coke?"

"Two," Saul interjected.

"Make that two orders. Identical. Medium." He nodded at Saul, and Saul nodded his approval.

"Forty minutes? Fine."

"Forty minutes for a hamburger?"

"A high-class hamburger, Saul. Got to give them time to make it look pretty."

"Oh, yeah. That's right. Can't just flip 'em and put 'em on a bun, right?"

Richard smiled. "Have they closed the schools and hotels?"

"Lincoln High School is closed till further notice. There are no services at the Barker Temple until further notice." Saul turned the page on his small notebook, took a deep breath, and sighed. "The businesses around Holmes Square have been evacuated. Hotel Savoy is closed until further notice. The federal courthouse has moved its operations to another location temporarily. The convention center has postponed all events until further notice. Union Station is closed until further notice. The Amtrak station is closed. That's going to be hell. And all the shops in Crown Center are closed until further notice. The Westin and Hyatt are open, but they don't have any customers."

"Here neither. Well done, Saul."

"I've already asked the mayor for a Jeep Cherokee."

"Good."

A knock on their door stopped Saul's report, and he opened the door to see who it was.

"Is this?"

"Yes, it is. Bring them right in please."

Two gentlemen in FedEx uniforms carried in ten white tanks and ten green tanks.

"Just set them over there against that wall," Saul said.

They were in a big hurry, and their uniforms were soaked with perspiration by the time they finished. "Sign here, please, sir." Seconds later, they were walking quickly down the hallway with their heads glued to the floor.

A moment later, there was another knock.

"Yes?" Saul asked.

"Sorry. Forgot to have you sign this other sheet. Which one is Saul?"

"I am." Saul grabbed the clipboard and signed.

"Thanks," he said as he sped down the hallway.

"Boy, they certainly were in a hurry," Richard said.

"Maybe because we're right in the center of the killer ant area," Saul answered.

"That'll do it," Richard said.

"So what do we do first, Chief?"

"Schools first, then the hospital, then churches, then the hotels, then Amtrak, then the shopping center, then the government buildings, and finally the cinema." Saul began numbering the locations in the order Richard mentioned.

"I'll check all the equipment if you'll write the agenda down so we can give a copy to the mayor in the morning."

"Sounds good, Saul. Let me unpack first. I have my lab equipment in my suitcase."

"These boxes are lab equipment too, Doc. I'll let you take care of those too."

"Got it. Wish those burgers would hurry up. I forgot to eat lunch."

"Doc?"

"Yeah?" Richard had started to unpack his bag. The desk would be his lab. "Great to be working with you again."

"Thanks. Same here."

"Who're you gonna call? The Ant Busters!"

"Oh, God!"

They both broke out in laughter, but Richard noted the nervousness in Saul's laugh. He knew this could be the final roundup—for both of them.

CHAPTER 37

━━ ━━ ▬ ━━ ▬ ▬ ━━

SAUL AND RICHARD WERE HAVING COFFEE WHEN A TALL man in a dark blue pinstriped suit and a yellow silk handkerchief that matched his tie entered the hotel's swanky restaurant. His dark blue dress shirt added to his Al Capone look.

"That's him," Saul announced.

"Spare me," Richard said.

"Be nice, Doc."

"Morning, gentlemen. You must be the famous Dr. Denton. Pleased to finally meet you." Mayor Alan Simpson took a seat.

Besides being impeccably dressed, the mayor's wavy hair didn't have a strand out of place. Richard could have sworn he noticed a touch of makeup too.

"Have you informed Dr. Denton of our situation, Saul?"

"Oh, yes, sir. Here is the order in which we will attack the problem."

The mayor looked over the list while the waiter took orders from Saul and Richard.

"I'll have the same," Mayor Alan said without looking at the waiter.

"Yes, sir. Thank you."

"I understand you are the ant expert, Dr. Denton."

"That seems to be the consensus, sir. Please call me Richard."

Alan nodded. "My city is in chaos, Richard. Children are losing education, and businesses are taking a shellacking, which causes my city to lose a lot of revenue. That will make it close to impossible to maintain the public aid programs we have. My phone's ringing off the hook, and there's a line of people a mile long who want to talk to me about how I'm going to fix this. I need answers, Richard. Can you enlighten me?"

"We should defuse your immediate problems within the next ten days, sir—and get your city back to normal. Solving the problem takes a little longer, and it's not just your problem."

"Ten days, you say. Can I quote you? When I walk out that door, I can guarantee you I will be mobbed by the media."

"You can quote me as estimating ten days, sir. I need to find the nests before we eliminate them. We may find more. We have prepared the substances and equipment. Saul tells me you are supplying us with a Jeep Cherokee?"

"Yes. As a matter of fact, here are the keys and the valet ticket. Is your room comfortable, gentlemen?"

"Quite, sir. Thank you."

"How exactly are you planning to solve the problem, which you say will take a while?"

"It's no more possible to eliminate these ants than it is the fire ant. However, we can change their habits and reduce their aggressiveness. Possibly make them just like ordinary ants, even less aggressive than the fire ant."

"And how do you do that?"

"Doc's going to change their DNA," Saul said.

"Change their DNA? Interesting. I guess that's possible. We can make human clones now, right?"

"In a way, you're right," Richard said. A thought flashed through Richard's mind of the possibility of cloning a dangerous species.

"And how long do you *estimate* it will take you to accomplish that *change*?"

"Actually, I believe I should have the answer within thirty days. Of course, being here and dealing with this emergency does delay my progress in that area. The real time will be in implementing the change. That will probably take at least a couple of years."

"Whoa. So the people's lives will be in danger for quite a while?"

"I believe things will be quieter after this. Saul has arranged a toll-free hotline to report any of the ants. We should be able to keep the incidents isolated for the most part."

"You may have the solution, Richard, but the timetable will be hard for the American public to swallow. I don't think your referral to isolated incidents will be popular either."

"I'm not a politician, sir. I tell things the way they are. I leave informing the public to experts like you. I just do the science."

"We each have our strengths."

The food arrived, and they enjoyed their breakfast with small talk. The mayor was interested in Richard's academic background.

"Is the list satisfactory to you, sir?" Saul asked, getting back to the business at hand.

"Yes. Here is my direct line and my e-mail. Please text me about your progress on a daily basis so I can keep the public informed."

"No problem," Saul said. "I'll be doing that."

Richard glanced over at Saul and nodded.

"Anything else you need, Richard?"

"Not right now, sir. Maybe some prayers?"

The mayor nodded. "I'll ask the public to help us there. Sure you don't need more people to help you?"

"They would just get in the way. More for me to worry about," Richard said.

"Whatever you may need, just let me know. You'll have it. You've got my word."

"Thank you, sir. I will." *I hope your word is better than most others I have known on the ladder of authority.*

"One more question."

"Shoot," Richard said.

"When do you start?"

"Right after breakfast," Saul answered.

"Great. Then I'll leave you two to it. Good luck, gentlemen. And be careful." The mayor stood, shook their hands, and left. A crowd was waiting for him when he left the hotel. Saul and Richard watched him soak in the limelight for a minute. They would watch and listen to his speech on the news later that night.

"Well, Doc. What do you say we get going?"

"Let's. And thank you for not mentioning the Ant Busters thing, okay?"

"Oh, that's common knowledge now, Doc," Saul said with a smile.

"Shit."

"Who're you gonna call?"

"Don't!" Richard waved his right index finger at him.

Saul put his arm around Richard's shoulder as they walked back to their hotel room.

CHAPTER 38

"HERE. TWENTY-FIRST STREET. NOW WE'RE LOOKING FOR Woodland."

"I see it, Doc." Saul nodded to the right.

"Yeah. Lincoln High School." Richard folded the map and put it in the glove compartment.

They pulled into a large empty parking lot, and Saul slowed to a crawl.

"To the back. There's a tree line."

"Got it." Saul sped up and stopped where the parking lot met the football field.

"Okay, Saul. You know the routine. Slowly from here."

"Don't have to tell me, Doc." Saul hesitated a moment, and they nodded to each other.

They inched across the field to the thirty-yard line and stopped thirty yards from the tree line. They kept checking the ground around them.

"Left or right, Doc."

Richard turned around and looked at the school. "They said the ants came in on the side of the cafeteria?"

"Yeah."

"Left. Real slow now, Saul. Keep your eyes on the ground."

"Don't have to tell me," Saul whispered, his heart pounding.

After twenty yards, Richard abruptly held up his hand.

Saul slammed on the brake and readied his hand to put the jeep in reverse.

"There," Richard whispered.

"Where? I can't see … oh, yeah. Got it."

Saul inched his way parallel to their nests from the tree line until they were in front of the siting.

They searched the ground for a minute before they stepped out of the jeep.

Richard pulled out binoculars and observed the ground before them, gradually continuing until he came to the mound.

"That's why."

"What's why?"

"They made their nest elongated and low instead of shaped like a cone—like they did in Custer. Smart. Less noticeable."

"God. You give me the creeps when you talk about them like that."

They went to the back of the Jeep and strapped the appropriate tanks to their backs. Richard checked Saul's tanks, and Saul checked Richard's tanks.

"Ready for battle?"

"Ready as I'm ever going to be." Saul sighed. There was no getting used to these confrontations. It would only take one sting to make it their last battle.

Without words, they spread out and slowly approached the nest.

When they got to the far end of the nest, they began to spray and walk. Richard was behind the tree line, and Saul was in front. When they got to the end of the nest, they hightailed it back to the Jeep.

Richard watched through his binoculars. They looked closely around them before pulling off their tanks and stowing them away.

"Okay." Richard was breathing heavily after they climbed into their seats. "Get us out of here."

"Don't have to tell me twice, Doc." Saul drove to the edge of the parking lot and turned them around to face the tree line.

Richard peered through his glasses again. "Looks good from here, Saul. Let's check the tree line to the right, just in case."

Saul put the Jeep in gear and took off. They toured the entire school. Richard felt satisfied they had taken care of the only nest there.

"This part doesn't bother me so much, Doc. It's coming back the next day and digging into the mound that scares the shit outta me."

"Ann seems to have done a good job on this formula. It's worked faster than any of the others."

"So far. What if it doesn't one time? The variables?" Saul asked.

"You're learning. I guess we just don't see the next time."

"Oh, thanks. I needed that."

"Okay. Children's Mercy Hospital next." Richard pulled the map out of the glove compartment and opened his notepad. "Should be close. Twenty-Second Street and Gillham Road."

They parked in front of the main entrance to the hospital. Nobody bothered to tell them they couldn't park there.

Richard went directly to the receptionist. "Thanks for being here. Do you have a map of your facilities?"

"Depends. What are you looking for?"

"This is Dr. Denton, young lady. We're here to take care of those pesky killer ants," Saul said.

"Oh, you're the Ant Busters!" The redheaded receptionist jumped to her feet. "Thank God you're here! I have been so scared."

"Told you I didn't have to tell anyone, Doc. See? You're famous."

"And so you must be Mr. Saul," the receptionist added.

"Looks like we made the hit list."

"Yeah. Great, huh?"

"I'm ecstatic." Richard took a deep breath and sighed.

"Let me see here. We don't have an actual map, but I can bring one up on the computer and print it for you. Is that all right?"

"Very resourceful, Valerie," Richard noted the name tag.

Once they had the map, they returned to the Jeep and studied it together.

"Wow. Big complex, isn't it?" Saul said.

"Strange."

"What?"

"Almost no grass. No trees."

"Yeah, you're right, Doc. Concrete city."

"Which building did they enter?"

"That one."

"That's the south side. Let's go around the block on the south side first to see if there's any trees across the street."

There were only buildings and concrete.

"What now, Doc?"

"We think." Richard pulled out the city map and spread it out in front of them.

"I can't believe how their locations so far are so strategically situated, Doc. Look at that."

"Yes. I think that very point is going to help me find them."

Saul silently looked around like a tourist. "Hey, Doc? Isn't that an ant path over there?" Saul pointed across the street at an abandoned building with a strip of grass between the sidewalk and the street.

"Drive over there. Let's take a closer look. Good eyes, Saul," Richard said when they stopped in front of the trail.

"But where do they go from here?"

"Inside."

"The building? There's no grass or trees."

"Adaptation, I'm afraid."

"I'll call the mayor. We need a key. Wouldn't want to break in."

In less than fifteen minutes, a young man arrived with a key to the building and opened the main door. "Just leave the key in the lock. I'm out of here."

Saul and Richard glanced at each other and shrugged.

"Let's suit up, Saul."

"Already? We really don't know if they're there."

"I don't want to get surprised. Do you?"

"Suiting up. Yes, sir. Suiting right up."

They slowly entered the building. A small crowd was gathering outside by the hospital.

As they entered, Saul made a cross in front of his face. Small beads of sweat began to form on his forehead.

"I'll be damned," Richard said.

"What?" Saul looked around.

"They have an atrium. Straight ahead."

They slowly approached the atrium. A two-foot wall bordered the open atrium, and two trees extended past the roofline. When they got close enough to see over the wall, the nest was obvious.

"Jesus!" Saul whispered. "It covers the entire atrium!"

"By far the largest nest so far. Has to be at least five million in that baby."

"How the hell we going to get around that? There's no room to go around it!"

Richard looked up. "How are you at climbing?"

"Maybe ladders would be easier."

"It would."

Saul got on the phone and asked for two twelve-foot ladders. Once in place, they cautiously climbed the ladders.

"Sure the spray will reach?" Saul asked.

"No."

"Thanks."

"Don't mention it."

Richard motioned for Saul to spray to his right and then nodded for him to begin.

The spray took longer to reach the ground, and many ants began to emerge.

"Don't stop!" Richard yelled. "Keep it coming!"

Saul sprayed like a marine with a machine gun. He couldn't stop the sound coming up from his throat.

"Ah!" Saul's teeth showed, and his eyes turned killer.

"All right! Let's go, Saul! Saul!"

Saul stopped and looked across the atrium at Richard.

"Move!" Richard said.

They climbed down their ladders and ran outside. They stopped at the entrance and watched the floor carefully.

After five minutes, Richard motioned for Saul to remain—and he slowly went back inside. When he got to the atrium, the nest surface was abandoned. They had gone deep.

When he emerged, he gave Saul a thumbs-up and a big smile.

As they drove off the crowd across the street cheered and chanted, "Ant Busters! Ant Busters!"

"Two down, eleven to go," Saul said. "Where to now, Doc?"

"Hotel. I've had enough excitement for one day."

"Roger that. I can't believe how hungry I am."

"I want to call Mary and tell her everything's all right."

"So where do we eat?"

"Room service. Restaurant's on the first floor. Can't enjoy the food if you're looking around on the floor all the time."

"Room service it is. A nice, thick, juicy New York strip sounds good, doesn't it?"

"Why not lobster and filet mignon?"

"Sounds even better."

"Order whatever you want. You deserve it. I'm going to see if they have linguine in Alfredo sauce, toasted garlic bread, and steamed, buttered cauliflower—maybe with cheese."

"God. You're making it difficult to choose, Doc."

CHAPTER 39

━━ ━━ ━━ ━━ ━━ ━━

"RALPH? SAM."

"Hi, Sam."

"You following this killer ant thing?"

"Yes. Interesting how they seem to have a lot more intelligence, isn't it?"

"Too interesting. Scares the hell out of me. What do you make of it, Ralph?"

"Hybrid, absolutely. The intelligence level has been brought up a notch, that's for sure. Be interesting to find out how."

"My thoughts also. And you're the man to do it."

"What? You want me to find out the how?"

"Right. We've got to find out if it's terrorism, some lunatic, or nature."

"It's not nature, I can assure you. I still think it's an experiment gone awry. Terrorists would have planted these in more than one place—and in places like New York City. It seems the Ant Busters are doing a good job eliminating them as fast as they find them though."

"Yes, thank God. I just hope Dr. Denton doesn't become one of their victims before he comes up with the solution."

"The gossip is there's a young lady by the name of Ann Kreindler who came up with the poison to kill these ants—working like a charm. I'd like to meet her someday too."

"Really? Maybe you should look her up. Know where she is?"

"Only that she went to the University of Kansas, was a student of Dr. Denton's, and is now working for him somewhere."

"She's working for Denton? Then I know where she is."

After a short silence, Ralph said, "You going to let me in on the secret, Sam?"

"What secret?"

"Where she is. You said you knew."

"I'm looking it up. Give me a minute. I know it's close to Lawrence. Here it is. A small town called Fisherman's Cove, North 1150 Road. It's by Clinton Lake, west of Lawrence, I believe."

"I'll take my fishing poles."

"Let's hope you catch more than fish. My biggest problem is whether this is a terrorist act or not. If not, we just let them take care of the problem. If it is, you have some really serious work to do."

"I've always had the fear of this kind of terrorism—or a deadly bacteria or virus attack—more than an atomic bomb. It would be almost impossible to stop."

"Yes. I follow your thoughts, Ralph. Family okay?"

"Yes. Little Ralph is becoming a real researcher. Spends almost every summer with me at the ranch now. Even has a lab in his bedroom, much to his mother's disliking, of course."

"Of course. I saw that picture of you and him you sent me a couple of months ago. Jesus, Ralph, he's a damn clone of you."

"Everyone says that. I just hope he's smarter than I am."

"Now that would be a challenge, I'm afraid. But if anyone can prepare him, you can. Obviously, there's no doubt where he is going to study."

"I have no control over that, Sam."

"Yeah, sure."

"Sam, they want you down the hall."

"Got to go, Ralph. Boss is calling. Stay in touch."

"I will. Just process the expense vouchers when you get them right away—not two months later, okay?"

227

"See you, Ralph. Roger and out."

Ralph looked at his phone after Sam hung up. *You never did answer me on the expenses, which means I will be out of pocket for at least sixty days, as usual.*

CHAPTER 40

━━ ━━ ━━ ━━ ━━ ━━ ━━ ━━

"THE BARKER TEMPLE AND HOTEL SAVOY." SAUL PLACED A check alongside his list. "That's four. Only nine more to go. Shouldn't we look for the nest by our hotel first?"

"Priorities are by number of people affected. There aren't many people at our hotel now. We'll go back to yesterday's locations next—and then we go to the Amtrak station."

They pulled around the Children's Mercy Hospital and parked in the same spot in front of the abandoned building across the street.

Richard checked to see if he had the test tubes and tweezers in his pocket. He noticed Saul digging in his satchel. "What is that? A slingshot?"

"I learned a couple of things on the other missions you weren't on."

"What are you going to do? Knock them off one by one?"

"You'll see," he said.

They walked through the doors and straight to the atrium. As they neared, their pace slowed and their eyes searched the floor carefully. Richard stopped and looked at the walls and ceiling.

"What? See something?" Saul asked.

"No. Just being careful."

"Oh. Please do." Saul glanced around at the ceiling too.

They inched forward and peered into the atrium. The huge mound was quiet. Not a single ant could be seen.

"Looks good, but let's be sure." Richard walked around to the glass door and opened it.

"Wait!" Saul said.

Richard froze and searched the ground.

Saul pulled out his slingshot and placed a pellet in its strap. He pulled hard and let go. The pellet disappeared into the mound. No response. He repeated his procedure, aiming at various locations.

"Okay, Doc. Now you can do your thing."

"That's ingenious. I never would've thought of that. Simple, yet effective."

"Gives us more time to run," Saul added.

Richard pulled out a small garden shovel and began to pull the dirt away in small amounts until he came to some ants. He took his tweezers and placed a few samples in a test tube. Then he kept on digging.

"What're you lookin' for, Doc? You got your samples. Let's get the hell out of here."

"I should find a nursery a little deeper."

"A nursery? You mean baby ants?"

"Eggs. See?" He took out another test tube and placed several eggs in it.

"They're dead too, aren't they?"

"Maybe, but I need them for my research."

"Can you hurry a little? I'm getting a little nervous here."

"Okay, Saul. Let's go."

▬ ▬ ▬ ▬ ▬ ▬

They pulled up to the Amtrak station and looked at the floor plans.

"Where do we start, Doc?"

"Don't know on this one. No vegetation at all."

"Maybe they have an atrium too."

"Not according to this."

"Let's drive around. Maybe there's something close by."

"Just concrete as far as I can see."

"Yeah." Saul sighed heavily.

They walked into the facilities, and their steps echoed on the tiled floors.

"The tracks." Richard stopped.

"The tracks?"

"What are the tracks built on, Saul?"

"Rocks, I guess."

"And under those rocks?"

"Good old dirt. Let's go."

Once on the platform, they stopped.

"Let's start at that end," Richard said.

"All right with me. Hey, Doc?"

"Yeah?"

Saul stopped in his tracks and looked both ways.

"It's shut down, Saul. There won't be any trains."

Saul shook his head. "It's not that, Doc. What if they come from both sides? I mean, they could trap us down here on the tracks. Know what I mean?"

Richard thought for a second. Saul had a good point

They stopped at the end of the platform and peered down onto the tracks.

"Look for some kind of indentation. Something they could use for cover, Saul."

They searched slowly, their flashlights fanning from left to right.

Saul grabbed Richard's arm and pointed at where the tracks ended.

"I see it. Good eye, Saul. Hard to notice under those railroad ties."

"Wow. How do we get to them?"

The nest rested under a mound of old discarded railroad ties. They couldn't just pull the ties away without disturbing the ants.

"Please don't tell me how intelligent these son of a bitches are, Doc. Please don't do that."

"But they are. Incredible," he whispered.

"What? Think of somethin'?" Saul asked.

"We get some of the commercial poison they're selling in Walmart."

"But that takes days to work. Why can't we use our stuff?"

"Won't get through the wood to the nest—and we can't move the ties." Richard shrugged.

"You've got to be kidding me."

"I'm open to a better idea?"

Saul sighed. "Let's go to Walmart."

"At least we know where they are."

"Whoopee," Saul whispered.

Richard told Saul not to bother strapping the tanks on his back. He would carry his. Saul would spread the granules, and Richard would man the spray gun.

They eased themselves off the platform and walked as quietly as possible on the loose stone.

Saul pulled on rubber gloves, dug out scoops of poison, and sprinkled the granules around. When he had formed a complete circle around the ties, he began to toss handfuls of granules on top of the ties.

"Oh shit!" Saul yelled. He dropped the bag of poison in his hands, ran, and jumped on the platform.

Richard covered a large area and retreated to the platform. Richard had enough time to climb the platform with his tank pack.

Saul gave him a hand. "My God! Look at them!"

In seconds, the tracks were totally covered. A blanket of black oozed toward them.

"Let's go, Doc!" Saul pulled at Richard's arm, and they ran to the doorway.

The ants had climbed the platform wall and were heading for the door; many were climbing on top of each other.

Richard and Saul ran down the corridor and checked their attackers' progress before they left the building.

"They're dispersing," Richard said.

"Giving up, right?"

"Yes. They're going back home." Richard took a couple of steps toward them.

"Oh no you don't." Saul grabbed his arm.

Richard looked Saul in the eye for a few seconds, and the tenseness left his body. He nodded.

"The disturbance will help get them to take the poison into the nest. Should speed up the process somewhat," Richard said.

"From your lips to God's ears. I'll call the mayor and let him know it won't be safe here for a few days. He's not going to like that. He was really anxious about this location. Referred to it as his money train."

———————

Back in their hotel room, Saul turned on the news.

Richard stopped writing his notes when he heard the mayor explaining the close call the Ant Busters had at the Amtrak station. He mentioned that it would not be safe for a couple of days. It would be a great test for the public, however, to see how well the granule poison worked on the killer ants.

"Oh shit, Saul! You told him?"

"Well, yeah. I mean. It was a close call—as he said."

Richard nodded and wasn't surprised when the phone rang.

"It's for you, Doc. Mary."

"Of course." He sent a hard look in Saul's direction and grabbed the phone. He took a deep breath and let it out slowly before he placed the receiver to his ear. "Hi, babe," he said, trying to be cheerful.

"Are you okay? I just saw the news. My God. I told you not to take any chances. How much longer are you going to be there?"

"Whoa! I can only answer one question at a time, hon. Slow down. First, we're fine. We've taken care of five of the thirteen nests already. Only eight to go. Probably four days."

"What happened? You told me it was pretty safe."

"They were in a really tough location. We couldn't use the gas."

"Gas? I thought you sprayed them with some kind of liquid?"

"Well, yes. But when the two liquids we spray at the same time mix, they form a gas that is heavier than air and travels down to all parts of their nests."

"I think you told me about that. I was so worried!"

"We're fine. Don't worry. Please. It wasn't as bad as the TV makes out." He looked over at Saul. "You know how the media loves to exaggerate? How's everything at the store?"

"Business as usual here."

"And Ann? Have you been going there?"

"Every evening. I take her dinner. I left her some sandwiches for tomorrow's lunch. She seems to be excited about something. I don't understand, of course. She says she has the solution. Something about your theory being right. She really thinks the world of you. Should I be jealous?"

"She's a bright girl—and no."

"And a nice one too. Her parents divorced when she was only six, and her mother died when she was eight?"

"I never really knew anything about her past."

"Men! You're so heartless. She lived with her grandmother until she was sixteen. She's had a tough life, but she never did the drug bit or turned to alcohol. Got to give her credit. She's a tough cookie."

"Sounds like you like her."

"I do. After dinner, we chat."

"Typical."

"That's how we find out things, Mr. Smarty-Pants."

"Whoa. I didn't mean to push any buttons there. I love you just the way you are, babe."

"I miss you, darling."

"I miss you, too."

"You taking the situation in hand?"

"What? Oh, no! Jesus! No, I'll wait till I get back. Just be ready, girl."

"You're the one who gets sore, remember?"

"Oh, do I."

"Are you done for the day?"

"Yes. We're in the room. Making my notes. You know."

"I don't know, but I believe you. Have you eaten?"

"Not yet. We'll order room service."

"Food good there?"

"Oh, yeah. Five star."

"Going to order pasta again?"

"Probably. You know me pretty well already, don't you?"

"Not as well as I'd like to."

"Well, you'll have plenty of time for that soon."

"As Mrs. Denton, you mean?"

"Yes, ma'am."

"You know, I never got one of those engagement rings."

"You'll get both rings at the same time."

"Okay. Get some dinner and get some sleep. I know you are going to be up for a while with your *notes*. Sweet dreams, darling."

"Sweet dreams."

As soon as Richard cradled the phone, Saul asked, "Where do we go tomorrow?"

"Maybe we can get three in: Union Station, the courthouse, and here."

"I'll feel better when we find the one here."

"I know. Maybe you won't spray around the door and the bed at night. What are you going to order today?" Richard asked.

"You noticed? Pork chops, mashed potatoes smothered in gravy, peas, salad, and clam chowder. I'll finish it off with a piece of hot apple pie a la mode."

"In that order?"

"No, I'll have the soup and ... Mary was right. Smarty-pants. And you?"

"Linguine with chicken and white cream sauce, salad, and clam chowder. Maybe a pecan pie. A la mode."

"In that order?"

"Touché."

They both chuckled, and Richard placed the order.

CHAPTER 41

AT THE REST OF THE LOCATIONS, THE NESTS WERE SMALL and fairly easy to find.

Pictures of the Ant Busters spread all over the world, mostly showing Saul and Richard with their twin tank packs. T-shirts were being sold, and dolls were being made. All types of merchants were jumping on the bandwagon.

Richard wanted to leave as soon as he was sure the nests were eliminated. He was tired, and he was anxious to get home to finish his research. He thought of calling Ann, but he had second thoughts. If he called, he would disturb her progress. If she told him something he didn't agree with, he wouldn't be able to concentrate on what he was doing right now. *It will all be there when you get back.*

Saul was enjoying the fame. "Can't leave yet, Doc."

"What do you mean? We're done. It's over."

"The mayor is having a ceremony at the federal courthouse in our honor."

"What for? Isn't there enough publicity about us now? Jesus! People are actually asking for our autographs, for crying out loud!"

"Isn't that neat? Hell, you deserve it. Why not enjoy it?"

Richard closed his eyes and sighed. *Because this whole thing is not your fault.* "I'll probably feel more like celebrating when we change the characteristics of the killer ants. That's when it'll be my Fourth of July, but that's still a couple of years off, Saul."

"I see what you mean. You really try hard to be a killjoy, don't you?"

Richard smiled, lowered his head, and nodded. "I don't mean to demean the task we just finished. You did a superb job, Saul, and you deserve all the credit you get, but try to understand. What we just did is temporary. There will be more. Hopefully only small cases until I change them."

"I see your point, Doc. Maybe I got a little wrapped up in all the hype."

"*You* deserve their recognition, Saul. Maybe I'm just a little too serious. Sorry. I don't mean to take the punch out of your fun."

"*We* deserve the recognition. And I want you to lighten up. Just for a little bit, okay? Twenty-four hours. Then you can go back to that lab of yours and your serious self."

"Okay, Saul. I give in. What time is the ceremony?"

"Five."

"I don't have a suit or tie. And I'm not buying one either."

"Don't have to. Just put on some clean slacks, a clean shirt, and that vest you always wear when we're out there working."

"The vest? What?"

"They eat that shit up, Doc. It looks cool on you. It's like your symbol."

"Cool. Right." Richard rolled his eyes. "It's 2:21. I can finish packing."

"You can pack tomorrow morning. Haven't heard from Dr. Morton or Larry on the news. Thought they would be soaking up all the credit on this, including themselves with the Ant Busters." He shrugged. "What's it going to take you, Doc? Thirty minutes? Tops? Relax."

"Let me put all my notes together at least. I think our friends are too busy enjoying their money."

"Or hiding their money, Doc. You're hopeless. I'm ordering myself a banana split." Saul picked up the phone and dialed.

"Hey, Saul? Make that two."

"Now you're talking."

"I'll have my notes together by the time it gets here."

"Ah, Jesus."

The federal courtroom was packed. Every seat was occupied, and the walls were thick with standing bodies. Cameras were set up everywhere. Five microphones were taped together at the podium like a bouquet of flowers.

Richard and Saul sat in front of the United States flag. When the mayor walked up to the podium, cameras clicked like machine guns and the flashes gave an aura of a Fourth of July celebration. Mayor Simpson took it all in stride.

Mayor Alan Simpson, impeccably dressed in a solid blue suit, a heavily starched pink shirt, and a blue silk Bill Miller tie with gold polka dots—began his speech by praising the city government. He mentioned how he reacted to the people's cry with the utmost haste, brought in the most qualified people to deal with the problem, and eliminated the threat to the people of Kansas City. He went on to say how business would return to normal soon and how, due to his quick response, the losses were minimal.

Finally, it was time to recognize Richard and Saul. "Ladies and gentlemen, members of the press, I have had the distinct pleasure of working with two of the bravest, most professional men I have ever met. They have worked relentlessly, risking their very lives to save the lives of the people of Kansas City."

The room burst into deafening applause.

The mayor smiled, nodded, and raised his hands. The applause subsided.

"These men deserve special recognition for their valor and work. It is with special pleasure that I give the key to Kansas City to both Saul Carrington and Dr. Richard Denton, known to all the world as the Ant Busters!"

Richard winced.

The applause became earsplitting as the audience stood to recognize the two men who walked to the podium to join the mayor.

The mayor gave a brown rectangular box to each man. Its contents revealed a large gold key set in dark brown silk.

Richard shook the mayor's hand and stepped back. Saul reveled in his moment of glory by waving at the cameras and public, his big whites beaming.

The mayor put his arm around Saul and waved at his public. The clicks of the cameras were drowned out by the continual applause. Richard was desperate for it all to end.

■ ■ ■ ■ ■ ■

When they finally got to their room, Richard collapsed on his bed. "Man, I am beat."

"How can you sleep after all that?" Saul asked. "I'm wound up tighter than a coil. I'm going down to the bar for a while. Let's have a couple of drinks. Tomorrow, you go home."

"No thanks, Saul. You go ahead. I've had enough signing autographs and pats on the back. I'm exhausted."

"Suit yourself, Doc." Saul almost ran out of the room. His public would be waiting.

CHAPTER 42

RICHARD WAS UP EARLY. WHILE HE WAITED FOR ROOM service to bring up his breakfast, he finished packing his small suitcase. His notes were in his briefcase. His lab equipment was stored in a larger briefcase.

Saul would take care of sending the tank equipment back to Dr. Morton whenever he decided to wake up. Richard's sleepy eyes focused on the white alarm clock when Saul stumbled in at 4:22.

Richard was leaving a note for Saul when his cell phone rang. "Hello?"

"Richard? Thank God! The ants! There's millions of 'em!"

"Ants? What ants?" He knew the answer to his question, but he wanted to be wrong.

"Killer ants! What do I do! They surrounded the whole store!"

"What are they doing?"

"What are they doing? What do I do?"

"Okay, okay. Calm down, dear." His mind raced and burned with the stress of coming up with a solution. His creation was about to take the life of the women he loved.

"Calm down? What the hell's the matter with you! Give me an answer, damn it! These are your creation, remember!"

Ouch. That truth pierced his heart so much his knees weakened.

"I know it's difficult. Listen, hon. Listen very carefully now. Go see what they are doing outside. Please!"

"God damn it!" She slammed the phone down and went to

240

her bedroom window. The ground looked like a large black tarp. It didn't move.

She went to the back bedroom and looked out the window. Another black tarp covered the yard, and it was growing.

"They're just kind of waiting out front. They're coming in hoards out back."

"They're coming toward the store from your tree line out back, but they're stopping at the house, right?"

"Yes. Now can you tell me what to do?"

"Richard! Where the hell are you? Answer me, damn it!"

"Okay, Mary. Listen carefully. I can never get there in time, but they're not ready to attack yet. You still have a little time."

"Sally taped the doors."

"Good. That won't stop them though. It might slow them down a little."

"Oh, thanks a whole freakin' lot, genius!"

"Mary! I have an answer. Are you listening?"

"Yes."

"Go downstairs, get two sleeping bags, and bring them up to the bedroom."

"I'm not going to be camping out with these things, Richard!"

"Hear me out, Mary. Pick up a bunch of straws and some duct tape. Are you listening?"

"Yes. Please, Richard. I don't want to die this way!"

"You're not going to die. Trust me. But you and Sally need to do exactly what I say. Sally is with you too, right?"

"Yes. Okay," she whispered through her tears. "They have us surrounded. We can't get out of here."

"I know. Now listen carefully, dear. Tape a group of straws together. Climb into the sleeping bag and zip it up, completely covering yourself. Leave an opening for the straws. Tape all around the straws from the inside."

"Then what?"

"You wait for them to come."

"Are you shitting me?"

"Mary, listen. The ants won't be able to get in. You'll be able to breath. Air will come in through the straws. The ants will search. It will take a little while. You'll have to be patient. They'll leave when they don't find anything."

"They're moving!" Sally screamed.

Mary threw the phone and screamed at Sally. "Grab two sleeping bags! Quick! Bring 'em upstairs!"

Mary was already flying down the stairs to get the straws and tape.

"Sleeping bags! What the hell?"

"Just do it!" Mary yelled.

In thirty seconds, they were back upstairs with the sleeping bags, straws, and tape.

"Put your sleeping bag right there so I can see you. Now get in it. Quick!"

"What are you doing?"

"Just do what I say, damn it!"

Mary got Sally in the bag and zipped her inside. She taped the straws and then taped around the straws.

"I can't breathe in here, Mary!"

"Yes, you will. Just be quiet and wait. And don't come out—whatever you do—until I tell you. Understand?"

"Oh, God. I'm going to die." Sally began weeping.

"No, you're not! Just don't move—no matter what! We'll get through this!"

Mary hurried to tape her straws and unzipped her sleeping bag. She looked around frantically. She climbed in, zipped herself up, and awkwardly taped around the straws. She was breathing heavily.

"Mary?"

Mary heard the muffled sound of her friend.

"I'm right here, Sally. Just try to stay calm."

When Mary peered through the straws, she could see Sally in her sleeping bag. The two sleeping bags formed a T.

"Mary? We're going to die, ain't we?"

"No, Sally. We are not going to die. Not today. We're going to die of old age."

"Yes, we are! Those ants are going to eat us. Just like all those other people. None of them escaped."

"We will be the first, Sally. Trust me. Richard told me how to do it. Now be quiet!" She desperately wished she could believe her own words. Visions of the ants biting through her sleeping bag haunted her mind. It was already getting stuffy breathing, and she was soaked with perspiration.

She peered through her straws. They were everywhere. The floor was painted black with them, and they covered Sally's sleeping bag.

"I can't do this! I gotta get out!"

"No, Sally! They're everywhere! Don't move! Breathe slowly!"

"I can't, Mary! I just can't!"

Mary could see the black mound in front of her move.

"No, Sally! No!"

Sally opened the zipper and popped out, but she never got to her feet to run. She screamed. They swarmed her, and she became another black mass that slumped to the floor.

There was silence except for Mary's weeping. She couldn't look anymore.

Mary sensed something with the straws. She peered through them and saw the ants trying to get inside the straws. One had put its head inside the straws. She squeezed the straws flat with her hand.

"Oh, please, God. Please make them go away." She began to sob violently, her whole body trembling.

She waited an eternity. The lack of fresh air became overwhelming—and then she passed out.

CHAPTER 43

RALPH LOOKED AT HIS MAP OF LAWRENCE, KANSAS. Unfortunately, his rental car didn't have navigation.

Why didn't Dr. Denton use the university's lab? He couldn't possibly have the facilities in his house, could he?

Ralph had his own lab at his home, and he understood the convenience of working at home instead of driving the distance, adhering to the protocol of a university, and navigating the red tape to get anything done.

Ralph nodded. *You still need specimens, Richard, and it would be too dangerous. That's it. He's keeping the danger away from the university. Good man.*

He stopped for lunch and called Sam. "On my way to his house, Sam. I think I figured out why he insisted on working from his house."

"Which is?"

"He's protecting the university from the danger of the ants."

"Why would they be in danger?"

"Need live specimens to work with, Sam."

"Oh. Gotcha. Good man."

"Besides, I would prefer working alone—without the red tape of some institution's lab. Too much interference."

"Makes sense. Any read on the source, yet?"

"Only a hunch, Sam. I really don't see this as terrorism. Wrong kind of people involved. What about the disappearance of our guys?"

"Checked them both out in detail. Both cleared. Absolutely no links to any Muslims or Europeans. Super-clean reps, well, except for Dr. Morton's philandering."

"Not good values, but not a crime."

"I'm getting the same vibes here, Ralph."

"I think we have a mistake here. Lab accident is my wild guess. No way these evolved this way. We would have heard about them a long time ago, and they would have been in South America or Africa—not here."

"I agree. Maybe Dr. Denton can help us out there too."

"I think we better give him time to solve the problem first. We need to find out how many people have the talent to play with the DNA like this."

"I'm on it. Only a handful in the US. We're checking Europe and South America now."

"Expect there won't be many. Shouldn't take you long to narrow it down."

"I'll let you know. Be ready to travel."

"Going to have to do something about the reimbursements, Sam."

"Actually, I have thought about that. Waiting for a piece of plastic now."

"About time."

"Okay, my lunch has arrived. I'll keep you informed, Sam."

"You do that, Ralph. Enjoy lunch."

Ralph drove toward Clinton Lake. When he was only a mile away, several police cars blocked the road. Up ahead, he could see ambulances. It was getting to be dusk, and the lights of the emergency vehicles and police cars made it look like the flashing lights on a Christmas tree.

Looks like a bad accident. He looked behind him. Cars had already blocked his only exit. He sighed. *This is going to be a while.* He changed the radio station, found some relaxing music, leaned back into the seat, and waited.

CHAPTER 44

"WHAT'S GOING ON?" SAUL ASKED SLEEPILY. "OH, MY freakin' head!"

"The ants are attacking Mary's store!"

Richard raced to prepare the last two tanks on the backpack.

Saul got up and began to throw on his clothes.

"I don't have time to wait for you, Saul."

"I'm going with you, Doc. And I'm not asking."

"Well, then move your ass! I'll wait in the truck."

"Oh, God. What a headache!"

Richard ignored Saul's comment and intently engaged himself in driving.

"If we get stopped for speeding, it will only take longer, Doc. We'll get there. And we'll get them."

"I need to get there in time. She and Sally are in sleeping bags covered with those ants. I hope they don't panic."

"In a sleeping bag? Oh, man. How long ago did they attack?"

"No more than ten minutes."

"All right. We're forty minutes out."

"Thirty," Richard corrected. The speedometer read eighty-five.

They ran into a roadblock at the entrance to town. The sheriff had his car blocking the road, and many people had gathered in the area.

"Great. How do I get through that?"

"Leave it to me," Saul said.

"Make room for the Ant Busters!"

The crowd dispersed, and the sheriff moved his car to let them through. They waved as they raced by. The small crowd cheered. There was at least half a mile of empty road ahead.

"Where are they?" Saul asked as they pulled up to the store.

"Upstairs." Richard jumped out of the truck and threw on his tank.

"Wait a minute. What are you thinking, Doc?"

"I've got to go in."

"That's suicide!"

He turned and stared Saul straight in the eye.

"You stay here. The ones I don't get, you get later, hear?"

"If Mary's in there, Doc, she's already dead."

"No!" Richard screamed. "Not if she did what I told her!"

"Wait! Look!"

"What?"

"No ants."

Richard scanned the area. Saul was right. They were gone. Was he too late? Richard cautiously went to the door of the store, opened it slowly, and eased his way inside. He made the moves he had learned from *CSI* and *SWAT* on television, except instead of a revolver, he had a wand.

His eyes roamed the floor, the walls, and the ceiling. The steps were in the back.

He spotted a black mass moving down and up the stairs at the same time. He could see small bits of red mass being carried down in a steady stream toward the rear. Tears began to blur his vision.

The back door was still taped shut, but the old doorframe had an opening that allowed them to pass through easily enough.

Richard dried his eyes, but his jaw tightened. He was frozen in place. He donned a small gas mask and aimed his nozzle. He gritted his teeth and sprayed at the stream of ants.

He fanned the spray quickly at first, and he repeated it slowly as far up the steps as possible.

He stepped back and waited, looking above him and around him for any possible stragglers.

They kept moving at first, seemingly disorientated, and then they stopped moving.

"Mary! Are you okay?"

There was no answer. He backpedaled and went out the front door and went around to the back. "It works!" he yelled at Saul as he hurried around the side of the house.

When he saw the huge blanket of ants, he stopped in his tracks. He couldn't possibly get to so many. He retreated. "I need a ladder," he said and entered the store once again. A moment later, he came through the front door with a large extension ladder, the price tag still tied on one of the rungs.

Saul helped him set it up to the upstairs window.

Richard looked around, grabbed a rock, climbed the ladder, and looked in the window. The window had been taped shut.

One sleeping bag was closed with a body still inside. The other was covered with killer ants that were busily working on an unrecognizable body.

The ants hesitated at the top of the stairs and began to bunch up.

He broke all the windowpanes and the wooden molding, pulled the harness off his back, and crawled inside.

Eyes locked on his enemy, he strapped the tank pack on and donned his gas mask once again. He inched forward, spraying small arcs of liquid in front of him as he went. He sprayed the first sleeping bag, and then he sprayed into the mass of killer ants.

They began to stir wildly, but they slowed and stopped in just a few seconds.

He grabbed the sleeping bag in front of him and dragged it to the window. He opened it and said, "Mary, please wake up!" He checked her pulse. "She's alive!"

Saul was already up the ladder.

"Hand her out, Doc. I'll put her on my back."

Richard looked behind him several times, and he was able to get Mary on Saul's back. Saul slowly got Mary down to safety.

"Let's get her to the hospital! You drive." Richard threw Saul the keys and carried Mary to the truck.

"Where?" Saul asked as he put the truck in gear.

"Back to Lawrence. I'm sorry, Mary. I'm so sorry, babe." Tears flowed down his cheeks as he hugged Mary's body close to his.

"You got here as fast as you could, Doc. She'll be all right. You wait and see. Did you give her the antidote?"

Richard reached into the glove compartment and pulled out a syringe and the antidote. He cradled her in his arms and rocked her in the front seat while he injected her.

━━ ━━ ━━ ━━ ━━ ━━

"She's going to be all right, Dr. Denton. She seems to be suffering from severe shock, but we couldn't find any evidence of ant bites. We have the appropriate people checking her out now."

"Great!" exclaimed Saul.

"Thank God," Richard said.

"We'll have to knock out that nest tomorrow," Saul said.

Richard nodded through watery eyes.

"You know she's the first survivor of the killer ants? That was really brilliant—that sleeping bag stuff. You literally saved her life."

"But not Sally's. She was Mary's best friend."

"Mary will take it pretty hard, huh?"

"I pray she didn't see Sally go down. It's bad enough she had to have heard it."

"You're right. That would be tough."

"You can go in and see her now, Dr. Denton."

"Thanks."

Richard rushed to her bedside and grabbed her hand. "Hi, babe." He smiled, but it slowly dissipated.

Mary just stared at the ceiling.

He moved his hand in front of her eyes, but she didn't blink. Richard looked over at the nurse.

"She's still in shock, sir," a woman behind him said.

Richard and Saul turned around and saw a tall, thin woman with long, straight auburn hair. "I'm Dr. Amelia McGregor."

"What?" Richard nodded in Mary's direction.

"She's in a traumatic trance. My immediate guess is she saw something really disturbing."

"How long will she be in a trance?"

"There's no telling. We can give her treatments to try to snap her out of it, but the chemicals are expensive. The other way is to put her in an institution—there's one in the city—and wait for her to snap out of it."

Richard turned to Saul and sighed heavily. "I don't have the money," he said softly.

"Yes, you do, Doc. Give her the best treatment money can buy, Dr. McGregor."

Richard looked at Saul.

"I'll tell you later. Just give her the okay to begin treatment."

"You'll need to sign these papers." She handed a clipboard to Richard. He signed them as if he were in a trance too.

Dr. McGregor disappeared as fast as she had appeared.

Saul said, " Remember all those T-shirts and dolls and stuff with the Ant Busters on them?"

"What do I have to do with that stuff?"

"I knew you wouldn't go for it, so I signed the contracts with various people to sell those things. We get 15 percent of the gross sales for the most part."

"I didn't sign anything."

"Yeah. But I put your name on it as a 50 percent partner."

"Son of a—"

"Easy, Doc. Dr. Morton hasn't given you one dime, has he? And, more importantly, you now have the means to take care of Mary."

Richard stared at Saul and then at Mary. He nodded. "Thanks, Saul. You're a real friend. Now I have two."

"Me and Bill in Kentucky?"

"Yeah."

"By the way, he called."

"When?"

"We were in the thick of things. I told him I'd have you call him back after this was over. Forgot. Sorry."

"I guess we did get kind of busy. Easy to forget."

CHAPTER 45

RALPH AWOKE WITH A START. PEOPLE HAD TURNED AROUND and left, and a police officer knocked on his window.

"Hello, officer."

"It's going to be quite a while, sir. Best you turn around."

"What happened? Bad accident?"

"Worse. Ants. The Ant Busters pulled one of the people out of the store. She's at the hospital now."

"My name is Dr. Ralph Mullen. I was sent here to see Dr. Denton."

"Dr. Denton is one of the Ant Busters. He's at the hospital with the lady they saved. At least, I think they saved her."

"I need to go to his house."

"Not now, sir."

Another officer joined his partner. "Everything all right here, Roger?"

"Yeah. This gentleman fell asleep waiting. He was just leaving, right, sir?"

Ralph nodded. He would have to go to the hospital first anyway. "What's the name of the hospital, officer?"

"Kansas Memorial, downtown Lawrence."

"Thanks, officer." Ralph turned his car around and headed downtown.

"These guys think they can fool us. Said he was sent to see Dr. Denton." Roger shook his head. "Glory seekers!"

When Ralph arrived at the hospital, he showed his identification at the front desk. A security officer showed him to Mary's hospital room. He knocked softly and pushed the door open. A tall bedragraggled man was snoring in a chair.

Ralph let the door close and walked to Mary's bedside. She was staring up at the ceiling, a look he had seen in combat.

He stepped over to the man in the chair. "Dr. Denton?"

Richard opened his eyes and was startled when he saw Ralph. "Who are you?" he whispered.

"My name is Ralph Mullen. Remember me?"

"Oh, yeah. Sorry. Been a tough day."

"I can see." Ralph noticed gray hairs in Richard's beard and his bloodshot eyes. "Looks like you've been through the wringer."

Richard rose to look at Mary. "That poor girl. It's all my fault."

"What's all your fault, Dr. Denton?"

Richard turned his head sharply, and his heart quickened. He shook his head. "I should've been there for her."

"From what I understand, you were busy saving quite a few other lives."

Richard nodded, sighed, and looked straight into Ralph's eyes. "Hers was the most important for me."

Ralph nodded, remembering his wife, and looked at Mary. "They told me you were single."

"We were to be married as soon as I got back from Kansas City."

Ralph closed his eyes, thinking of Stephanie again. He nodded. "Sorry. What do the doctor's say?"

They're giving her chemicals. Don't know how long." Richard's voice broke.

"The government sent me to see how you are doing with your research."

Richard nodded. "Of course. It's possible we have the solution, Dr. Mullen. Saul and I will take care of the nest tomorrow, and I'll go back to the lab. I can let you know within a couple of days."

Ralph wanted to insist on going with him, but he felt the timing was bad. He would know soon enough. Richard wasn't the one responsible for the ants. He didn't seem the type and would never have endangered the woman he was to marry.

"I look forward to hearing from you, Richard. And please call me Ralph."

Richard nodded and kept staring at Mary.

"If you need anything, don't hesitate to call me. I can pull some strings." He handed Richard his card.

Richard was as still as a statue.

Ralph understood and sympathized. He turned and left. He knew it would take a while for her to recover—if she ever did.

CHAPTER 46

Three Months Later

EVERY MONDAY, WEDNESDAY, AND FRIDAY, RICHARD DROVE to Lawrence to see Mary. She had made some improvement. All her faculties had returned, but she only had memory from the time she broke her trance in the hospital.

She accepted Richard's visits, but she didn't understand his interest in her. The doctors hoped she would regain the memory, expecting the more distant memories to return first.

Richard asked them if it was possible to remember everything— while leaving the incident that caused her memory loss to sink into the abyss of her mind forever.

They understood his desire, but there was no way they could control such an outcome.

After his visits to Mary, he would return to Mary's Family Groceries and relieve Ann, who voluntarily looked after the store when Richard couldn't.

Ann continued to work in his lab, testing the work Richard had done after making final changes to her work. The only real challenge left was figuring out how to implement their work in the field. Ann could handle that. Maybe Saul would be willing to help her.

The rest of the time, Richard got up at six, ate a bowl of cereal, and opened Mary's Family Groceries.

He had become quite good at merchandising her products,

eliminating the slow movers, and adding others that would turn more rapidly. He sold all the camping gear at 75 percent off. What he couldn't sell, he gave away.

Between customers, he remodeled the store, doing all the work himself.

Every penny the store generated, he left in the bank, using only the funds necessary to run the business. Each time the funds accumulated to fifteen grand, he pulled five out and bought a certificate of deposit.

He told Washington that Ann would finish the work—and that he was retiring from entomology. They insisted that he continue as an advisor for the same pay. He had shrugged and said, "It's your money."

Ann visited almost daily.

Saul called once a week. He had been given Larry's position at the same pay.

Bill called once a month, insisting in vain that Richard come down to visit so Mary Sue could fatten him up again. He was sure Richard was losing weight and not taking care of himself, and he was right.

Larry had taken off to Barcelona. He bought himself a nice condo on the northern side.

Dr. Morton had retired to West Palm Beach. He lived in a two million-dollar condo, drove a fire-red Lotus, and was the proud owner of an eighty-foot yacht. He was a member of an exclusive yacht club. His life was what he always dreamed it would be—at least two voluptuous girls at a time at all times. On the yacht, he would bring four or five girls— for himself.

A Year Later

Mary and Richard drove up to Mary's Family Groceries, and a smile filled Mary's face. "Wow. It looks fantastic, Richard. Bigger, somehow."

"It's the white paint, sweetheart."

"The dark green trim really sets it off well."

A large sign hung above the doorway: Welcome Home, Mary.

Mary stopped in front of the door and looked at Richard. "That's really sweet of you, darling."

Richard smiled. Her calling him darling again over the last two months was so gratifying to his heart.

When she opened the door and stepped in, the lights went on—and more than fifty people yelled, "Surprise!"

Mary held her cheeks with her hands, her mouth agape. All her customers crowded the aisles and the displays. Tears rolled down her eyes as she soaked in the applause. She turned to Richard and embraced him with all her strength, whispering, "I love you, darling. More than anything else in the world."

Richard looked into her eyes and said, "And I love you."

Ann embraced Mary. "It's so good to have you back home, Mary. We all missed you, especially your cooking."

They chuckled as all the customers gathered around her and began to shake her hand and wish her well. Over the next two hours, the customers filed out and left Richard, Mary, and Ann alone in the store.

"Didn't Richard do a great job with this place?" Ann said.

"Yes. My God, dear. You fixed the whole place up. The displays—wow—I don't know what to say. And you did this all by yourself?"

Richard nodded proudly.

"I got myself a real handyman, don't I?"

"You sure do," Ann said.

"And how are things in the lab?"

"Good," Ann said. "It'll be time for me to leave in about three months."

Mary looked at Richard.

He nodded. "It's her baby now. I retired. I am dedicating the rest of my life to Mary—my wife."

"You sure? I won't hold you to that, you know."

Richard nodded.

"I can't believe you married me in that place."

"I think it was very romantic," Ann said.

"Maybe so, but I was hoping for something a little different."

"Oh, there will be," Ann said.

Richard winced.

"Oops. I blew it, didn't I?"

Richard nodded.

"What are you all talking about?"

"We're going on a cruise. The Mediterranean. We're going to be married again on board."

"Again? So soon, darling? We haven't even had our first honeymoon."

"Well, now you get two for the price of one."

"You're getting away cheap, mister," she said.

"I'm sure you'll get your money's worth. Sorry I let the cat out of the bag, Doc. I thought you told her when you two married last week."

"My fault. I should've told you."

Mary turned around and looked at the store. She took a deep breath and sighed.

"What's the matter?" Ann asked.

"Would you be really angry with me if I told you I didn't want to be here anymore?"

"No, babe. Actually, I half-expected it."

"And you fixed it all up anyway?"

"I figured if you decided to sell it—and I guess that's what I'd do with it—at least you'll get more for it this way, especially now that I got the sales up another 40 percent. Actually, I got a buyer waiting to see what you want to do."

"And I thought you'd be a zero in business!"

"So did I," Ann said.

"Thanks a lot, girls."

"And a businessman to boot. So where do we go, Richard?" Mary asked.

"Someplace where there's a beach, fishing, and golfing."

"Golfing! You don't golf," Mary said.

"Hey, I'm retired now. I can start. *We* can start."

"You're right. Galveston, Texas."

"Galveston?"

"Has everything you mentioned. And not a lot of people."

"Galveston, here we come," Richard said.

"Looks like we'll both have to buy some golf clubs."

"And a boat."

"Oh my. The cost is already going up, but I'm not complaining." She wrapped her arms around his neck.

— — — — — —

"Larry!"

"Michael?"

"Yeah! Did you hear the news?"

"What news? I don't have any idea what you're talking about."

"The bottom is about to fall out. Already has!"

"Michael, talk sense."

"Walmart canceled the poison sales! Says there's no market anymore."

"No market? What do you mean?"

"That son of a bitch *changed* them."

"Who changed what, Michael?"

"Richard! He and Ann changed the killer ants. They don't attack anymore. They're even foraging on vegetation now!"

"Well, that's good, isn't it?"

"Don't you get it? Boy, are you dense! No sales. No money. Your income just dried up."

"You mean the well dried up. It had to sooner or later, Michael. We knew that. I got no problem with that. I don't owe anything, and I put some aside for a rainy day. I'm okay."

"I've got millions in debt. I'm going to lose my condo, my car, and my yacht!"

"You shouldn't have spent all that money, Michael. What can I tell you?"

"That's it? After all I did for you, that's it?"

"After all you did for me?"

"Yes. You're living high on the hog because of me!"

"Michael. Listen—and listen carefully. One: I'm not living high on the hog. I'm not stupid. Two: I knew this day would come. So did you! Three: It was my connections that had just as much to do with your success as your science. Four: I am not responsible for your squandering your money on the expensive condos, cars, boats, and broads. You have a problem. You fix it."

"You've got to help me! You need to loan … hello? Hello! Ungrateful son of a bitch hung up!"

Dr. Michael Morton lost everything and filed bankruptcy. No university would hire him. A year later, he started working as a cashier at a supermarket—without any good-looking dames on either arm.

Printed in the United States
By Bookmasters